HOMESTEAD

HOMESTEAD

MELINDA MOUSTAKIS

FLATIRON
BOOKS
NEW YORK

HOMESTEAD. Copyright © 2023 by Melinda Moustakis. All rights reserved. Printed in the United States of America. For information, address Flatiron Books, 120 Broadway, New York, NY 10271.

www.flatironbooks.com

Designed by Jen Edwards

Library of Congress Cataloging-in-Publication Data

Names: Moustakis, Melinda, 1982– author.
Title: Homestead / Melinda Moustakis.
Description: First. | New York : Flatiron Books, [2023]
Identifiers: LCCN 2022041931 | ISBN 9781250845559
    (hardcover) | ISBN 9781250845566 (ebook)
Classification: LCC PS3613.O88 H66 2023 | DDC 813/.6—dc22
LC record available at https://lccn.loc.gov/2022041931

Our books may be purchased in bulk for promotional, educational, or business use. Please contact your local bookseller or the Macmillan Corporate and Premium Sales Department at 1-800-221-7945, extension 5442, or by email at MacmillanSpecialMarkets@macmillan.com.

First Edition: 2023

10 9 8 7 6 5 4 3 2 1

For those who wander

So my life was split up. The logic of it also. This is my proof. We lived at our homestead, well rid of the world.

—WILLIAM CARLOS WILLIAMS,
IN THE AMERICAN GRAIN

CHAPTER 1

PIONEER PEAK

JUNE 1956

GOD MADE THE TREES and men make the kindling, they say. One hundred and fifty acres of white spruce and paper birch, alder, aspen, cottonwood, and willow—spears of evergreen pointed at the sky, and the pale and peeling bark, and the leaves of every branch—all for the taking if the acres are proved. Fell the trees and clear twenty acres of land to seed a crop, raise a cabin with nails and timber, and weather the seasons. This is the way to earn and own the deed.

Lawrence stands where the cabin will stand, the marsh and muskeg easing miles toward the marine inlet of Knik Arm, and beyond, the sloped rock of the Chugach Mountains, and the soaring crest of Pioneer Peak cragged in snow, the highest point on the horizon. Here, in this place, the low rising to meet the bluff on the northern ridgeline, and to the south, the thick-lain woods that lead to the lake that has water for hauling. On these acres in Point MacKenzie, in the territory of Alaska, is where he will homestead.

He had considered the map at the Bureau of Land Management as the man looked on, the parcels divided and numbered, free, and no price to be paid, though there were conditions. Traced his hand over the paper and waited for a feeling, a jolt of decision. So many prospects before him, and he closed his eyes, and asked for a sign, and when he looked again everything in him aimed toward the dot of a small lake. "You sure?" said the man, stern. "Most take more than a glance." He was certain. With the weight of his left hand he wrote his signature, Lawrence J. Beringer, on the promissory title for lot 041180. Took the map he was given, and as he was leaving Lawrence heard the man say, "Bastard won't survive the winter." Grit in his teeth, the official papers in his grasp, and he drove to Point MacKenzie, the miles ticking, that man saying he would amount to nothing up here, that he would abandon and forfeit his claim. Had taken stock of him, lean and slight, and passed judgment, quick as that. Happened all his life.

He drove for hours and the gravel road turned to mud and then there was not an access road that he knew, or any sense of a living. When there was a path no farther, he headed into the thick trees with a pistol and a compass, his rucksack filled with painted wooden stakes to mark the edges of his property. He unrolled the map and could not find the plot number or the terrain, and he blamed himself, and then he understood the wrong that had been committed against him—and he tore it in half.

Should have checked the map, not trusted the man to do his job, this was not an honest mistake. Had it in mind to drive to the bureau and confront him. But he would not turn back now. He walked through the woods, the sweat of the search on his neck as the time wore, and the mosquitoes swarmed, and when he slapped the sting, the blood ran down, and he had to look away. Washed out the faint taste of metal in his mouth with water from his canteen, swished and spat, quickly dabbed his arm with a handkerchief. He went farther in, making his own trail, the needle on the compass his only direction. He crossed bear tracks dry in the dirt, the claws short of the length of his boot, bigger than a black bear's. He knew to heed the signs of grizzlies, and he checked the bullets in the pistol, made his steps light. The ground edged to swamp with shallows, dark earth and muck, and he pressed on to find the lake. In the brush a cow moose grazed with twin calves flanked at her side, their downy heads poking through the low shrubs, and though he was quiet, the cow herded the yearlings back into the thicket. At a pass he came to a meadow, and in the open view of the grass, far in the climbing distance, a large white sphere, masted and man-made, a question. He drank more water from the canteen, leaned against a birch tree. Could belong to him, for all he knew, this birch, the dewed ferns bright in the blind of the woods, the sodden ground under his boots, the bloodthirsty mosquitoes.

A chop in the air, and he searched the sky above, and he knew the sound, but out in this wilderness it could not be, and he sickened at the thought that what he heard was not of the world. Then a shadow appeared, and circled him, and a helicopter landed soft in the clearing, silver with a red nose and tail, a white star circled in blue painted on the side, air force. The engine tuned and the blades slowed, and he waited. The pilot opened a door and waved him over, and with caution, he approached. There were two men in the front.

"Where you going?" asked the pilot. "You don't seem like you know."

Lawrence showed him the title and the torn and useless map and did not mention his service.

"One of those tenderfoots," said the other pilot. He knew of a trail leading off the landing field at the outpost and could show him. "Looks like you could take that and drive through the marsh to your land. Lucky I spotted you," he said.

Lawrence pointed and asked about the white sphere and the outpost. The pilot said he had stumbled on a radar tower for Site Bay, Nike Missile Defense. Lawrence clenched his fist. Missiles, when he had tried to find a place far away from everything. "You won't even know we're here," said the pilot. Lawrence almost laughed. He took in a breath. He had chosen the lot and he would find it.

And so Lawrence was lifted up and flown into the sky, as he had been in the war, above the ridgelines and the jagged face of Pioneer, above the wide green of the trees, and he was lost, straining and searching, the stock of his life held up to clouds and air, his feet afloat, a pressure at his temples, his arms heavy and empty, and suddenly a bullet of light in the acreage below, the sharp gleam of a lake, his lake. There, his land, his homestead, where his children will call the years. Where he will cut the timber and till the ground and build a cabin of his own measure. He will claim what he is owed.

And by the work of his hands this will all be his.

CHAPTER 2

MOOSE LODGE

JULY

THERE ARE SCORES OF men in Alaska, their faces a worn stare, and the first man Marie likes the look of who has prospects and could be tied down long enough to marry, she will have him. Visiting her sister and brother-in-law, Sheila and Sly, all the way from Conroe, Texas, with the money they sent and no return date, she walks with them into the Moose Lodge and mouths open and forks hang in the air. Talking to Sly is a way to be closer to her, be a big man and offer what before was a hassle, a favor to have hers. Marie laughs too much and too easily, the charm of being the shiniest thing in the room, and sips her beer to be polite and to avoid the swarm of do-gooders if her glass becomes empty. Two women at a table are collecting signatures for the support of statehood—now that there is an Alaska Constitution this should follow—and one talks about how Alaskans should be able to vote for the President and for their governor, who currently is chosen by the President, which is *just not how things should be done, we're taxpayers, after all*. Sly and Sheila add their names and Marie takes a pamphlet, and then the raffle is announced. They bustle over to the buffet and fill their plates and sit down.

To her left, a table over, is a man with a shadow on the sharp line of his jaw. The other men at his table steal glimpses of her but not this man, his hair black as polish, and he puts his knife down after each bite, and chews with care, and clears his plate. He fills his plate again, and the raffle ends, and the other men around him get up and return with dessert, bread pudding, but he eats his helping of pot roast and potatoes and gravy. She has a feeling about him, about the hunger he is slow to fill, and the edges of his face that cut the air, and she says, "Mister, they ever feed you 'round here?" with a hint of a drawl. He knows she is speaking to him, his back tenses, and he glances over. And nothing more. He does not answer her and stands up to leave. He is not wide or tall in strap, but wiry, a spine set straight. She dares not turn her head around and sinks into her seat. Then a tap on her shoulder. On a scrap of paper he has written: *150 ACRES*.

"Tomorrow," he says, a rasp in his deep voice.

That night she waits for Sheila and Sly to retire to their bedroom and she studies his handwriting, the lean to the right, steep and falling, the letters squared and pained. In this she sees a man with a will that defies his size. A man making his way. A man, and not the boys she knew in Conroe. And not the old getter who thought he was waiting for her. She rolls the note and places the paper underneath her tongue, holds the promise there. Land. Acre by acre. This one she would endure.

—+—

ANY WOMAN NOT A wife—a sister, or cousin—is a welcomed change to the company of drillers and carpenters and diggers and mechanics at the Moose Lodge, the tired and hungry scraping of forks, the talk of too many hours, bosses with big mouths, the grind of frontier life. The first woman Lawrence reckons can winter in a cabin, he will ask her. There is an empty seat beside him in the '53 Mercury he drove up to Alaska, and in the truck he bought once he'd saved enough, and room beside him where he sleeps, on a couch in a bus he has lived in for a year. He could have dragged the bus out to his claim, but is working and saving over the summer. His father, Joseph, drove up from Blackduck, Minnesota, to visit and had brought him a bed, made from carved oak and passed down, for when he settled. Joseph schemed a business for him—an old school bus, a 1945 International Harvester, outfitted with a woodstove for heat and a propane one for cooking and a counter inside, a diner on wheels, and he fashioned a wooden sign that said JOE's and fixed it to the top, *Don't matter where you are, people need to eat.* Which was why Joseph had opened his own diner some years ago in Blackduck, the Atomic Café. Lawrence had preferred working the farm to busing tables and washing dishes and having to listen to his father tell the same stories to the same customers. He found the bus suited him as living quarters and left the sign and stored the bed and what it was for.

A young, dark-haired woman arrives with Sheila and Sly, who he met once before at the lodge, and with that a promise has walked through the door, of someone to give him a reason to suffer the long shifts and cockeyed work of a drunk man with a hammer. And, for him, a wife for the sake of children. Mechanics and drillers who know Sly are the first to introduce themselves with hearty slaps on the back, offers not asked for or needed. "Borrow my tools, my lift, my haul trailer, anytime. You take care, now. You take care of this one, too." Weasels, all of them. She can have her pick, but what pickings they are, hard-worn, wind-slapped, smelling of sweat and grease and damp. She smiles but makes no promises, laughs loud. Says, "How about we see?" The rush dies down only when the Luck of the Moose drawing starts and everyone is asked to take their seats and listen to the numbers for the winning raffle tickets, but it is not the raffle that interests the men. Her name is Marie, he overhears. She will be in Anchorage a week or two visiting Sheila, her sister.

He watches her without staring. He downs his scalding coffee, holds the liquid in his mouth with the burn, shows neither pain nor weakness. There is a glass of water in front of him and he does not allow himself to reach out and drink—no comfort, no righting of his mistake. He bites down on his tongue. *Take it easy.* Bernie is talking and he wants to say, *Shut the hell up, I'm trying to think.* Bernie, a Moose Lodge member and carpenter he met at one of his first construction jobs, and brought him here for a home-cooked meal, and he's been coming here ever since. Bernie also knew who to ask for more work, and at one remote build told him all he knew about grizzlies. Lawrence eats his plate of food, piled high, and he does not know what else to do, he needs more time, and he buys another. For every bite he cuts a square of pot roast with his knife and fork, the roast not as tender as the last, and covers the square with mashed potatoes and drags the mouthful through the brown gravy.

When he finishes another plate, she turns from the table over and asks him a question. He catches a hook in her voice, and the way she says "Mister" sends a pain straight through his throat. She laughs, her mouth wide on her small face, her hair dark against her skin. Words, he hates them, how they fail to come out of his mouth and make happen what he wants to happen, and he nods in reply. Another man talks and takes her attention away.

Bernie glances over at them. "There's about three women up here in Alaska, it seems. And he just got one of them."

Lawrence will lose his chance, he knows, and grabs the pencil out of Bernie's shirt pocket. He writes on a scrap of paper and stands up and taps her on the shoulder. She reads the message. She understands.

"We're at the end of Clay Street, a green trailer," she says.

He nods. "Tomorrow evening, six," he says. It is done.

———

MARIE TELLS SHEILA SHE has a date. A man from last night. He had not given his name, and he left after handing her the note. So she asked around, and someone called Bernie told her: Lawrence.

"Do I know him?" says Sheila. "Should Sly and I tag along?"

"I don't think he'd want a crowd," says Marie. "Seemed shy."

He has to see she is worthy of those acres, that she is as serious as he is, no time to waste. In this trailer she is Sheila's little sister who might still return to Texas. But out there, on that land, there is a chance for more.

"Wait a minute, we're supposed to go dancing at the Panhandle," says Sheila. "Could join us."

Marie shakes her head.

"Where's he taking you, then?"

"He didn't say, now that I think of it," says Marie, and knows Sheila will be concerned. "I have a time and I know he's coming here."

"Not sure I like this," says Sheila. "We'll be gone before he arrives. Sly has an early day."

"One evening," says Marie. "He knows I have family."

"He knows you're young and you just got here. Men are the same no matter what fence they're leaning on."

"Isn't that what Valera used to say?"

"It's true even if she did," says Sheila, of their grandmother. "I guess you can go. Besides, won't be dark til midnight."

"I promise I'll be back hours before then," says Marie.

"What will you wear?"

"What would you let me wear?" says Marie.

Sheila laughs. "I see nothing has changed."

But it could, and as soon as tonight, a beginning. Sheila heads to her closet in the back of the trailer. She has two new getups she will allow Marie to try on, if she is careful. He will take her to dinner. Though she loves to dance, he does not seem the type.

Marie turns on the radio and the announcer says the next song is "Everything I Have Is Yours" by Billie Holiday, *who was right here in Anchorage for a few concerts in 1954.* The slow, dreamy music starts with the rain, and she opens the window and leans on the sill and drops fall on her outstretched hands. They were always praying for rain back in Conroe, looking to a blue and cloudless sky, and she was tired of waiting.

———

HE ARRIVES IN THE two-door Mercury and his hand shakes as he holds out the wildflowers he picked, the blossoms of fireweed so bright and purple they embarrass him.

"For me?" she says.

"Who else?" he says.

She wears a peach dress and boots. The boots are a good omen. He drives in the rain. She fills the silence, tells him she is eighteen and finished high school, though her grandmother almost kept her back on account that Crockett, where she went, and Booker T. Washington might not be separate anymore, and Sheila made the dress, her sister can sew most anything and she, herself, not a stitch. He does not mind her talking. The roundness of her face, her eyes golden in the summer light, and in those eyes, he sees the children he is set on having.

"You going to say something?" she says. "How old are you? Where you from? Where's your family?"

She, he could sense, is looking at him, the whole side of his face, waiting, and would wait until he opens his mouth. He grips the steering wheel. "Why don't we get married?"

She cracks into laughter, gasping and kicking the dash. "You don't have a ring."

"I'm twenty-seven," he says. "You know what I have and what I got to offer."

"Pull over," she says, breathless, "I need the ladies' room."

He turns into the soggy lot of the Buckaroo Club, crowded on a Friday night. She runs out and yanks open the Buck's double doors. He slaps his face. He should leave her there, drive away, and she would return to Texas. But she would tell Sheila, who would tell Sly, and he would never be able to show his face at the Moose Lodge again.

The Mercury rolls a few feet and stalls. He is too late. She is running back to him, holding up her dress and splashing with each step. She jumps in and slams the door shut. "You ain't leaving without me," she says.

He reaches over to touch her hand, and her staying is an answer.

CHAPTER 3

NORTH, TWO CROSSINGS

AUGUST

SPARE TIRES TIED TO the top of the Mercury and fitted in the trunk, they will burn through them driving across Canada. Sheila and Sly follow in a loaned car, and Lawrence drives because Marie has never learned. She has sent a letter to Valera saying her visit in Alaska will be longer, and in a few days she will send another to tell her she is staying. And Sly had a buddy at Fort Richardson's army surplus send a letter Lawrence wrote with news of the wedding to Minnesota so it would arrive in time. Lawrence asked his parents, Joseph and Lois, to prepare for their arrival and the ceremony, and to give a tithe of cherry and dandelion wine to the priest at St. Michael's so he would paper the bride as Catholic. Marie and Sheila were raised Baptist, though they did attend a Catholic boarding school for girls in Houston for half a year, sent there by their mother, Rosalie, with the money of one of her suitors. She and her sister did not have a mother and a father in the way Lawrence could call on his. Rosalie, sick and pale and always leaving her daughters if a man came about, that paleness no amount of sun could shake, *mind yourself, mind your sister, mind your grandmother,* and if she was home with them she was frail and resting in bed. Rosalie had come to Sheila's wedding and played the doting mother-of-the-bride, but Marie did not need her—Sheila would be there. Rosalie had given Sheila her wedding dress, which Sheila hemmed for herself, and now had given to Marie.

On the long drive, when the radio skips with static, Marie tells Lawrence that Valera, her grandmother, took her and Sheila in time and time again and told them they were charity, *You two are not blood kin, and girls besides, your mother was adopted from the orphan train that came from New York, three boys and we lost one and a girl sounded right, she had that brown hair silk as a horse's tail and skinny little thing, survived rheumatic fever.* And how did Rosalie repay them? By running off to Houston with a roughneck, and no one heard neither hide nor hair of her til a letter came saying she had married a man, Julius Kubala, and had a baby girl, and then Julius enlisted in the Second World War and died. Rosalie showed up with suitcases and a black mourning dress and little Sheila and a baby, Colleen Marie, christened after his Irish mother's side. Kubala, that unusual surname, was Czech, as his father sailed from Moravia to Galveston as a boy. Rosalie came back to Conroe because she said her in-laws did not approve of her. And that was the first of their many returns to Valera and the clapboard house with the sagging porch, and then being left behind as Rosalie chased a promising new something, one after the other. And then Marie shut her mouth, having said too much, because Lawrence could stop at any moment and call off the wedding, but he listened and did not flinch, nodded whenever she turned to study his face.

When Marie imagines being married, she sees herself having a life like Sheila's for a while, without children, though that has not been her sister's choice. She will need time to know Lawrence. And as for his family, would they accept her? Only Sheila there to stand and Sly to give her away. Maybe Lois was what she fancied mothers were, apron in a warm kitchen, generous and patient. And in regards to becoming a mother herself, Marie only knew it would happen someday. Any know-how she had from her sister, who spent time with their neighbor, a midwife long ago, and all those tales of birth and death. Sheila had wanted to be a nurse and then she met Sly and wanted what he wanted. There were jobs in Alaska and he had just been fired again. Marie found that life in Conroe without Sheila was unbearable and had to leave Texas before Valera married her off. But her sister was not surprised she left. All the swimming holes they went to, before drought and polio closed them, and Sheila never lasted as long as she did, called her a water baby. Said she swam like she thought she was going somewhere.

—+—

MARRIAGE WAS A MEANS to have children, and then he filed on the homestead and the land would require many helping hands. So he needed a wife, and when Marie accepted him he had a vision of St. Michael's, the church of his First Communion and confirmation, the red brick and the bell tower, polished pine covering the rafters and fashioned into pews, two hymnals in each rack, and the altar in the center, the piano and pulpit on either side, every line true and level, everything knowing its place, and as a child he felt a peace there.

On their way to Blackduck, tired and sore from hours of driving southward, the car parked on the Alcan Highway and covered in dust, he kisses her good night. For longer each time. Then he sprawls in the front seat and she crawls over to the back, and before he falls asleep she asks him about his life, she wants to know who she is marrying, after all. *Tell me about your parents, your kin.* She tried when he was driving but he had to watch the road, the strain of finding the words, and so she waits for the end of a long day, when he is, as he says, *pert'nere slack to the world.* And this is how she learns he was born in Herreid, South Dakota, and named after a saint. His grandfather came to this country from Germany, a Beringer. He grew up picking potatoes and chopping wood to sell. Has three brothers and a sister and they moved to Blackduck where they could afford land sold to them by another German family. Enlisted and served in the Korean War and became a paratrooper because he would be paid fifty more dollars a month if he learned to jump out of planes with a parachute. He was sent home, a hardship discharge Joseph had filed when one of his brothers came down with polio, as Lawrence was the oldest son and was needed on the farm.

—+—

SHE MEETS THE FAMILY, the three brothers and the sister, the husbands and wives and children, and Joseph and Lois, at the cabin the morning they arrive. A stock of thin men, the one brother with a marked limp, standing on the covered porch, and the women round-faced and hen-clucked in the kitchen. Joseph offers a handshake and then an embrace. Lois stands at the sink busy with the dishes until Joseph ushers everyone outside, the kitchen was the whole cabin for years before he could build on, and shows them the barn, the few goats and cows that are left, the vegetable garden that Lois planted. But this is not the land that Marie is wanting to see. There was not time, in the rush to marry, but she had the promise of the homestead, had seen the claim number with her own eyes. The ceremony is tomorrow and they will leave soon after.

Supper is corn, carrots, meat loaf, rolls, and chocolate cream pie, and the adults sit around a large wooden table, crowded, another table for the children. Joseph touches his forehead, the sign of the cross, *In the name of the father,* and Sheila and Marie follow, they know the words, *and of the son, and of the holy spirit. Amen. Bless us, oh Lord* . . . When Marie looks up, she catches Lois watching her from across the table. Through her nerves, she smiles at her. But Lois remains tight-lipped.

"So why'd you say yes to this brother of mine?" says one of the younger brothers, John if she remembers. And the table laughs, all but Lois, who refolds the cloth napkin on her lap.

Marie glances at Lawrence. "Because he asked," she says.

And Joseph slaps the table in delight.

"Aren't there men up in Alaska not half as scrawny as him?" says John.

"John Jacob," says Lois. "You mind your manners."

"Yes, ma'am." John passes a plate of beans. "I'm just thinking if he can find a wife in Alaska then maybe I should go and try my luck."

Joseph wipes his mouth with a napkin, covers his laughter for a bit. "He means you did well, son," he says, "and Marie, we're happy to have you join our family."

"So am I," says Lawrence, and his brothers repeat after him, teasing, and his face turns red.

"Time for dessert," says Lois, tense, and she busies herself in the kitchen even though no one has finished.

After Lois would not let them help with the dishes, Marie and Sheila retreat to a bedroom for a fitting. There had been time for a few alterations before leaving, but not all. A line of worry crosses Sheila's brow.

"You sure about this, about him?" she says. "You ain't got to marry the first man that asks."

"I'm getting married," Marie says to the mirror.

"I said before," says Sheila, "just doesn't sit right by me. Engaged the day after you met." The dress is lace and tulle and Sheila pins the shoulders to take it in, a pinch and a stitch. "But what do I know?"

"I know for the both of us," says Marie.

"Then that's the last you'll hear of it," says Sheila. "And he is handsome." Marie blushes.

Then Sheila whispers, "Much more so than any of the brothers."

"Hush, they'll hear you," says Marie, though she was not mistaken. The strong angles of his profile and his thick black hair.

Then Sheila holds up a scalloped veil. "Lois offered something old."

"She did?" says Marie, as Sheila places the veil with the comb.

"She's doing her best," says Sheila.

"Is she?" says Marie. Her own mother would not be here and she had expected a little more warmth from his. At the least.

Marie slips on the white satin gloves and swooshes the skirt. Sheila pats a tear from her eye and says, "You're a bride."

Marie thought that the night before her wedding, standing in a white dress, she would have a feeling like Sheila's, happiness or joy and wondering where have the years gone. With time, she could say. Though endless hours in the car became nothing when Lawrence kissed her, and the sound of his voice, low and dignified, yet a softness, she would know it was him in one spoken moment. But what is she certain of? She pulls the veil over her face. Hidden, she mouths the reason, the answer, *One hundred and fifty acres,* and with this confession she is ready for her new life.

—+—

LAWRENCE SLEEPS IN THE hayloft out in the barn, away from his brothers, who have that wishing look but call him foolish, and from his mother, who wrings her hands and wipes the table. Lois had begged him not to leave Minnesota again—the war had already taken him from her and the family, and Joseph had his head in the clouds enough for the lot of them. His brothers said she prayed for him every evening he was away, the rosary beads in her clasp, the creak on the stairs as Joseph helped her to bed, the quiet when she finally fell asleep. These prayers were answered when he returned. And what of his? Other soldiers and other prayers, and holy books, and charms, and those who believed in nothing, in dust and worms, and bullets killed them all.

Four years he was home, scratching at the dirt, the rest of the country waiting for rain, and though he would inherit the farm as the oldest son he did not want the small plot, did not want the work of bringing the land back to its prime. Besides, the best days of his childhood were on road trips away when his father bought their first car, and never told them where they were going. He sat in the front seat because Lois stayed behind worrying of the expense, and his siblings always loud or complaining, and he would open the windows so he could drown them out with the rush of air. He wanted to stretch out his arms and know miles and acres were beyond him in every direction, untouched, and overgrown. And so he headed north, saved and filed on the homestead. Faith in the blind choice, and in Marie. And the children yet to come. Twelve of his own, he decides, a good round number of mouths to feed who will learn to feed themselves, work the land, and one day carry him to his grave. His father had wanted a farmer's dozen and had five children, and Lawrence would surpass him, in land and name.

———+———

THE CHURCH, RUDDY WITH brick on the outside, shines with the gloss of a wooden ceiling and sparse-filled pews on one side, and the piano melody begins the procession. Sly offers his arm to Marie and they walk down the aisle, and she is glad for the veil as she is beaming at Lawrence, standing at the front in his navy blue suit. Sly lifts the sheer and Lawrence only nods when she is presented. Perhaps he is as nervous as she is. In a whirl of Latin she does not understand, they exchanges rings, which are borrowed, a small diamond from Sheila, and a gold band from Joseph. She takes Communion, the holy wafer on her tongue. Then a feather of a kiss, fast and embarrassed. The priest whispers, "Come with me," and they both follow him to a back room and he recites the vows again, in plain-spoken verse, to affirm the bride's commitment, and she says, *I have, I am.*

There is a document to sign. Lawrence takes the pen and then hands it to her. He has written *Lawrence Joseph Beringer* and she writes *Colleen*

Marie Kubala, her maiden name, and then, finally, *Colleen Marie Beringer.* Lawrence holds her hand as they leave the church, and, as Marie passes the candles lit for the dead and dying and sick, she turns back, a farewell to her past, and with this turn the veil catches the tip of a flame and Marie snuffs the burn with her hands, but it is too late—the edge is singed. She removes the covering and says, "Will your mother forgive me?"

"I'll ask my father to tell her," he says.

Sly and Sheila are waiting for them, and as they drive to the farm, Lawrence is silent as Marie tells them of the misfortune. An accident, but is he angry with her? And is this one kindness from Lois ruined, as if Lois knew the truth of her heart? But already, that truth was becoming another, despite every sensible notion. Sheila says not to worry, *this is your wedding day, after all.* The cabin is bustling with greetings and well-wishes. Joseph gives Marie a consoling smile, Lawrence must have already told him. His toast is short, about love and grace, and he dabs at his eyes with a handkerchief. Then he takes photos of them with a new camera and Lois shies away from being in a picture, but relents. Marie and Lawrence cut the chiffon cake together, and Lois serves slices with cream and strawberry preserves but will not look at her. She should say something to Lois, thank her, or apologize. But they have to be on the road, Lawrence announces, and the well-wishers celebrate his eagerness to leave though Marie knows there is no honeymoon, no money for one. Sheila packs the dress and then holds her too tight in goodbye, *and now your life is changed forever,* she says. She helps Marie gather her belongings on the stoop as Lawrence readies the car, the gifts still wrapped. Joseph, left to give the goodbye, leans in and pecks her cheek. "Lois is Lois," he says. "But don't you worry, I mean that. We'll send you the photographs. And have a safe journey."

They leave, one last wave to Sheila, who is trying not to cry, which will surely bring tears to Marie's own eyes if she is not careful. Husband and wife, alone after the wedding, and tin cans are tied to the bumper of the Mercury and trailing them. She laughs along with the clatter. But Lawrence is bothered. He stops and cuts the strings.

"Where are we going?" she asks, when he returns. The map and the signs tell her south.

And he says, "We're heading where we need to go."

"We lost?"

He grips her knee as he drives. "What did I say? You want north, or my north?"

His voice is stern. And she crosses her arms, she knows how to read a map. Why has he changed so suddenly? The veil, but before the veil. The sweetness of preserves still on her teeth. She takes off the white gloves and places them beside her. She could not drive away if she wanted to. Or tell him to turn around. Or undo what has been done in the church, signatures in black ink. He stares ahead at the road that is taking her farther and farther away from Sheila. And the hours pass in silence, the hum on the road. Neither one willing, and the sun fades and she takes the backseat and stretches out her legs and leans her head against the window.

In the night she wakes and the Mercury has stopped and he is asleep in the front. She rolls down the quarter window and leans out, the air is cool and damp as they are near water, a dark slick stretched out before her, and there is something to be done before they are really married, Sheila had explained this to her, but he has not asked and she has not asked and, *Where's he taken us?* His strange manners at the wedding, his face a blank stare, as if he could not muster more than being there in a suit. She lies down on her side, a mirror of him. He is so close, lying there under a blanket, and yet. A seat between.

Early, he is already driving and stops and she pretends she is still sleeping, but then he nudges her and has coffee from the gas station and holds a cup out to her. "Time to get," he says, and starts up the Mercury and drives to the road, and then he says, "Sit by me? Help with the map?" and she hesitates, then climbs to the front. A weight has lifted from him, and this is the man she remembers. He drives over the long expanse of a bridge, the rising sun on the horizon, gold shining the river's water, every wave and wavering bright and lit, and the clouds are soaked with the morning and he counts, *One, two,* and by *three* she is counting with him and there is a flicker of a smile on her face and they reach the end after nine, and that feeling has returned, newness, and the luck of those young in their luck. He turns the car off the highway onto a road in the woods, parks far enough to not be seen.

"I came here as a kid," he says, "on a road trip with my father. And I was so happy to be away from the farm, for once." His face is turned away. "He never told us where we were going." She waits for him to say more, her palms clasped on the knee over her crossed legs. And then his hand, unsteady, reaches for her, he is her first, and his mouth, and the pulling, and the undressing, and the weight of him, this stranger who is her husband, and after, he rests his head on her chest, eyes closed and heavy, and she is worn thin, as if she has been swimming underwater and holding her breath for too long before coming up for air, that gasp and lightness. The windows are fogged over and a coldness settles, and what was is leaving, and in that place there is a pain buried deep, there might be a child, please not yet. "Some whiskey?" he says. "Been saving it." And she takes a swig, wraps a blanket around her shoulders, and rushes out of the car, into the woods, her knees shaking, the piss and blood.

—+—

LAWRENCE HAD BEEN WITH a girl a day shy of shipping out, that fumbling in a field, and then as a recruit in training stationed in Japan waiting to be sent to the reserve, out drinking one night with the nurses, but not after, until Marie, his wife, and he knew the sign of purity, and he had to look away. The sight of blood, even before the war, sickened him, and life on a farm is a test, the birth and death and slaughter. Even more, the feeling he is losing his hold and the solid ground he found in the years since the war, how the time slowly passed until he could trust his senses, and the return of an old dream, the waking to a swarm of mayflies, the cling and covering and flutter, wings as numerous as leaves, the crawl on his skin, the window open as they pour in, a thick flock, the crush of them in his hands and Marie says he is shouting, and he opens his eyes, the Mercury, the driving back, and he remembers where he is. She asks him what he was dreaming of, but he shakes his head. Mayflies came to Blackduck every year in the early summer. The only person he dared to tell was his father, who found him sleeping in the barn and asked for an honest answer. And no one else needed to know.

Hours on the road, the radio in and out, through towns and fields, and he has to rest to drive another day, and sometimes he pulls over to doze a little in the afternoon, just enough to keep on. He tries to talk more, to give her that, at least, to point out a beautiful quarter horse at a fence, and waits for their return to Anchorage, the moving into the bus, to be with her again. She did not have much to bring beyond a suitcase and the wedding gifts in the trunk. A couch, instead of the narrow seat of a car, and Marie lies beneath him, the release, and a dreamless night. And he wakes with Marie curled up at his side.

They gather supplies and tools from army surplus at Fort Rich, and, for a steal, buy an army ambulance with big airplane tires and chains, thanks to Sly knowing someone, and he said, "If anything could pull an old school bus, this is the ticket." Then Marie asks Lawrence to teach her to drive. Sheila left and Valera would not let her near her car, she says. Learning, at first, is shaky, is stop and start and start again. This is something she will need to know, forget the wearing of the brakes. He remembers all his buddies had girls in their trucks, told him what a time. The Mercury obeys her sharp turns and she wants to take a main road and he says, "Not on your life." And her laugh rings out, and so does his.

A honk behind them and she hits the gas at the crook of a turn and they run into the brush.

The driver, an older man, slows and pauses with the window down. "Should she be driving?" he shouts.

Lawrence leans past her. "She has to learn," he says.

"Brave man," says the driver, with a knowing eye.

"He's right," she says, holding her hands over the steering wheel. "If I can drive, who knows what I can do, or where I can go?"

"I'll know," he says.

She bites her lip and shakes her head.

He takes her to see the land, a trip to build the outhouse, found in the scrap of a torn-down saloon, the rusted antique hinges on the door from a steamer ship. On the way he tries to listen to her, but there are knots in his hands. He fidgets with the steering wheel. This is what will matter, and will she believe what he believes, that a life can be made here? The sky turns as they reach the outskirts of Point MacKenzie after three hours.

The sound of gravel drowns out the quiet, and he takes smaller dirt roads, and then he stops. She walks down the hill, arms crossed. This is not how he wanted her to see the homestead. Low clouds surrounding them, rain in the air, the woods shined and wet. "On a clear day, ocean and mountains," Lawrence says. He watches her face, and she says nothing of her feelings for the hundred and fifty acres, of the shrouded view.

The lake, why he made his choice, he says, and leads the way. He would show her the map if he had it. "Up here now," and he taps his forehead, "the one I'm making as I go along." They reach the clearing and stand near the edge. Beginning of rain patters the surface. "Water for drinking," he says.

"For swimming," she says. She undoes the laces on her boots.

"Too cold," says Lawrence.

She tosses her dungarees on the ground under a tree. "Come on."

"We better get going before there's a storm," he says.

She reaches for a button on her blouse.

He shakes his head, unmoved.

"Why not?" she says.

"I'm headed back," he says, and walks away. Together, as husband and wife, and he does not know what this will require. How to keep himself? How to keep her? She hurries into her clothes and runs to catch him as the rain breaks, a hiss in the air.

One last look before he starts the truck. But he has to ask, "What do you think?"

"This will do," she says, a wide smile. And gone, for this moment, is every doubt of what all this could be.

—+—

THE DAY ARRIVES AND the bus is hitched to the army ambulance, Lawrence at the wheel, and Marie tails in the Mercury. Moving to live on the land, and Sheila said she will give her a little time and then make the trip to see her, *Be good for you, you'll see.*

They stop at Teeland's Country Store in Wasilla, the nearest one they will have at the homestead, says the owner, Walt. Rows and shelves of staples, and Lawrence picks out a large bag of oatmeal. A man walks in, and Marie finds herself staring, his plaid shirt is one any man might wear, leather shoes and belt, and he nods, and she returns the gesture, and he has tanned skin and black hair, and none of the stores here have signs saying WHITES ONLY as they do back in Conroe, and he could be a Native she decides, and her nerves quicken. But the man knows Walt, his voice clear and strong, and he buys a box of nails.

An errand, ordinary, there for the same reason they are, and yet Marie is relieved when the man leaves. She had been holding herself still. "Was that man Native?" she asks Walt.

"Athabascan. From Knik-Fairview," he says. "This place used to be down in Knik years ago, a trading post called Herning's. And Herning moved the original logs up here, he told me, when he realized railroad construction was stopping in Wasilla. No one opened another store, so folks come from all over, but the Knik Bar and post office are still there."

"That's where we'll be getting our mail," says Lawrence.

"Might at as well stop at the bar while you're there," says Walt. "Tell Jones I sent you. He's been around about as long as me."

After their purchase Lawrence loads the Mercury.

"Athabascan," says Marie, to hear the sound.

"Heard of Tlingit, too," says Lawrence. "Bernie said they've been here a long time. Keep to themselves."

An older man walking up to the storefront says, "Tlingit. Athabascan. All thieves, if you ask me. And then you people keep coming up here ruining the place. I've been here forty years and I never—" The man throws open the door and turns his head. "I'd go home to the States if I were you."

Marie looks at Lawrence, who shrugs. "This could be our home," he says to her. "If all goes."

As Marie drives, she wonders if the man tells everyone to leave, and she wonders where the Athabascan man lives, if he has a cabin, a family, and what other ways she will have to learn. In Conroe everything was segregated, schools and the lot, but not the movie theater, because the one for Negroes burned down, and they sat in the back. Valera said no use changing what had always been. She was unsure of what would be asked of her by this unfamiliar place, by the acres, by Lawrence, who was accustomed, and she was determined in this new life to stand and take what she could, earn her right. The stakes are laid out before her—though she knows Lawrence had brought her along, and would be ahead of her in the while, older and knowing the land and that the homestead would be his. He moved to Alaska a year or two earlier. Same as Sheila. And what if she had come then? Would she have still met Lawrence at the Moose Lodge that night in July? One folded note, and here she is, following a man to a place she has seen once.

A turn onto Knik Road, and then a curved and winding offshoot, and Lawrence pulls over and military trucks pass on a small bridge, coming from the Nike missile site. Lawrence stops to fit chains on the tires to cross the marsh, and they carry on. At the airstrip, they are flagged by a man in uniform who talks to Lawrence and points to the trail. They follow his directions and Marie waves as she passes. Now the path is downhill and she keeps her foot on the brake.

Eyes on the back of the bus and a lurch and tires spinning, Marie yells for Lawrence, for help, as if he can hear her. Deep trenches of mud and muck, an uneven scrape, the car weighed down with tools and canned goods and sacks of flour and potatoes, 6–12 repellent, wooden boxes of Blazo kerosene. Lawrence will have to drop off the bus and come back, she knows. A relief to be alone, as long as Lawrence will come for her, here on a cut through the wilderness.

In waiting there is a giving in, she learned this as a child, not to expect her mother to return, *to hell with that woman,* she and Sheila would say in secret, and there was comfort in the riddance of what they wanted most and could not have, but Lawrence would return, how could he not, though this surety begins to stretch with time. She needs him, and the simple fact of it bites at her, and would he ever say the same? *He will,* she whispers, *he will.* Another hour passes into the summer evening and a moose crosses in front of the car, taller than any horse she has ever seen, a lazy gait without care that she is there, and slips into the trees. And she will tell Lawrence, though he would have seen so many, and this is new to her, wanting to tell someone besides Sheila. Then the army rig appears and she opens the door and then closes it to calm herself. Rig hitches up to the Mercury, which means he drove this way backward, for a long stretch.

Lawrence comes to the side and she rolls down the window. "Figured you would need help," he says. "Had some trouble myself."

"Was wondering," she says, composed.

"You didn't think I'd leave you out here, did you?" he says.

"Never," she says.

After the tow she steers the Mercury and they make their way, each turn a slow gain, the way furrowed, then through the open marsh, and a climb of a sloping hill to the parked bus. Inside, soot and ash has spilled from the stove and the couch is buried in the pack. Lawrence throws down paper mail bags for them to sleep on and this is how they spend their first night, apart, tired, she covering her eyes from the midnight sun. This does not trouble Lawrence, though he mutters in his sleep and then gasps awake, and she hears his steps as he leaves. He does not speak of what ails him, and what else has he not told her, this man she married?

He returns, and there are streaks of soot on his face. Then he grins when he sees her. "Looks like you've been mining coal."

"Should see yourself," she says. "You sleeping at all?"

"Enough," he says.

He settles on the floor and crosses his arms. She puts on her boots and heads to the outhouse, the day breaking. How long had Lawrence left her alone? And then, by the lake? Were these signs, or passing trials? Valera once said a man is nothing without land. And land is nothing without water. Mist in her hair. Trees and leaves, ferns and dew. This after the dust and sun beating down, the drought and dry for six years and counting. She will breathe it in, every acre. She stops in her tracks, high mountains on the horizon before her, towering and tipped in pink snow, and she had seen snow once in Texas, covered the dirt in a sheet of white. She believes for a moment, pink snow, and then the color bleeds through the low clouds and disappears—a trick of the light.

CHAPTER 4

AGAINST THE LEAN

SEPTEMBER

CHAINSAW IN HAND AND the felled trees are for firewood. Spruce for logs should be close to the eight-inch mark in diameter, straight, strong, and these he leaves standing, and scores, cuts a ring into the bark so the sap will run out as the tree dries. By his figures, he needs one hundred logs, give or take, a cabin a child can learn to walk in, first steps across the floor. He knows a smaller dwelling would be wise, but drags a boot in the hard dirt, walks and measures thirty-by-thirty feet. The cabin will overlook the low.

He crouches and rests a knee on the ground. A skiff of early snow, white salting the spruces, every acre touched. The aspen and birch leaves painted gold as sudden as this, and winter came late October the past year. In the hazed light, three bull moose move slowly through the trees, the bone of their antlers a wide sprawl. No hunting til the cabin stands. How to drag the kill? Haul the meat? Put the meat away for keeping? Ain't a deer. One moose, reckon, the meat of ten. Good meat, too. Bernie had given him a moose steak, nothing better, no fear in this animal, he said. Two eggs swimming in butter, the yolk running down the side of the steak—what he could eat for every meal. Worth the trouble of gutting and skinning, even for him. He holds his hands up near his face, fingers pointed in one line, his thumb the sight. He triggers the air and follows the shot to the moose on the left, will wait for hunting season to come around again.

When he returns to the bus to fill his thermos with coffee, Marie is sitting on the couch, says she is feeling unwell. She asks him to sit down. She says she has all the signs and, "I think I'm with child." There are tears in her eyes. He nods, he kisses both of her hands. A baby already, according to his plan. He laughs, he can scarce believe it. He is going to be a father, and he wants to write a letter to Joseph. But not til she can talk to Sheila, she says, and is more than sure. He jumps up and pencils a circle around the day's date on the Moose Lodge calendar nailed to the wall. We have to mark this occasion, he says, we have to do something, and he grabs a wooden spoon and bangs it against the pot on the stove as if he is telling the whole world.

———+———

MARIE IS WITH CHILD, she has no doubt, the bleeding has stopped. Days of sick and spit and sucking on pilot bread, the slow softening of hardtack on her tongue as she breathes through her nose, not again, oh for Lord's sake, and her mouth warms and she runs out of the bus.

Air is cold, fresh, and she breathes it in. She grips her belly and the yellow of her sickness is a stain on the new, thin snow that covers the ground. That damn chainsaw. Buzzes loud enough to ruin being alone, the wild of nowhere near. She wipes her mouth on her scarf and breathes through the blue yarn. Sheila had knitted and sent it, set the date for her visit the next week. Maybe a letter with news of the baby would be better, not having to see her sister's face, who has been waiting for her own, a kindness. But she has to see Sheila to tell her, to share this. Pain in her head throbs and she rubs her temples. Chainsaw her in half so she cannot hear that buzzing.

Cooped up here and sleeping in a bus. She wipes the slush off the side mirror. Dark circles under her dark eyes, and red spots again, from the strain of being sick. She swishes out her mouth with the last of the boiled water in the pot on the stove. One jerry can is empty and she should hold off until they use up the other. Easier to carry one in each hand. She sprinkles salt, too much salt, on the tack of pilot bread and shoves it into her mouth and takes a breath. Her belly growls, and she slips some into her pocket and licks her fingers. She picks up the jerry can and heads toward the lake, away from the buzzing.

She closes her eyes when the chainsaw stalls, quiet, and then a choke and pull and the buzzing again, louder for the moments of calm. Clamps her mouth closed and the pilot bread softens and she swallows, slowly as her belly aches, with hunger, with sickness, with hunger. Nothing sticks, not oatmeal or sips of water. A little water sloshes around so she has been drinking til she is full and pissing a river. Pilot bread settles on a good morning, and this ain't a good morning. Down near the low, three moose graze. Blood and meat, that is what her belly needs. Have to learn the land to set traps, find a way to keep and store the meat. Could shoot and take a moose down right here, make no mistake. Her eyes narrow in on the shot. She forgot the pistol for scaring off bears—they are saving for hunting rifles. Shotgun would be better protection, but Lawrence has it, and she has enough to carry with the jerry can and the baby on the way. She knew a baby could take, Sheila told her, but she thought there would be time to want one.

Lake is rimmed with a shock of melting snow. Water is clear near the edge and Marie steps in to fill up the jerry can. She hauls it out and sits down to rest, fishes the pilot bread from her pocket. A hush, the lake is far enough away that she cannot hear the chainsaw, but a knocking hammers the air, and another. A woodpecker hangs off the trunk of a tree, a bright red spot on the head, a mark if she had the pistol and wanted to kill and eat a woodpecker. Carver Calhoun, one of Rosalie's suitors, perhaps the only good one, had taught her to shoot. *Here,* she would say to Lawrence. *Woodpecker stew.* Little bird bones and scant bird meat. She would laugh but he might just look at her as if asking, *Who are you? So go on now,* she says to the woodpecker, *bang your head against that tree.* She pulls out her mittens from her pocket and there is only one. Other she spots in the shallow of the lake. The mud is silky, and covers her hand in a smooth, dark film, and she wrings out the mitten and then bends down to wash off the mud, but licks her palm first. Salt, and sweet, and bitter and blood and dirt and gravy burned at the bottom of the pan, and she scoops up more and eats the mud, grit dribbling down her chin. Water has to be boiled, and she squeezes the mud dry, handful after handful, and her belly groans, and she shoves both hands into the mud and then a quiet, that's enough now, she has filled the gnawing hole in her gut.

She wipes her mouth. What's to come of eating all this dirt? But no one's to know the wiser. Jerry can is heavy, should have brought two for balance, and she switches hands and the sweat cools on the sides of her face. Stubborn as the day is long is what Sheila always says. But gone are the long summer days here. Each night darker than the last. The sun does not keep her awake as before, and she is bone-tired besides. She could sleep here in the trees, curl up and turn into a stone. But there is washing to be done. She had helped Valera with laundry after Sheila left and now she is on her own. Dinners and suppers, too. Heating tins in a pot most of the time. Sheila was the cook, taught her a bit. And when she left, Marie and Valera ate a lot of fried eggs, and there are no eggs to be had out here. But she couldn't stomach an egg today, not on her life.

She knows she is near, through the woods and into a clear, and still takes her breath—the white mountain that breaks the sky, Pioneer Peak. She sets down the can. Watching, waiting, and what has this mountain seen? How many years? And has it seen the likes of her—a married woman eating mud?

—+—

LAST TREE BEFORE HE breaks, a leaner, dead and dry and near the bus. So it has to come down. A large spruce, could be a hundred years old, and he will use the axe, how he felled for years. Lawrence saws a small cut near the base, in the direction he wants the tree to fall. He walks around to the other side and punches in. In this cut he wedges a shim and hammers with the sledge. Three shims and the tree does not fall. He crosses the shims and they double in height and he hammers them. There is a crack, but not at the base where he is hammering, at the top of the spruce, and a big branch falls and he scurries out of the way. Too close. Spruce teeters back toward the lean without the weight and all the wedged shims are for nothing as the tree falls in the wrong. Crash of metal and another thud and he runs. Marie and the baby, by his own hand. How could this be? He reaches the clearing and the spruce has fallen on the front of the bus, the large windshield cracked. Marie, he yells. He rushes inside, her boots are there, and the fixings for dinner, beans and hash and coffee, are sizzling around the stove and splattered on the floor. Marie, he yells. He circles the bus and finds footprints in the frost of snow, headed out into the woods, and he kneels down to touch them, gasping with relief. How small her tracks—slivers that disappear at the arch, only a half touches the ground. He runs, crazed and breathless, until he finds her. He grabs her shoulders. The shock in her eyes. "What happened?" she asks. "What did you do?"

———+———

THEY STAND IN FRONT of the bus and the crashed tree. "Damn branch," he says, and does not offer an apology.

"Is that all you can say?" And she turns away from him. Tree could have killed her and trees ain't falling by themselves, are they, and she is sick. All that running, and her belly. He has to take her elbow so she can walk. Steady, maybe she wants him to leave her alone. Or she wants to leave and go see Sheila. But she would be sick on the way. And Sheila is visiting soon. She lies down on the brown cord couch, her arm over her eyes. Sweat, dirt. She asks for warm water to wash her feet, to see if he will, and he fills a basin. This test, of him. "Bring me the bucket," she says, and he does. What else will she ask? When the heat cools and her feet are clean she places them on the towel and reaches down. "Let me," he says, and kneels, and wraps the towel around her ankles. She knows this is as gentle as he can be, his palms hard and callused. A shaking comes over her, and she needs the touching, and nothing else will help or ease, and she takes in a breath and another, please, she says, and her hands caress his face.

———+———

IN THE NIGHT SHE draws him close, as if she would be reconciled to only that, but this is not enough, and he is taken in, again. Nature, he supposes, but if he could resist, think on what kind of man he wants to be. One who is sure, and does not bend, who remembers who he is, who does not make mistakes, whose hands obey his will. And what does he owe her, for the cut and the tree and the fall? He is sorry, but she should know, and what of this weakness for her?

"What happened in the war?" she says, in the after, that drowse and sigh, certain he will answer. "You don't have any scars." Her fingers on his skin.

"Nothing to say."

"That can't be," she says.

"You want to talk?" And he kisses her mouth until she forgets.

When she is asleep he pulls away and leaves the couch. He could walk outside but does not want to wake her. This can't go on. She will find every part of him and then that will be the end. So he lies down on the floor of the bus to settle his thoughts. Down, to the ground, the earth, and below. But he wants to be near her. How this happened, this pull, he does not know.

———+———

SHE WAKES EARLY, ALONE on the couch again, and she does not have time to wonder why—Sheila and Sly will be arriving in the afternoon. Yesterday was for bathing. All day to haul and heat enough water for her and then Lawrence when he came in after felling trees. She sat outside on a stump near a campfire, read a dime novel, and let him be. The windows of the bus foggy with the heat, and they had, without even talking, some-how agreed on this politeness.

She washes all the windows inside and out and wonders if Sheila will know she is with child just by looking at her, if she will be sick, if she should tell her sister, who has been wanting a baby since she married Sly and is not sure what is the matter. She cooks dinner, a can of beans and a can of bacon, she soaks the strips in water first because they are too salty even for her, before adding them to the pot. Lawrence comes in and sits down and says, "Didn't know the windows had gotten so dirty," the sun streaming in. She wrings her hands. "Please don't say anything about the baby til I can tell Sheila."

"You don't have to worry about me talking," he says.

"That's true," she says.

They hear the truck before they see it, and then go outside. Sheila is waving as Sly drives. When the truck stops, Sheila climbs out and Marie rushes to hug her and Sheila whispers in her ear, "You're in that way, aren't you?" And Marie pulls back and nods, and Sheila cups Marie's chin in her hands. The men shake hands and unload. Sheila has brought fresh eggs and oatmeal raisin cookies she used to always make and Marie eats one on the spot. She could cry, having Sheila here.

Sly is asking too many questions in his excitement, his voice fills up the bus. Marie can tell Lawrence is annoyed, by the way he cocks his head to the side.

"Sylvester, take a breath," says Sheila.

He laughs. "Sorry, got carried away." He runs his hand through his curly blond hair, which he has tried, in vain, to slick down. "We've been thinking about homesteading for a little while. Just wanted to see how it's done."

"I didn't know that," says Marie, and looks at Sheila.

"We've only talked about it here and there," says Sheila.

"Well, come see the lay of the land," says Lawrence. He shows them the spot where he is planning to build the cabin, the size.

"Even I know that's a big place," says Sly.

They walk the property and he points out the mountains, how on a clear day the view is something to see.

"It is now," says Sheila, "clouds and all."

Geese in the two lines of an arrow fly overhead and point south, squawking and flapping their wings.

Lawrence leads them to the lake and tells them the story of being lifted in the helicopter and finding what was on the map, this water is why he chose the lot.

"And you got your swimming hole," says Sheila, to Marie.

"I'm of mind to go in now," says Marie, who is feeling heated even in the cool of autumn.

"I'll go in with you long as I can stand it," says Sheila.

"Crazy women," says Sly. "Us men are going to have some whiskey." He and Lawrence head back.

Marie and Sheila undress. Marie looks down at her stomach. "Can't tell yet."

"Was your face," says Sheila. "Only one thing makes that shine, how I knew."

Sheila gasps when she steps in the water and then rushes in and Marie takes her time. Sheila turns and splashes her and Marie lunges to grab her foot and pull her under. Sheila comes up for air and shrieks. Then they float, moving their hands back and forth at their sides.

"Looks like you have everything," says Sheila. "Land and a baby. How'd you manage that before me?" She smiles, but there's a pain behind her eyes.

"Not everything," says Marie, thinking of Lawrence sleeping on the floor.

"We're trying to get ahead," says Sheila. "But you know Sly. Can't help himself. Gets caught up and before he knows it he's bought a round for everyone. Was something I loved about him."

And there, the one question that she has about Lawrence. Sheila knows Sly, his reasons and faults, and who she is to him. And for this, Marie has to wait.

CHAPTER 5

RUT

OCTOBER

SNOW CAME AND WENT, a promise and a lie, and the turned trees lose their finest gold and yellow leaves to the wind. The scrape of moose antlers on branches and the rustle of willow shrub, the rut, and the bulls in a fight over the cows, the hollow racket of antler thrown against antler, the echo through the low. And the thud of a tree as it lands, Lawrence at work all this morning, before she made the coffee. She stirs in powdered creamer. She is keeping food down, hungry for everything, on her feet most of the hours.

He comes in early, before midday, for dinner. Sweat shining on his brow.

"How's the felling?" She slides a plate over to him.

Silence. He sits on the stool near the counter and winces. She places her hands on his sore shoulders to work out the knots and he moves away.

"What's the matter?" she says.

"Can't I eat in peace?" he says.

She grips the heavy handle of the skillet, heavy cast-iron, a wedding present from Sheila and Sly—she could knock him one over. "Don't bother about me," she says. She sucks in a breath and opens a can of beans and grabs a spoon, the holster with the pistol.

"It's cold out," he says.

"Colder in here," she says as she steps out of the bus.

She walks and eats spoonfuls of beans from the can, show him who's not speaking, and the tin that boils off by cooking coats her mouth and her belly sours. She scrapes the taste off her tongue with peeling birch bark, crushes spruce needles in her palm and covers her mouth and nose, breathes in the sharp smell of green. Then she arrives at a meadow surrounded by brown and withered ferns, the grass tipped in a sweep of rust. A place she had come to before and picked white flowers, and a bull moose had wandered into the clear, his open-palmed antlers shedding their velvet, the long tatters hanging off the points, one in the corner of his mouth, and the furred strip torn from the bone, the velvet dark and veined, the raw antler pinked with blood—a moose standing there eating its own skin.

———+———

HE SHOULD RUN AFTER her, but this is a notion he must stamp out before it burns him alive. Her touching his shoulder is more than he can handle, and he does not know the reason. This is the allowance of a marriage, this is how children are born, and what brought the one that is coming into the world. What clock has he begun, and it was time for all of this, but he is not prepared. A cold sweat at the back of his neck creeps down, and he is somewhere else, his blood drained and spilling, and he is there in that pouring out, trying to find his way back. Happened at the wedding, and he does not remember the words of the ceremony, though he spoke, though he signed the certificate that Marie has with her papers. Discipline is what he will find again, so he stays, standing in his boots, solid and sure.

He commits to working, the cutting of trees. This month, every year, he allows himself to remember the days of his only mission, that he is lucky to be alive. A payment, in a way, for the sacrifice of others, while he is here.

He sits on a stump with his coffee. A cow walks slowly across his felling path, tall and brown, a golden graze on her back. A bull moose follows, darker and racked, and rests his heavy chin on her backside, and then circles her. They do not see him, and wouldn't care that he is watching. Bull circles the cow, sniffing her, and the cow rubs her head along his side, under and over his haunch and down his back leg. They turn around and around each other, moving toward the cover of the trees. Even the moose, he thinks. But he is no animal.

———+———

WATER AT THE LAKE has thin-edged ice that breaks under her feet as she walks in. Her clothes are a pile on the ground near her boots. A fever in her mouth, the heat of it sweet and thick. She reaches down and picks up a shard of ice and rubs it over her open lips. No more eating mud, that need went away. She shivers in the air and steps farther into the lake, knees, hips, takes a breath, shoulders and neck. Waits for the calm in her bones.

She floats and holds her hands out of the water and her fingertips are white and pinched. Presses her cold fingers against the sides of her face, and slides them down to her stomach, which is warm and round and growing. Maybe Lawrence does not want her now because of the baby. She would have to ask Sheila, but would she know? Early evening and a yawn of sun hangs low in the sky.

Drags herself back to the bus, chokes down a supper of hash, and this is where the day ends when Lawrence returns—his eyes heavy, her blood racing. He nods and washes his face, says he will not eat. Bet Lawrence is the only one sleeping for miles, the crook of his arm covers his face. She leaves the dishes and wipes the table. Restless, the woods, the air. A low wail, strong and strained, sounds through the woods, a moose calling, calling.

In his sprawl one hand reaches out, not to her, or for her. Night the tree smashed the bus, Lawrence pulled her close and kissed her and was sorry and sorry again, and she fell asleep nestled into his neck, thinking those feelings for her had returned. But come morning, he was on the floor, and there since. She drinks a cup of water and fills another, this man and living on a bus. Pour the water on his face, now that would be something to tell Sheila. *You did what? Lordamercy,* and that is what she is wanting, the Lordamercy. Can't quite figure why, with the way he's been acting, he wanted a wife. Why her? Why carry the bucket if you ain't gonna fill it? She didn't know what she was missing until that night after the wedding, that touch what having skin and bones was for. Weren't for this baby, she would run into the dark as fast as her legs could carry her, find another life. But would she? Lawrence sighs and she turns around and crawls over to him. His fingers twitch as he chews the corner of a dream. She holds her hand to feel the warmth of his breath, hovers above his mouth. His eyes open and she snatches her hand away and he grabs her arm. "What are you doing?" he says. He is holding her too tight

"What you won't."

"Go on back," he says. "Leave me be."

She buries herself in the couch and *don't you dare cry with him listening, don't you dare, it's too late, you married him with your head spinning.*

———+———

EARLY TO RISE, AND he cannot lie still any longer. His day has begun, his steps lighter. That he could refuse her, deny himself, means the world is what he says it is. He holds the reins and beckons, rather than being dragged along—he slept sound with the knowledge of his own strength. What is all his training for if not for that sense of discipline, a call to order, and falling in line? He will not apologize for doing what has to be done. For them both. How small she seems, curled up on the couch, to have asked so much of him. Only a number of hours left to stockpile firewood. Before winter sets, the termination dust on the mountain peaks a warning, and then how much longer can he work in the cold before having to be inside? But not today, the weather is fine for a song of victory.

———+———

A SLAM OF THE coffeepot on the stove and Marie wills herself not to flinch. Can opener bites a top, a grind. Go ahead and have beans for breakfast. World don't move to feed that empty belly. He stirs and whistles, *Oh when the saints come marching in,* and let the damn saints come marching, one by one, let them march, she will lie here dead as he goes on. When he leaves she waits for the chainsaw buzz to start. Can't hear nothing. No sign of him out in the woods. One of those brimming days, sun bright in the blue glass of the sky. Wish Sheila was here. She would know what to do. Heat the water. Wash the morning off your face—the night, too. His hand, the way he grabbed her, still tender on her arm. Feeling the ghost, as Sheila would say. What's wrong with a man if he don't want the loving and fussing? All the questions she wants to ask Sheila are weighing her down. Sly, Sheila said, didn't let her sleep when they were newlyweds. *That man acted like I was the only water that could keep him alive.* Lawrence is not that man, what she can tell. What does he need her for? Washing and cooking and carrying this child? Just so he's not alone? He'd be well as can be if he was. And better company to the trees he's cutting. As for her, could she outrun this ache that, because of him, had grown and deepened, the drowning that is living? Another branch falls. What did she know of this wanting before, and now she could not know, it was done, and left to spoil. But luck's for the birds or luck's for the choosing, and she chose Lawrence, simple as that. And each day she has a choice. This claim on the land, a place of her own where she can build a life that won't be knocked down.

———+———

WHAT HE IS SURE of is this child, the purpose of bringing one into the world, the same knowing in seeing the lake and making the choice. Though he tries to have that same feeling about Marie, and he cannot find the handle, the aim, the mark is always moving. This felling and cutting, the work, is for her, for them. *But how could she know if you don't tell her?* is what his father would say. Start at the beginning, before the logs, before the cut into the trunk of a spruce tree, further and further back, to the farmhouse, and before then. And his father said he learned to walk in a field, in the cold, because they were all living together in one small room with a roof, before the rest could be saved for and built. Was the youngest two who learned to walk on a floor, inside, and Joseph said he could rest easy knowing that.

So Lawrence turns in for coffee and he says he wants to show Marie something, and she drags her feet, but follows him out of the bus. He makes thirty steps and then marks the line with his boot, and has her do the same across.

"I already know this is where the cabin is going," says Marie.

When the four lines are met and closed, he turns to look her into her eyes and tells her he had done the same thing the day she told him they were going to have a baby. "I'll never forget," he says. He tells her about the one room. "There's something in knowing that this cabin will be big enough for all my children, our children, to learn to walk."

"You were the happiest I've seen you that day," says Marie.

He nods. "I can count on one hand days like that," he says.

"Well, let's keep counting," she says.

CHAPTER 6

FOOLS FALL
NOVEMBER

IN AN OLD HATBOX she keeps the promissory title for the land that Lawrence signed, his handwriting she would know anywhere, their marriage license and certificate, the pamphlets on Alaska statehood, old letters—the one from Carver Calhoun who had tried to be a father, past and recent letters from Sheila because neither has a telephone, the latest with the news she is pushing back her visit, the tracing Marie made as a child of her mother's birth certificate that Rosalie said was issued when she was adopted into the Snider family and somewhere her real one was with whoever bore her, and these she stole from Valera before she left, the scrap of fabric pinned on Rosalie's coat when she arrived in Houston on the train, her own birth certificate, a few photographs, her high school diploma, and the rest are ribbons and cards and ticket stubs from the Lion's Club Carnival and the Hi-Y Drive-in, where she went with Bobby, who was in Sheila's year. He was sweet on her, would let them in the back to play billiards at the pool hall where he worked, the first round of soda pop on him. And when Sheila left he kept his eye out for her, even after he started at the Dr Pepper Bottling Company. She never said goodbye to him when she moved, she told no one of her plan to never come back to Conroe.

Valera had a spell, did she ever, and all her hopes were on Marie to marry well and save her and her sons. Years before they sold off the biggest parcel to pay their gambling debts and it was that land that struck black gold, and they lost a fortune as others prospered in the oil boom. Valera schemed with one, an uncle who started coming around and said, drunk to high heaven, he could have Marie for himself, but Valera's sights were on Mr. Raymond Peyton, an old widower who made a mint owning general stores, who came to the shabby house with his tobacco-stained teeth, and at first Marie thought he took a shine to Valera, the way they laughed on the porch. But then Valera told her she needed to forget Bobby and think about settling down, and Marie said she wanted to finish high school first, and she smiled through their card games and refilled their glasses of lemonade. In Sheila's wanting her to visit Anchorage she saw her chance, and questioned whether she should go so as not to sound eager, and Valera nodded as Raymond warned of the dangers and what could she want in the land of igloos and Eskimos, though he had never been there. She wanted to say Sheila was well enough but she held her tongue, and packed enough for two weeks and no more so there were things to come back to though she knew she would not be returning.

Rosalie had been invited to the graduation, and though Marie secretly hoped she would come, she chose to believe she did not want her mother there, and then a card with money arrived in the mail. After the ceremony in a cap and gown, she flew on a plane, and then a smaller one, having never flown before, her blouse soaked in sweat under her cardigan, snow and mountains at a height beyond her understanding, but her own life began on that flight. She would decide who she needed in order to survive, to stay, and then she met Lawrence, and is now having a child.

But she wonders about Bobby now, who told her his feelings, his dreams, what he wanted for himself. In the silences of her life here, even as Lawrence spends more of his day at the bus, she has time to remember and regret. Bobby's light hair and good-natured smile, and she never had to bother about him, he was plain as a sun-dripped day. And would never have slept away from her on the floor. And who would listen, would hear and not just nod, when she says she misses Sheila. She is sure a letter is waiting from her at the post office. And today they are headed there, she asked Lawrence. She had told Sheila most everything all her life, but her correspondence was becoming more and more about the weather, the cold. She could not bring herself to reveal the trouble with Lawrence, not in a letter, as if the words could burn through paper.

—+—

MARSH IS FROZEN, A gamble, and the airplane tires on the army ambulance should hold in a deep slog of slush and ice and mud. Marie draws a line in the fog of the glass as Lawrence drives.

"Can't see nothing," he says. Rig slows and he unrolls the window on his side and the front lurches and he punches the gas. "I'm not sinking us," he says. "Take the wheel." He cranes his head out of the window to see their route. "Keep straight," he says. "Faster. There's a dip ahead."

He hears her foot tap for the pedal. "That's all I can do," she says.

"Turn right," he says. "More," he shouts. "A log."

She cranks the wheel and the army rig rattles and he flails and holds on.

"You trying to toss me?" His eyes are bright.

"You said more. More is what you got."

She drives blind, the windshield covered in frost. Lawrence slides out on the sill to sit on the spare tire tied to the door and anchors his boots underneath her leg. He bangs on the metal top. "Faster." And she punches the gas. "Left," he shouts. "Now straight for a while. I'll tell you when. Give it some more." He releases his grip, crosses his hands over his chest, and leans back. She holds the wheel—one wrong move and he could tumble out into the snow, if she willed it to happen. He is smiling, his hair wild in the wind, his arms reaching out, palms facing the sky, floating, the air moving and still, a patch of smooth ground underneath as they race across.

"Slow down," he says. "We're almost there."

She brakes. Their tracks trace the path, two lines of every turn and waver. He takes over the wheel. *Trusted her with my life*, he thinks. *Now, that's something.* The speed and the rush, the holding in the air with the parachute, the silence lifting before the burden of the pack weighing down, before the fear of falling, of landing, of the mission. That is what he missed, though he would never have to jump from the sky again.

And what has stayed is the shaky feeling on the ground. Every piece of him scattered in the air. But he will not speak of this, and has written his father announcing that there will be a baby. The letter is short, to the point— Marie is with child. And strange to think that a child is with them, each day.

—+—

AT THE KNIK BAR Marie spots their truck, which Lawrence left when the weather turned. A float plane appears over the trees and lands on the road, and parks in the empty corner of the lot.

"Would like to have one of those someday," says Lawrence.

"I'd fly you around," says Marie.

"You just did," he says.

Her mouth wrinkles into an almost smile.

The bar is a narrow house with a wide, blank face, eight trucks wide, and stark gray-white paint. That cheap paint she recognizes, buckets at salvage and army surplus. She has not been inside and there is a small bar with stools, and a few tables. Three men turn to see who has come in and fix their eyes on her. No curtains on the windows, no deer or moose heads on the wall, and, glowing under the dim lights, a jukebox.

Lawrence nods at the men and says, "Jones around?"

No one answers him.

"You want a seat, darling?" says one in a red flannel shirt. He offers the empty barstool beside him.

Marie takes off her woolen cap and smooths her hair and leaves her parka on to hide her belly. A big, stocky bald man comes through the back door near the bar, singing along to the music. "Lawrence," he says, "you need your keys? And this your little woman? Marie is what he calls you?" He reaches out his hand. "How'd you end up here?"

"There's a story," says Marie. His large hand mitts her own.

"Every homesteader has one. And if we ever become a state I reckon there'll be more of you," Jones says.

"I wouldn't mind one bit," says the man next to her.

"There will be more of everything," says another. "More jobs, roads. Be another gold rush, some say. And maybe Eisenhower will listen now that he has four more years."

"Would've voted for him if I could," says the man.

She had forgotten there was an election, Valera had talked of Eisenhower being born in Texas, so she had to vote for him that first time in 1952, and then his heart attack a few years later, and Marie would have heard more if she had stayed in Texas—her old life.

"So this here's Rex, Wayne, Martin," says Jones. A man with white-blond hair comes from another room. "And that's Pete," Jones says. "Has to write his messages to his sweetheart in private. Though they'll be read over the radio in Anchorage."

"Have to make sure she stays my sweetheart," says Pete, and he winks at Marie. Her face smiles in reply, a big naked grin, and Lawrence catches her and narrows his eyes.

"Martin takes messages once a week up to that Nike site and they relay them," says Jones. "You're just in time."

"Any way to get a message farther? Down to Minnesota?" says Lawrence. "Fort Rich sent a letter for me once."

Martin nods. "Only in emergencies. If you know a guy. And I know a guy at the site, says that his only job is minding those missiles just in case the commies get out of line. They'll let me take a letter bound for the States every once in a while, so it won't take ages and ages."

"Good to know," says Lawrence. "I'll take those keys." He turns to Marie. "I'll warm up the engine and come get you."

When he leaves, Jones turns to Marie. "That his way, or did something bite his ass?"

"Besides you?" says Rex.

"That man of yours don't how lucky he is," says Pete.

"I can have my pick, is that what they say?" says Marie.

Jones slaps the bar. "Let the lady sit down," he says.

"Let the lady have a drink," says Pete. He beckons to his barstool and stands near.

"We got beer or beer," says Jones.

"I think I know what I'm having," says Marie. Though she does not have the taste for beer these days, bitter as backwater.

Jones pours. "I always say, you stay out here long enough and you'll start dreaming about eggs, soap, and women."

"I once dreamt of all three," says Wayne, the oldest of the bunch, and they laugh.

"Let's drink to you," says Pete, and he clinks Marie's glass. She nips her smile.

Beer is dark and smooth. She gulps a long swig, and another.

"You like that?" says Jones. "Made it myself."

"With a secret ingredient," Rex says.

Pete leans in to her ear. "Birch syrup," he whispers.

"Hey, don't ruin my fun," says Jones.

"The Soviets already ruined it," says Wayne.

And the jukebox switches to a new song, fast and catchy. "I know what will warm up this Cold War," says Pete. He grabs Marie and sweeps her into his arms. He smells of smoke and hard work. "You know how to two-step?" and she says she's from Texas and he leads her around the room, a small circle, and a kid too young to know anything sings, "Why do fools fall in love?" Song breaks for a wailing horn and Pete spins her around and around, pushes her away and brings her in close. "Now we're swinging," he says. In spite of the parka to hide the baby, the big boots on her feet, she is as light as air, warm and tipsy from the beer. Kid comes back into the song, crooning, and Pete clutches her hand to his chest. A man is touching her, a man not her husband, and this is a thrill, and she steps to the music without a thought or count or care. Spinning again, and each turn is a breath to catch and the song ends with a blast on the horn and she is still laughing. A slow one starts and Pete sways with her, his arm tight around her waist.

"That's enough," says Lawrence.

She closes her eyes.

"Just one more," says Pete. "Haven't had a proper dance partner in a while. My gal won't move out here."

"We're leaving," says Lawrence.

She knows the leaving he means—the first punch, the last word—between men.

"Let them dance," Jones says. "Don't be a killjoy."

—+—

LAWRENCE LEANS AGAINST THE wall and crosses his arms. *Killjoy*—what his father calls him. But that's his wife. What kind of man do they take him for? He waits for them to sway near. Taps Pete on the shoulder. "Can I cut in?" he says.

"She's all yours," says Pete. "Thank you, darling," he says to Marie.

Lawrence wipes his palms on the front of his shirt. Her arms are rigid and at her sides, her chin up—*I dare you*. He places a hand on her shoulder and she steps back.

"What'd you do?" yells Rex over the music. He laughs.

"Give him a chance," shouts Martin.

"Give her a spin," says Pete.

Lawrence shoves his hands into his pockets—keys and *I'll leave you here* on the tip of his tongue. Before he can speak, her mouth is on his, pressing hard, and he braces against her, *not here,* and then gives in, and the jukebox sings, "So why don't you pretend?" and the men at the bar cheer and drum the counter.

Lawrence leads her by the hand to leave so he is sure she will follow, his face red as a fool's. The truck idles and she swipes the heater switch and a blast of hot air fills the cab.

"Wait," says Lawrence. He turns the heater down.

Marie slides the heat up. "This way's faster," she says.

He could argue and force his way, and the want to do so burns his throat.

"I'm starving," says Marie. She searches her pockets. "Forgot to bring pilot bread."

"Glove box," says Lawrence. "For emergencies."

"Thank the Lord," she says.

He wraps his fingers tight around the steering wheel. The heat in the cab is stifling, but he is cold.

"Feel my hands," says Marie. She leans over and covers his hands with hers, and they are warm. "You're ice," she says. "You sure you're alive?"

"I'm sure," he says.

He drives along the Knik Arm, and crosses the Matanuska, and the Knik River, the waters low, stranded in snow and mud.

She taps the window. Sighs. "Will we ever—" she says. "You know?"

"Don't," he says. He had not told his father about the lack, the sweating through his shirts at night, he could not wrestle the words out of his head.

"Sorry," she says, and rubs the swell of her belly.

At the post office Marie has a package from Sheila with a letter and three books. Sly was ill, she says, but he is on the mend. Nothing a soup with boiled bones won't cure. So they will come a different time, but Sheila does not say when. Lawrence has a letter from Joseph and then holds up the envelope he has stamped. "My father will be pleased to hear about the baby."

"Will Lois?" says Marie, before she can stop herself.

"Nothing else to be," says Lawrence.

Marie nods.

Family in mind, and his father's letter to him, and he says, "I know what we need."

"And what is that?" she says.

"Been cooped up too long on our own," he says. "How about we head into Anchorage so you can visit your sister?" And the light in her eyes tells him he is right.

———+———

SHEILA IS HOME. SHE hugs Marie and places her hands under her chin, and has a knowing flash in her soft brown eyes. "What is the matter?" she says, when Lawrence heads out the door to stop by the Moose Lodge and the general store. She pours them both coffee and the steam hovers.

"Why didn't you come to see us?" says Marie. She has tears in her eyes.

"You need to learn to be on your own," said Sheila, a hardness in her face. Her hands are clasped around the mug.

"You visited before," says Marie.

They both sit down.

"I didn't want to see you," says Sheila. She stares out the frosted trailer window.

"Because I'm having a baby?" says Marie.

"Because I wanted to be happy for you." Sheila leans over and touches Marie's arm. "And I am." She retrieves her knitting needles and holds them up. "Started a baby blanket."

Marie leans over to touch the yarn of purples and blues and greens. "Will be beautiful," she says.

"How you been feeling?" says Sheila. She leans toward Marie with concern. "How's married life?"

Marie shakes her head. And she cannot help herself, she tells her sister all, he doesn't talk, the silence and no radio the whole way out there, he doesn't let her, he doesn't—

"If he's not talking, he should be doing. And anyone can see he's not much for conversation."

"I thought he was shy, but only at first," says Marie.

"He is first a man," says Sheila. She laughs.

"I needed you," says Marie.

Sheila sinks in her chair. "I'm here," she says. "I'm always here."

———

HE READS JOSEPH'S LETTER twice more. *Takes time. You don't talk much and she's willing to live out in the woods with you, in a bus for all's sake.* How his father always knew what to say.

He does not want to head back to the trailer yet and stops by his old post office in Spenard, where he still has a P.O. Box from when he first moved and lived outside Anchorage, a forgotten detail in the rush to move out to the homestead. He stands in line and means to close the account, but then decides to keep it, for no reason he can bring to mind. Then he finds Bernie at the Moose Lodge and asks him to mail notice of work when he can. And he drives to Fort Rich, to see what they have at army surplus. The gear, the best for our boys, as they say. Lawrence spots a pair of thick white bunny boots, as they were called in Korea, though he preferred to call them barrier boots, didn't want to think of himself as helpless, as easily shot as a rabbit, fur as soft as snow covered in blood. He and his brothers hunted cottontails, pelts tallied and strung up at the end of winter, and he would shoot but left them to the dressing and butchering. And after the war and coming home, he could not bring himself to shoot for some years. But those ugly boots, rubber with wool inside, were the darn warmest things he ever wore on his feet. He had only brought home a rucksack, and back in the cold of Minnesota he had thought of these boots. He tries them on, a slim chance they will fit his smaller size, and they are not too big. He can double his socks. So he will buy them.

The man at the counter says, "Were you in Korea?"

Lawrence shakes his head no.

"Well, if you were, you would swear by these," says the man.

"Heard as much," says Lawrence, and he pays.

He suspects the man was in the war and does not want to have that understanding, that nod. That part of his life is in the past, and he needs no ties. Marie had pried few details out of him on the road in all those miles, a paratrooper for the money, the hardship discharge, and that was more than he wanted to share.

—+—

BY THE TIME LAWRENCE returns, Sly has come home and suggests they go to the Lucky Wishbone for supper. He convinces them to stay the night if they need. They have been to the restaurant before, but not Lawrence.

"How could you not have gone?" says Sheila.

"Saving up money," says Lawrence.

They squeeze into Sly's truck and drive downtown, Sly singing too loudly along with the radio on purpose. Sheila laughs at him. Lawrence shakes his head and Marie sings along, too, glad for the company. She had been a few times with Sheila, where they walked and looked in at the shops, had a drink at Rosetta's Bar if Sly met them.

They pass the signs for B&B Liquor and the Fourth Avenue Theatre, before turning onto Fifth street and parking. The smell of fried chicken hits them a block away. Inside, they are seated at a booth, and one of the waiters from behind the counter in a grease-splattered white apron and a paper hat comes to take their order. "We'll have four chicken dinners and four blueberry milkshakes," Sly says. "We're celebrating."

"We are?" says Sheila.

"Got a raise at the shop today," he says.

Sheila leans into him with her shoulder. "Sly, what a guy," she says.

When the waiter leaves, he fishes cash out of his wallet and says, "And I got a little bonus for fixing this one truck even the owner couldn't figure out. So this one's on me."

"I can't let you," says Lawrence, embarrassed.

"You can," says Sly. "Today I'm a rich man."

They eat themselves sick, and Lawrence finishes what Sheila and Marie have left over and the owner, Peggy, comes by to say hello. Sly introduces her to Lawrence and when Peggy sees the stack of bones in front of him, she says, "Looks like someone is still hungry." There is no hiding his skinny build. And Lawrence says he isn't but Sly orders him more. Marie is worried there will be a scene and stares down at the melt of her milkshake. Sheila tries to distract them all by asking Lawrence what he has been up to out at the homestead.

"Same as always," is his short answer.

But when the waiter returns, Lawrence eats what is served, every morsel.

"Told you," says Sly.

And Lawrence dabs his mouth with a napkin and finally admits, "I could have another."

Sly looks around the diner, about to wave down the same waiter, when Lawrence says, "But I won't."

Back at the trailer, the men sit outside to smoke cigars and Sheila says, "Here, you can have this," and hands her a white silky nightgown, cut low at the top. "I think it will help with your problem."

"I have another I wear," says Marie.

"No, this is the one," says Sheila. "Trust me."

Marie hides the nightgown in her bag.

"And I hate to ask, are you feeding that poor man enough?"

"Of course." She thinks for a moment. "But I could make more."

"Make more to get more," says Sheila.

Marie groans and pats her belly. "So full."

"Whiskey will take care of that," says Sheila, and hands her the bottle the men left on the table.

They each lie on a bench seat and drowsiness takes over until the men come in. Sly places all the cushions on the floor for a makeshift bed and heads to the end of the trailer with Sheila. They close the door to their room. Marie takes one side and leaves the other for Lawrence, if he chooses, and he lies down, and then Sheila bursts out laughing, tells Sly to stop, to be quiet, and there is whispering. Lawrence pulls on the blanket and Marie turns to face his back and shoulders, the smell of cigar smoke, an old fire.

CHAPTER 7

BITE THE DAY

DECEMBER

A NIGHT OF SNOW falling, spruce branches heavy with powder. Sunup at ten and breakfast and dishes washed and dried, and Marie, though rested through, yawns for bed as the clock ticks past eleven. Buckets of snow boil down as she reads on the couch, another dime novel from the stack Sheila gave her, and the ending is the same as the one before, and Marie tosses the book into the kindling box. Back in Conroe, they had read through the ones about Buffalo Bill and Calamity Jane and rangers and cowboys and Sheila still bought them by the box at thrift, the one expense Valera allowed. The latest were tales about women and how their marriages turned out to be mistakes, the priest a swindler in disguise, or the groom already married to someone else. Sheila thought they were amusing because who were these men who would go to all this trouble—certainly not Sly.

Christmas Eve supper is canned green beans and canned corn and mashed potatoes and flour gravy and corn cakes. Last slog into town she and Lawrence had stocked up on supplies for the winter, more cans than what she imagines ten people could eat in a few months. No hash today. Every smell is too strong, coffee and sweat and dirt, and a hint of smoke when the wind changes. Lawrence fells trees when the weather allows, there's no such thing as fair weather, only fair warning, he says. Short of a blizzard or snow too deep for walking, cuts down or chops firewood and kindling and has a fire stoked and flamed to warm his hands and heat up the coffee from the thermos Marie fills in the morning.

She should peel the potatoes, get a move on, bite the day back. She says this out loud looking down at her belly, she talks to the baby now. When did this happen? She could not remember when it started, could not point to the day. Sheila is bringing a ham and molasses cookies tomorrow. When she told Sheila that she and Lawrence agreed not to waste money on presents, Sheila said this would not stop her from knitting.

One spruce tree rains powder—a black bird's head pokes out of a branch. Marie wipes the window with her sleeve. Bird bobs his head and pecks at the spruce needles. A roasting bird for the taking and she has practiced her pistol shot on empty tin cans. Bus windows, if the freezing metal latches open, will make a ruckus and scare off this fat little bird for her gravy. Marie opens the side door and waits on the step in a gust of cold air. She cocks the pistol and the bird moves in, taking shelter underneath an overhanging branch, and snow shakes loose. In her socks she walks the shoveled path and steps closer to the tree, the pistol in her coat pocket. Her breath is white and steaming and her eyes tear up in the sharp, bright sunlight. Her feet slip on a small patch of ice. Damn bird could be the end of her. She aims again for the head, too far, and the bird picks at the needles on the branch it is standing on. How close can she sneak before the bird scares? She shuffles a few feet more and steadies the pistol on her forearm, and not a bird in sight. She will wait. She will be right and ready when he shows himself again.

Bottom of her socks are wet and heavy and losing track. A few more steps on the hardpack and she will stop and scope out one good shot, but she slides, and wobbles, and she throws herself backward to avoid landing belly-and-baby-first, her tailbone, and then her shoulders. The pistol is still in her hand, and did not fire, and she places the gun on top of her stomach. She smooths the back of her skull to make sure she has not cracked her head open. Fine, fine, and the throb of pain is not in her head but everywhere, warm and aching. A rustle in the spruce tree, and she sits up, one arm propped behind her, cradles the pistol in the other. Bird is eating in full view, with nothing to fear, and glossy black feathers with small white markings gleaming in the sun. She raises the pistol, shaking, her eye finds the sight, and she counts, tenses her grip, and fires. Bird falls out of the tree, and she cannot believe her luck. She throws back her head and laughs. "Would you look at that?" she says to the growing baby, and pats her stomach. She crawls toward her kill. Bird is a beauty, a red arch for a brow, white lid that folds up over the eye, feathers soft and sleek, a fan at the tail, and white tips pattern the chest. She holds him up by the feet. "Hope you're good eating," she says.

Engine hum turns her head, and Sly's truck drives toward her, a day early.

Sly opens his door. "Nice shot."

"Weather was turning, so his boss closed the shop and we got a move on," says Sheila.

Here she is, standing there with a dead bird in one hand, a pistol in the other, no boots on her feet, wet snow on the knees of her pants, with her hair a flying mess, with child, and wild as they come.

"You get a spruce hen?" says Sheila.

"Looks to be that way," says Marie.

"Neighbor just showed me a better way to skin those bastards," says Sly. "Feathers off in one swoop."

"Could use a hand," says Marie, after he tells her how.

"Have to warm mine," says Sly. "You kill it, you clean it."

"Coffee on the stove," says Marie.

"Bless you, darling," says Sly.

"And throw me my darned boots," says Marie.

"And a knife," Sheila yells.

Marie places the hen on the ground and steps on the wings, close to the body, and leans over her belly and grabs the feet and pulls straight up and she feels a rip and the feet and legs and feathers and skin around the body peel off the meat in one piece, a shell. Head dangles and tears off at the neck. She reaches into the chest and drags out the bloody guts, stomach and entrails, and there—the dark heart in the shape of a bullet.

"Save that," says Sheila, "for roasting."

Marie rolls the warm, raw heart in her palm and blood seeps out in a small gush with one last pulse, and she swallows it whole.

"You're not having your way with the rest of this bird," says Sheila. She saws at the wings and twists the shoulder joints to loosen their grip on the smooth, pink meat around the breastbone. "We're cooking this proper," she says. They make a fire outside and Sheila shoves a stick through and holds the meat over the flames.

"You think you can last out here all winter?" says Sheila. "You look a fright."

"Fixing to wash today," says Marie. "You were coming tomorrow."

Lawrence walks up, surprised, and gives a small wave. "Heard a shot," he says. "And what you got cooking?"

"Look at what Marie killed," says Sheila. She pokes the roasting meat. Then gives Marie a turn with the stick. "Sly," she shouts after a while, "come on out here."

Sheila carves the hen and gives Marie a portion, then Lawrence. Mud and meat is the taste.

"Better than squirrel," says Sheila. "I'll say that."

"God, anything is," says Marie.

Sly appears finally and greets Lawrence with a handshake and a Merry Christmas.

"Sly, I know you heard me," says Sheila. "Bring out what we brought from the truck."

"A gift?" says Marie. "But we said."

"Was old," Sheila says. "Close your eyes and wait."

Music sounds from an old windup Victrola playing a big band record.

"Like the one at Valera's," Marie says. She laughs and embraces her sister.

Sly dances a little jig and Lawrence once-overs the Victrola sitting on a stump. "Look at them," says Sheila. "Our men." This is what they have always wanted—the keeping, the staying. Tell that to the winter sun, lying low and tilting toward night in the middle of the afternoon, the light a burning on the snow.

After Christmas Eve dinner and playing cards, Lawrence sleeps on the floor, as do Sheila and Sly. Marie has the couch, and is lying on her side, her belly in the way, she can no longer rest on her back in comfort. She listens to their breathing, the snores, the crackling of wood in the stove.

But she can be still not a second more and she rises and walks to the out-house. The pale sun begins the morning.

When she opens the door, Sheila is waiting for her turn and asks her to stay until she is done.

"So tell me," says Sheila. "Did the nightgown work like a charm?"

"I've been tired," says Marie. "All those feelings, just gone. Don't know why I was the way I was."

"Those feelings will come back. And you'll be ready," says Sheila.

Marie rubs her stomach, and then places her hands at the ache in her back. "I have other things to be ready for."

Back at the bus, everyone is awake and Marie makes breakfast. Then they open the presents Sheila wrapped, a crocheted afghan blanket for the couch and mittens. Sly has bundles of wool yarn and new needles for Marie, and a pot roast pan. For Lawrence, Sheila has a pair of blue coveralls that she embroidered with his name. Coffee and flapjacks and fried eggs, Sly had brought a few dozen, and then they pile into the army ambulance. Lawrence drives too fast, and three deer run across their path, hurried and leaping in the blinding sun, and he chases them in the rig, their hooves and white tails in sight, Sheila telling him to leave them alone, until they reach the trees and he slams on the brakes, and they fall forward, laughing.

They walk the rest of the way to the lake, Marie and Sheila trailing the men. The air thin and nipping, the sky opening for the sun. The white tip of Pioneer Peak visible above a ring of clouds. "My favorite mountain," Marie tells Sheila. "Makes me feel small, but then all the more reason to earn the right to stand here."

"You have," says Sheila.

"Not yet," says Marie.

The lake is frozen and patched with new snowfall. Sly walks along the edge, sliding in his boots. Lawrence shakes his head.

Sheila takes Marie's arm. "Remember that time we went skating in Houston?" A school trip, and Sheila had held her hand as they glided across the ice. One of the few good memories after being sent away to Houston. Sheila was always with her, until she moved to Anchorage. But they are both here now, finding their footing. At the edge of the lake

Lawrence stands apart, hands in his pockets, and she waves at him. And then Sly picks up a large stump, raises it above him, and they are telling him not to, but he throws, a heave with both hands, and the sound is a crack and a skip, past and beyond them, branching out across the surface.

The stump is a dark ruin on the snowy ice, a mistake. Sly laughs as Lawrence marches out onto what is shattered, without care of the danger, and throws the stump back onto the bank. Marie knows the offense: this is their lake, their land, theirs to alter as they see fit.

The men are outside, sharing a flask at Sheila's prodding, a fire for heating water, and Marie has a pot on the stove in the bus. She carves a small piece of ham, which is for supper. Sheila says, "Make sure to boil that bone tomorrow for a broth and save the drippings," already giving instructions for when she leaves. Salt and grease agree with Marie, and the baby, and the taste brings tears to her eyes.

Lawrence brings in the hot water and fills the metal tub and leaves. Marie pours the pot and then steps in. "Forgot the soap," she says to Sheila, who brings over the bar wrapped in a washing cloth.

"You always send Lawrence out when you bathe?" says Sheila.

"Of course," says Marie.

"Maybe you don't," says Sheila, and she laughs. "Could be a fix."

"Quiet," says Marie. "So is Sly always causing trouble?"

"He doesn't mean to," Sheila says. She tsks. "Look at your hair."

"I've been so tired," says Marie. "And then I'll have a good day. Catch up on chores. Just haven't had one lately."

"Here," says Sheila. "Let me." She brings a stool over and sits behind Marie. She rubs soap into her hair and scrubs her scalp with her fingertips. "Your hair is slick," says Sheila.

"But look at me," says Marie. "Tell me, how am I different?" The only mirrors are the ones on the side of the bus.

"You're a little softer in your face," says Sheila. "And I can see your belly."

"That all?"

"You're more sure and less sure," says Sheila. "Even in your letters."

"I know you've prayed for a baby," says Marie. "And I didn't."

s a little something by carrying this child. Left of the line,
a small rise, a kick, the first she has felt, and she places her
spot. *Are you there?* she whispers, and waits. Baby has been,
ng and gaining, but she has worries, and questions. Sheila
much. And there are moments when she wishes for Rosalie,
ows as a mother, the changes that are coming. Another kick,
stomach, and she says, *Lawrence, the baby, come quick,* and
feet and says, "Already?"

s, "The baby's kicking. Come here," and he does, and she
s and pulls off his gloves, and places his rough, callused
ft skin of her belly.

———

WARMER than he remembers, the heat of a new life, of
e soil holds the burn of the sun around a seedling. A kick
he lifts his hand, a shock.
ready to come out and see us," he says.
she says. "Don't say such a thing," but her eyes are smil-
casting over the gold and brown, the brightness of tears.
pples—the force of a little foot.
p a storm," he says. "Does it hurt?"
she says. "Though I feel it. No mistake."
, feeling either way?" he says.
w when the time comes," she says.
n the farm called Sonny," he says, and kneels down. "First-
the sound of that."
es we'll know," she says.
iver, and his fingertips trace the spot. She places both her
. He presses his ear to her side. "Sonny?" he says. "Sonny,
e? This is your pa."

———

HER FINGERS through his hair and he does not flinch
his is how they could be, in the waiting in the last months.

Sheila's hands stop. "That's life," she says. "Praying doesn't mean getting."

Marie reaches behind her and clasps Sheila's hands in hers. She hears Sheila sigh.

"How about that music?" says Sheila. "And you can rinse."

She winds the Victrola and then sits, lights a cigarette. Taps the ashes into an empty tin can. She hands the smoke to Marie, and their old times waft in the air, and things are as they should be.

CHAPTER 8

WINTER CIRCLE

JANUARY 1957

BLIZZARD WIND A HOWL and rack for days, and the blessed quiet when a storm lies down. Lawrence steps out in the dark, and the sharp sound of the shovel begins, can't it wait, they're not being buried alive, and she opens her eyes to the lazy blue of moonlight. When he has circled the bus, he rests, and she slinks down on the couch, but no need, as his steps hurry past the door, and how is he running laps in those heavy white boots in this cold? Then his pace slows and he stands, his back to her, and the low and the marsh and the trees with their backs to him, and he waves his arms, here, over here, trying to wake the winter moon.

———

THIS AIN'T NOTHING HE can't handle, ain't nothing to fuss around, and if he can work his hands, tire himself out, then this, too, shall pass. Have a reason to be soaked in sweat and shaking. Not the crawl of a swarm of mayflies when he knows he is safe, on the floor of a bus on land covered in the snow. A choking in his chest, and the faster, faster beating of his heart—no use to him if he is no use. Grip of the shovel, the weight of snow on the blade, the break of the path, the whistle of cold air

through his teeth, the wh
he is alive.

WHEN TO BEGIN THE
the quilt and covers and
around her body, and wa
of carrying this baby and
sopping laundry, twist and
traces the dark line that cu
toward her ribs, and, as Sh
and that's what she had th
shot so high, and she knew
a boy is coming. But she c
secret to keep for herself, ar
thinking when he swings tl
around the bus in the mid

HIS ANKLES TURNED OI
boots are still on his feet. His
and warms his face and he k
life to, and coffee is the cure,
and coffee just doesn't make i
hot steaming cup to appear t
his head, and he is still in his
and she is sleeping for two, sh
she will not ask him why he i

A FLUTTER, AND SHE slid
over the swell. Could have s

think she know
left of her navel
hands over the
all along, growi
only knows so
for what she kn
the ripple in he
he springs to hi
    And she say
grabs his hand
hands on the s

HER SKIN IS
waiting, how t
to his palm an
    "This one's
    "Too early,
ing, the green
Her stomach
    "Kicking u
    "Not yet,"
    "Boy or gir
    "We'll kno
    "First boy
born son. Lik
    "Time con
    Another q
hands over his
can you hear

SHE SWEEP
or pull away.

Sheila's hands stop. "That's life," she says. "Praying doesn't mean getting."

Marie reaches behind her and clasps Sheila's hands in hers. She hears Sheila sigh.

"How about that music?" says Sheila. "And you can rinse."

She winds the Victrola and then sits, lights a cigarette. Taps the ashes into an empty tin can. She hands the smoke to Marie, and their old times waft in the air, and things are as they should be.

CHAPTER 8

WINTER CIRCLE
JANUARY 1957

BLIZZARD WIND A HOWL and rack for days, and the blessed quiet when a storm lies down. Lawrence steps out in the dark, and the sharp sound of the shovel begins, can't it wait, they're not being buried alive, and she opens her eyes to the lazy blue of moonlight. When he has circled the bus, he rests, and she slinks down on the couch, but no need, as his steps hurry past the door, and how is he running laps in those heavy white boots in this cold? Then his pace slows and he stands, his back to her, and the low and the marsh and the trees with their backs to him, and he waves his arms, here, over here, trying to wake the winter moon.

—+—

THIS AIN'T NOTHING HE can't handle, ain't nothing to fuss around, and if he can work his hands, tire himself out, then this, too, shall pass. Have a reason to be soaked in sweat and shaking. Not the crawl of a swarm of mayflies when he knows he is safe, on the floor of a bus on land covered in the snow. A choking in his chest, and the faster, faster beating of his heart—no use to him if he is no use. Grip of the shovel, the weight of snow on the blade, the break of the path, the whistle of cold air through his teeth, the white mist of his breath that tells him he is awake, he is alive.

—+—

WHEN TO BEGIN THE day, and when to open her eyes and throw back the quilt and covers and let the winter air take the pocket of warmth around her body, and wake to the swollen feet and the weighted steps of carrying this baby and wishing she could wring herself out with the sopping laundry, twist and press away the too much here and there. She traces the dark line that cuts her in half, cuts through her navel and up toward her ribs, and, as Sheila said, the line stops at the navel if it is a girl and that's what she had the hoping for, and then the line appeared and shot so high, and she knew even for how wide and black the line became, a boy is coming. But she did not tell Lawrence and still hasn't, this is a secret to keep for herself, and how many secrets does he hide, where is his thinking when he swings the axe and stacks the firewood, when he runs around the bus in the middle of the night?

—+—

HIS ANKLES TURNED OUT while he slept on his back, and the white boots are still on his feet. His knees ache. Sun streams through the window and warms his face and he knows he has slept past every alarm he sets his life to, and coffee is the cure, but she is not awake yet, and he is not moving, and coffee just doesn't make itself, now, does it? What he wouldn't give for a hot steaming cup to appear to wash away this tight, punched-out feeling in his head, and he is still in his coat and gloves, and he tried not to wake her and she is sleeping for two, she says, and if she sleeps til the morning maybe she will not ask him why he is digging in circles at all hours.

—+—

A FLUTTER, AND SHE slides her shirt up over her belly. Runs her hands over the swell. Could have sworn, and no, nothing, a trick to make her think she knows a little something by carrying this child. Left of the line, left of her navel, a small rise, a kick, the first she has felt, and she places her hands over the spot. *Are you there?* she whispers, and waits. Baby has been, all along, growing and gaining, but she has worries, and questions. Sheila only knows so much. And there are moments when she wishes for Rosalie, for what she knows as a mother, the changes that are coming. Another kick, the ripple in her stomach, and she says, *Lawrence, the baby, come quick,* and he springs to his feet and says, "Already?"

And she says, "The baby's kicking. Come here," and he does, and she grabs his hands and pulls off his gloves, and places his rough, callused hands on the soft skin of her belly.

———

HER SKIN IS WARMER than he remembers, the heat of a new life, of waiting, how the soil holds the burn of the sun around a seedling. A kick to his palm and he lifts his hand, a shock.

"This one's ready to come out and see us," he says.

"Too early," she says. "Don't say such a thing," but her eyes are smiling, the green casting over the gold and brown, the brightness of tears. Her stomach ripples—the force of a little foot.

"Kicking up a storm," he says. "Does it hurt?"

"Not yet," she says. "Though I feel it. No mistake."

"Boy or girl, feeling either way?" he says.

"We'll know when the time comes," she says.

"First boy on the farm called Sonny," he says, and kneels down. "First-born son. Like the sound of that."

"Time comes we'll know," she says.

Another quiver, and his fingertips trace the spot. She places both her hands over his. He presses his ear to her side. "Sonny?" he says. "Sonny, can you hear me? This is your pa."

———

SHE SWEEPS HER FINGERS through his hair and he does not flinch or pull away. This is how they could be, in the waiting in the last months.

Could a child bring them around? Tie down what needs to be tied, the promises they break over each other in the words of the priest. *Will you honor each other? Will you accept children lovingly? Your lawfully wedded husband? Will you take him all the days of your life? Will you take him? Will he take all the days of your life? For what God has joined. For what you will.* What she knows now, would she have answered the same? There is a rattling in Lawrence, a broken piece, and is this child what has been missing.

———

THE BABY STOPS KICKING and he slips his hand out from under hers before she can ask him what happened in the night, him shoveling snow when he should be asleep, running under the moon's watch. *You'll catch your death,* she will say. But maybe that's his aim. Run hard to kill the shivering he wakes from, the sinking ground, and the seconds he counts flat on the floor, a whisper: *This is winter, Alaska, my land, my homestead, my wife, my child to be.*

———

WINDOWS ARE FOGGED AND frosted-over and lit with sun. She could ask him but she wants him to tell her, to trust her. What more can she give, these months, this baby?

"Let's take a look outside," he says.

"Coffee first," she says. "Can't move my bones."

"Guess I'm already up."

"Guess?" she says, a little snap in her voice. "Guess we're living in a bus. Guess I'm having this child."

"Guess I'm making breakfast, too," he says, in time to keep the ease in the room.

"Wait til I tell Sheila," she says. She sits up and he shakes his head, his shoulders rising with laughter, as if he might cry. And he is altered, and she wants this to last. "I'd like eggs and pancakes and bacon," she says.

"High-and-mighty," he says. "And I'd like to be filthy, stinkin' rich."

"You are filthy," she says.

"Now, wait a minute."

"I'm waiting, all right," she says. "Resting here, waiting for a cup of joe."

"Hold your horses," he says.

"Those are some dead horses," she says, a wink in her eye. And why is this not their way, every morning?

———+———

SNOW AS WHITE AS the sky is blue. Zero degrees, says the Old Cabin Still thermometer, the red a bright slash.

"Never been zero," she says.

She walks ahead and he walks over her tracks, the heavy boot prints trench through the path. *Don't ask, please, don't ask me,* and this life, living with someone who knows every coming and going. Different in the army, in bunks, with a call and mission, and no one caring a whit about you as long as you did your duty. Duty isn't it, not quite. Beholden. Not once in his life did he want to have a debt he could not repay. Yet, Marie and this child, his child, and is this his debt? She gives him a child and what can he give in return and who is to say she is owed for what he is owed? Is it belonging? *Her ways are my ways,* is what his father says after a spat with his mother, and how can that be the reckoning of them?

———+———

FEATHERS OF ICE COVER every tree branch, every drift, in a downy white.

"Frost flowers," says Lawrence. "Haven't seen them in a long while."

Dazzle of sun, so bright after the storm, catches diamonds in the snow.

"I wish you could see this," she whispers to the baby.

This miracle of a morning, as fine as can be, right here, no bother about before or after, or how she married a man so she could be on her own and have her own, and this is zero and nothing counted, nothing borrowed and nothing owed, no account to be taken from her, the balance is made and the balance is in her favor and ain't it the truth, to be told, that God favors those who help themselves?

—+—

NIGHTFALL, A CLEAR WINTER sky. Bright star edging left of the moon, Aldebaran. And north is the Big Dipper, whose handle is the tail of the bear, Ursa Major, whose face points to Capella. How long since he looked up and found the Winter Circle? As a boy he learned the stars for every season from his father.

"Wake up," he says. "I want to show you something."

She rubs her eyes. "What time is it?"

"Not late," he says.

"You shoveling again?"

"Just come," he says.

She is slow to find her boots and her parka and she grumbles as she steps outside.

"See that star by the moon?" he says. He stands behind her and reaches for her hand and points where to look, Alderbaran to Capella, to Pollux, to Procyon, to Sirius, to Rigel, each of the six.

"You've been keeping this from me all this time?" she says. She leans her back into his embrace.

"Saving, not keeping," he says.

You coming to bed? is what she will ask.

A choice hangs in the air, the floor where he has been sleeping or the couch where she sprawls and lifts her shirt over the hill of her belly.

"Show me again," she says. "The stars. Show us both."

He kneels down and traces the crown of her stomach with a fingertip. Capella to Pollux, and so on. And another loop around his map, *Look me in the eye, son. Howl at the moon and the moon howls back.*

CHAPTER 9

COLD TIL MORNING COME

FEBRUARY

BULLETHEART, DARK AND SWIMMING in her blood, a silver fever inching closer and closer to her stomach. Her hands rush to her arm, dig with her fingernails. A cry in her throat, and sweat and tears sting her eyes. Fresh scratch marks near the old scabs of the same dream, and the heat burns when she is awake.

Why isn't the baby kicking? Making a fuss and keeping her up all night? She presses her hand to her belly. Why the quiet? Why here? Why this land, and why this man? She knows why. What if a tree falls and kills him and she finds his body smashed and bloody and has this baby alone, and what then? What happens to the land and the bus and the scored trees for the cabin that hasn't been built? Don't know the first thing about building a cabin. Tree that fell almost killed her, and not one tree would dare fall on him. How the world works. But he could be shoveling at night and keel over dead as a rock. Maybe he is dead now, on the floor, because her big belly takes up the couch and she does not want anyone near her, she's an oven, he says, and soon they won't have to burn firewood, she will dry the wet clothes just standing there. Weather turned for the worse, and she waited on the wash, for a day, and then five, and then she wore everything she owned, and the last clean thing she had hidden and stashed away until her shirt slicked at the collar, and so she wore the white nightgown Sheila had given her that gathers with enough fabric to swell over her belly, and cuts low at the bust, and hikes the hem over her knees. "Ain't that the way," said Sheila. "How you wearing white'll make him want to roll in the mud?" Lawrence came in for supper and said he was starving, just same of the same, no care that she was wearing the nightgown. And she had been meaning to ask him, when should they leave to stay with Sheila and Sly in time for the baby coming, the hospital?

"The hospital?" he said. "Can't Sheila?"

"That's not how things are done. I'll be going," she said.

"What about the money?" he said.

"Is that what you're worried about?" she said. And he did not answer her and they ate in silence and she watched the darkness move past the windows.

Hunger she knows, but what this is, this bite-down-on-her-hand-and-breathe, worse than any hankering, this is a warmth under her skin and a boil in her blood. Lake is frozen, or she would swim, even in the dead of night, and drown this heat. If the noise would not wake Lawrence, she would fill the tub with snow and stay there, on a bed of slush, til the morning comes.

You awake, little one? She holds her stomach and tiptoes past Lawrence and the bus creaks under her feet. The door is the trouble, the swing and shut, but Lawrence has, this night, slipped into the hard sleep of a hard man. She listens for a rustling after the closing, and then walks into the cold air. Beyond the path is the clean fall, and this snow she presses to her mouth and holds against the back of her neck. Fire in the stove keeps the bus so warm, and she breathes in the air. Can't be gone long, wearing only this, but she has to move, and then maybe the baby will follow and kick, or flutter. No one has a baby outside of a hospital anymore, that much she knows. What was he thinking? She might never know because when she asks he will not tell, and what he does say is not enough. She rests and catches her breath. Looking back, he was this way when they met, watching her with that pain set in his jaw.

She should turn back, but above the ridge is a distant glow, as if from another, fuller moon. A soft *tick, tick, tick* crackles in her ears, the break of a radio, and she moves toward the ticking and the rise, lifts the nightgown up to her hips, and her bare legs slice through the snow. She feels nothing change with the baby, not with the cold, with the walking. She wants an answer. As she crests the top, the air thickens, a charge runs up her spine and hums at the back of her skull, and the nightgown clings, molds to her body as a sheen of skin. A green blaze is twisting and roping in the sky, a witching spell threading through the stars and coming for her. Waves of light above and below and then all around, pulsing and pressing in on her throat, for a moment she cannot breathe, and a ringing and a throb in her head, faint rush after the crush of pine needles, how bitter, how bright, to behold.

—+—

HOW LONG HAS SHE been gone? The outhouse, a walk to stretch her legs, the minutes tick by and weigh in the air. He has never worried be-fore. She could, he supposes, decide to never come back one day, and how strange that she could, with his child, their child-to-be, but she would not, this he knows in as little as he knows her. He lights the lantern, and her parka hangs on a nail near the door from when she wore it last—in December? Burning up, is what she says, hand to her stomach, when she opens a bus window and breathes in the cold, her face and hair slick with sweat.

At this hour? Dead of winter, dead of night. He sits on the couch and taps the top of the worn-out cushion. She will come through the door and laugh at his waiting up and the lantern lit with his concern. And where is she? Not work that kills, but worry, as his father says. Worry rusts the blade. He did not know how to explain, the hospital where there is blood, not wanting to be anywhere nearby when the baby is born. So he asked about the money to cover his fear. And where did that lead? But if he gives her everything she asks, she will have everything of him. He will not know the end or beginning, in the way he does not have the map for the land, the drawn lines, or stakes driven at the edges.

Marie has been gone too long. He shoves a cap on his head, buttons his coat. His wife and his child—one of his choosing and one of his making. Both god knows where. He carries the lantern and the shotgun outside, and the sky is alight with an eerie cast, and the peel of the moon is caught in the sweep.

He shadows her trail in the snow, a bend and a sharp lean toward the ridge. As he walks, the lantern dims and flickers and the air shifts. A pulse thrums in his ears, and a warmth flushes his face, creeps down his neck and back. And then waves of green light are snaking through the darkness, tangling and trembling in a fury across the sky, shining gold in the heat of each flare. A blinding, shimmering star appears on the trail, closer and brighter and closer. He shields his eyes, the line of her form, her night-gown a white flame, her hair loose, her skin glowing, her swollen breasts, the curve of her belly, the dark between her legs—she is where the light begins. A cold shiver comes over him, this wanting to touch her, and in wanting her knowing his life is already hers.

CHAPTER 10

HOWL OF THE BLIZZARD

MARCH

WEATHERHELD, THE OLD CABIN Still thermometer forecasts the day: ten below and your breath will freeze before the air leaves your mouth. In the howl of the blizzard, the ramping swirl of wind and snow, they listen to the windup Victrola and roll cigarettes and smoke with the windows closed.

Lawrence points at the cribbage board on the table near the couch.

"Cut," says Marie.

He holds up the ace of spades from the card deck, low card deals and has the first crib.

"Aren't you lucky."

Marie throws two cards to his crib pile. He lays down a four and she a king, fourteen, and he pairs her king for two points, twenty-four, and she lays down a five. She sits up straight and braces her back against the weight of her belly, which is low and heavy near her hips.

"This blizzard passes," she says, "we're going to Anchorage."

"Already?" says Lawrence.

"I'm having this baby in a hospital, that's how these things are done. And not out here or in a trailer. You think Sheila would let that happen?"

Lawrence will not look up from his cards.

"I know you're worried about the money. I don't know what we have," she says.

"I get checks from the army and had unemployment through December," he says. "And been saving for the cabin."

"We can borrow. It can't be much. Sheila would—"

"We don't borrow," says Lawrence, steel in his eyes.

Her throat catches. "You ever seen a baby born?" she says.

"On the farm we—"

"I'm not talking about animals." She throws her hand down.

"I ain't, either."

"I'm the one carrying this child," she says. "I have a say."

"You might," he says. "And that depends. But Sheila doesn't."

She stands but has nowhere to run, no escape in the blizzard. Lawrence collects his cards into a neat, sharp stack, and places them on the table. "We'll drive there after the storm," he says. He stoops to his sleeping spot on the floor, punches his pillow down, and pulls the blanket over his head.

What can she say, how could he, and the record scratches. And does he remember that night, the green ribbons in the sky, and does he remember the way he looked at her then, and every day since a little less, and the storm is a clatter of questions.

———

HE HAD PROMISED HIMSELF he would be a different man after he saw Marie on the ridge, the strange light all around them. Could feel the word *yes* in his mouth, waiting there for whenever she asked, but heard himself argue, fight, for unsound reasons, could imagine Joseph chastising him, *these are not the ways of a father and husband, you must become what is asked of you, what is required,* and what if he could not? The dark morning, the snow still falling. He knows he is late to rise, and so is she, and he makes the coffee and she stirs from the couch. They will start again, he decides. And he will try. He pours the oats into the water and waits. She says she isn't hungry, she feels sick.

"You should eat," he says. He holds out a bowl to her.

She waves him away. Then grimaces and touches her back.

"What's the matter?" says Lawrence.

"Nothing," says Marie, through her teeth. "But this is the third one in the hour."

Lawrence scrapes the last of the oatmeal from the pot.

"This can't be," says Marie. "Coming too early."

Lawrence turns. "Here?"

Marie breathes through another. "I'm not having this baby on a bus," she says. "Not now."

Lawrence pales and the handle of the pot shakes in his hand. They cannot drive in the blizzard, and he boils more water and the water cools on the stove, and he dabs her forehead with a wet rag, and the truth is, he knows to boil water but has not seen how a child is brought into the world, always in another room, or outside on the porch waiting for his mother to be herself again, or clenching his eyes shut and clutching his stomach as his father tended to a goat in the barn, her swelling bleats loud and urgent and the *Come help me, boy, come on now,* and him burying himself in the hay until the quiet and the strain were over. His father is not here. Sheila is not here. Of course Marie should be in a hospital, and he should be far away from all of this. He could have Sheila take her there and he would be waiting at the trailer. Marie, on the floor, grips a pillow with her hands, sweat on her brow and crowning her hair, and she struggles to take in air, and he says, *Breathe, breathe.*

———

THE HOURS CRAWL TOWARD darkness in the afternoon. The pain, hot and sharp, and then a dull ache, comes and comes, a tightening, and her belly is a stone. What did she know of the world? Of the pain of mothers? Sheila could not tell her. Valera, and Rosalie, spoke little of these things, only if necessary, the bleeding, and when to know you were bleeding, at least Sheila had married before her, so she could know but not really know the ways between a husband and wife, and this, to not know but every person is born, ain't that the truth. She was and Sheila was, and on and on. Even the Lord Jesus was born, and Marie laughs. Soft at first, and then in fits, tears slipping from the corners of her eyes, and then the stitch, stronger, sharper, and she turns on her side, the weight lifts, and a calm, the hours stretch as she breathes, and a rag dabs at her temples, and then the sound of cracking glass, and a rush of warm water, and she crouches on her hands and knees, the nightgown wet and pink near her ankles. She presses her forehead to her wrist and wails.

"Baby's coming," she says.

Lawrence drops the firewood he has brought in for the stove. He stands empty-handed, unable to move.

"Something's not right," she says.

"Should I look?" he says, a waver in his voice.

"Burning, God," and she cries into the floor.

He composes himself. Kneels behind her. "I'm right here," he says. He lifts the nightgown and gathers it at her waist. "I can see the head," he says.

"Help me," she says. She tenses and pushes and the head stays.

He feels around the skull and a cord is around the neck and one shoulder, the other shoulder is still under.

"Please," she says. "Please."

He bears down on the shoulder and she screams and there is a snap, a give, and he holds the infant in his hands, skin blue and purple and peeling and blistered, dark red lips and nails, blood trickling from the nose, the brown cord wrapped three times around the neck. His hands tremble as he cuts the cord with a knife.

"Let me see," she says, facedown, eyes closed to the world. He dries his mouth on his rolled sleeve, the infant still in his hands, it was a boy, but now a limp and flopping shadow cast from the light of the lantern, some dead, fallen thing. He wretches, choking vomit on his hands, and he walks on his knees to the pot of water and wrings a rag to clean the infant and then swaddles him in a towel. "Marie," he says, "wake up." She whimpers, and a gush of blood soaks the floor and the afterbirth comes, a flat snarl of dark veins, with the root of the cord. She is still breathing but her eyes are shut to him, and what has happened? He places the infant near her. Opens the door of the bus, the day is just starting to dawn, and the snow of the blizzard has settled, and he shovels a path to the army rig, and clears one around the airplane tires, Sheila will know what to do, if he can drive them to Anchorage she will know, and he carries Marie to the rig and she sprawls across the seat and the infant he wraps in a blanket, and he prays the tires will last and he prays Marie will survive and he prays for the boy, he prays to be forgiven, in the name of the Father and the Son.

CHAPTER 11

SWING HIGH, SWING TRUE

APRIL

WHAT A TERRIBLE THING it is to be born, the scream and mess. On the long drive to Anchorage, Lawrence searched the small face for a cry, as if shaken and come back to life, and he thought if he reached down, he might find a reason to say the hours that had passed were only a beginning—a story he could tell, and then the boy lived. But it was not to be. And now what did he call himself, a father to a child who never took in a gasp of this world? Who died strangled and choked and drowned? No, he could not.

But the boy was his. And Marie was his, and now she is with Sheila and Sly. He stopped by the trailer but she did not want to see him—Sheila in the kitchen and Marie in bed. *Marie eats what she can stomach, which is little,* Sheila said, *and the ashes are buried in the snow but you will have a proper burial at the homestead, good of you to give her time, work and make yourself useful out there, and she will come back to us.* He fells trees, chops wood, axes wood into kindling, tool in hand and devil be damned, he will quiet his mind.

Saw the spruce and push and pull and the wood cracks and god help him, forgive him, the falling timber, how quick to touch the dirt, and his hands tangled in her hair, her belly with child, his child, and he is losing his hold, the ache in his bones in his teeth, weak at the knees and he is never weak, damn the fool once, goddamn the fool twice, but it was not a mistake, he does not make mistakes, and he cannot undo what is already done. How many times had he felled trees without an accident, not by axe or saw or chain? Ain't no luck. Just hard work. And a man makes his luck, good or bad. Trick was to think, to choose. And what of dying? The others in the war, and he came home early. And what of a child dying? Was this his punishment? Should be more careful. Will be more careful.

Axe in hand, axe over his head, swing down and wait for the break, throb of the edge on the stump, the hot callus burn under the leather gloves, the crack and the new log and the new start, bark facing in, and swing high, swing true, the splintering, by his own hands, by his aim, and he stumbles, weak at the knees, and slumps to the muddy snow. His eyes on the ground. Then the fluttering under his skin, he is having one of his fits, another bootshaker, and he lies on his back, spreads his arms, and his head weighs down, his shoulders, body to the earth so what sense is leaving him will return. His teeth chatter, his chest heaves, ragged and slow. What of Marie, what of them? A gray, flat sky above, a thick and heavy slab, and the light is dull but sharp, and wincing. Two birds appear, high and aloft, and as they descend, their wings span and lengthen, the white crowns become visible, and the eagles glide, slow and loose and free. One breaks and flaps its wings and chases, and they swoop toward each other, talons out for the kill, and then they are caught and clawed together, talon to talon, and flip over in the air, falling backward, wings overthrown by wings, pitching handle over blade, and they twirl into a spiral, a headfirst dive, beaks bowed and still, wingtips flared and arched, and around and around they spin, one talon hooked between them, the pull and weight of a tightening circle, two black flames burning the air.

He sits up to follow their flight, down, and down, and they should let go, so close to a crash, and he holds his breath as they disappear below his range, and he waits, and then, no longer bound, the two eagles fly away together, westward shadows crossing the horizon. And so he will tell his father, send a letter and ask him to come. They will bring Marie home.

CHAPTER 12

FIT TO BE TIED

MAY

EVERYTHING IS PASTE IN her mouth, but she eats, or Sheila sighs, a hand to her forehead, *How you feeling, running a fever?* And they have already given her the bedroom and so they sleep under a table and she cannot abide, cannot abide that man, this dead and buried baby, living in this trailer a burden. Sheila with the boy, leaning down, and, *So sorry, honey,* and his face with black lips, and, *Do you want to hold him?* And in the crook of her arms she runs a fingertip across his mouth and the milk comes, and there he stays, bundled in an old, soft bedsheet, a hat Sheila knitted, and the days pass in whispers, and she sleeps and the baby sleeps and Sheila says *this can't go on,* but if she sleeps, the baby sleeps, and one morning, the baby is gone, and *had been,* Sheila says, she had taken them both to the hospital to register the death. Sheila steers her elbow, *Come on, now, the neighbors will wonder, you walking around in a nightgown,* and the sky is too bright, and she follows Sheila back to the trailer and the bed is warm and the room is dark, and the ground is frozen so the burial would have had to wait and there is a metal can with ashes deep in the snow for now, until the right time, there has been enough death in this house. Marie curls her fingernails into the pillow and waits for the calm of night and the marker is in the yard, a white wooden cross, and the snow is wet and cold under her fingers and she digs and a flash of light and Sheila says, *In god's name what are you doing?* And the slap across her cheek, *Leave him be,* and Sheila crying, *Stop this, you hear me?* Sheila washes her hands in the sink scrubbing harsh but she keeps quiet and the milk runs and Sheila curls up in the bed beside her and strokes her hair, *We're through the thick, don't you worry,* and she whispers as she falls asleep, *Don't you worry,* and her arm is light, floating, and she slides her wrist under Sheila's waist, and with that weight and warmth, she closes her eyes, and they are girls with braids down their backs running in a field, Sheila in front of her always in front and faster and taller and dirt black on the bottoms of her bare feet. If she can she will catch her and they are girls running away, Sheila's legs angry red marks from the switch her dress too small soon a rag and washed-out blue skirt flying, and, *Sheila, wait, wait for me,* and a gasp of breath and black birds in a fit to be tied and the sun going down the last of the light in the shade of the woods and, *Where are you?* And her voice is an echo that knocks on the branches and finds not a soul and keep looking and maybe this turn and she is lost and Sheila is lost and the ground sways and she holds steady against a tree and the darkness has footsteps and eyes and teeth and, *Sheila,* she screams and screams again, and the hot tears and snot drip from her chin and there she is, Sheila smiling her crooked smile, *Wanted to know you'd look for me,* and all is forgiven.

Sheila stays with her that night, *Go to sleep crying and you'll wake up crying, and we can't have that, can we?* And Sly in the kitchen washing dishes and her unbraiding and braiding Sheila's hair and Sheila telling her their life, the one only they know, the little jam frogs in the ditch jumping out of their hands and the cartwheels in the air as she tossed them to Sheila who batted them as far as she could and bringing more home in a jar that was kicked over loose, and when Sheila tires of the braiding she turns on her side and goes on telling, a balm over them both, this and every night after.

One day oatmeal is oatmeal, bread is bread, and her milk dries up. And then she makes a stew thick on the spoon and Sheila rolls out the biscuits and says, "Snow in May," and snowflakes fall in a whisper. Gravel on the icy road, and she says, "Sly forget his dinner again?" But there is a knock and Sly never knocks and Sheila wipes the flour on her apron and answers the door. Marie stirs the stew, and who else but Lawrence, wringing his woolen hat in his hands. "My father," he says, "you remember," and Joseph, blue eyes smiling, brown leather bolo tie, wiry hand with a pat on her shoulder, "Thought I'd come see you need any help," he says. "Seems I left a little sun back in Minnesota for snow." Stew swirls in the pot.

"Well, that's something," says Sheila, and she takes away the spoon dripping on the floor.

"You coming?" says Lawrence, gruff and loud.

Marie crosses her arms.

Joseph clears his throat. "If you're ready," he says.

"If you are," says Lawrence, and Joseph nods. "We sure'd like you to come on home."

"So you know, you can stay here as long as you need," says Sheila, but there is a weariness in her voice.

"Got a cabin to build," says Lawrence, and he stares at his boots.

"Could sure use the company," says Joseph, and he side-eyes Lawrence, and winks.

Sheila covers her mouth to stifle a laugh.

"It's time," Marie says, and turns toward the bedroom at the back of the trailer. She cannot stay, not with this offer and kindness poured out for so long.

Sheila helps her fold. When everything is found and packed, Sheila leans over and reaches for her hand, *Take care of yourself, take care, take what you need.*

Bring down the axe and the round splits, one leads to the other, hours to work, build the cabin—the men clearing. She is of a mind to make them give her more to do. But not yet. Something's not right—and she wipes the sweat from her neck and the beating in her chest is not hers. Has a will of its own, tearing on without her. Raise the axe handle, the blade, that weight, because her arms are free, arms that should be holding a child. Weight of an axe ain't enough. Though what had been soft and swollen, a reminder, is becoming taut and lean.

Why gain light if only to lose the light? Worse than not having is the having and the taking away. Not having, there is the want and waiting of having. *We want everything because we got nothing,* Sheila would say. *Think*

75

of how good the biscuits with butter will be. She chewed the air. *Not as good if you're not hungry. Just wait, ours is coming.*

She knew what chance Sheila saw in Sly, and how they deserved to make their life. And what she saw in Lawrence, the acres, the stalks of fireweed shaking in his hands. She married him, and would she have done the same if she knew his stubbornness, his lack of regard? If she knew what was coming?

She raises the axe and swings. Lawrence knotted up thinking he would have a firstborn son, but he didn't carry a child. Doesn't have a part of himself waiting to be buried, and is she wandering closer to the grave and to those in the great blue yonder? *If you keep on this way,* Sheila would say. *If you won't stop feeling sorry for nobody but yourself.* She turns because Sheila was here, and could be sitting there behind her, saying these things, all the days are one day to her, but she is alone.

A pile of firewood, and she steadies one cut on the block, and the axe bites into the wood, and she strikes for the splinter beneath the blade.

On the sill, the metal can filled with ashes a reminder, a blinding when the light catches. For over two months it has stood there, without dignity. And so she has none, her hair unwashed, and Joseph handles the laundry and the meals, she suspects. Sheila visits again, and sits with her, brings a pot of stew. Food appears and she eats without hunger. All that chopping of wood, that will to do so, is gone, and what is left is a callus on her right hand. There is another Marie who lives and breathes and sleeps, and she is where the wondering is, how he would have grown, what sounds and cries. Why would God take him? Had he known her uncertainty? And the singed veil, was that her warning? And why not take her as well? If only they had been in Anchorage, near a hospital. And for this she blames Lawrence. For the miracles the doctors could have tried.

One morning Lawrence shows her the wooden box he has carved and says the ground has a little give under the snow. Joseph stays behind, the sadness in his face, and says they need to carry each other through this. But there is nothing she can carry. And Lawrence has hot water in a bucket to soften the ground. They head to the woods, and he asks her to choose a tree, and she does not want to but points to the tallest in her view. Under this spruce he digs, the dirt half-frozen, and the water steams, and the hole is small, but deep. He opens the box and scatters a wisp of ashes and offers it to her, and she shakes her head. She had held her baby, and that is how she wants to remember him. Lawrence closes the lid and places the box in the hole. Words in the air, a prayer written by hand, copied and given to him by Joseph, and she hears him say, *Tender mercy,* and she whispers these two words under her breath over and over, until he says, *Amen,* and he throws a handful of cold dirt, and she does the same. But she has no tears for this, still, no prayers, for how is this tender and how is this mercy?

CHAPTER 13

HANDS GOD GAVE US

JUNE

A COME-ALONG WIND NIPS through the trees. Marie sits in the rocking chair Joseph made, a knitted afghan for a shawl, the sun warm on her face. That tip back and forth soothes what ails you, gives the bones a rest, he says. Not what she needs. Bones break and heal, and the thick-shined scar on her arm is proof, the snap of white sticking out of her skin after falling from a tree and Valera pulling back and sewing the hole with needle and thread, and Sheila, against Valera's wishes, running for the doctor. But the small grave for the wooden box dug near the roots of a spruce, the ashes scattered, numbers carved into the bark, the tallest spike of green in the low, is a hitch and a hold. A little dirt moved and shoveled and marked, that dirt is hers, a blood-rotting spot as the living go on. And all these acres, when the land is proved, will be theirs, but what is her stake, her claim—a child buried in the mud?

Wind blows and branches nod and a rustling comes down the ridge as the leaves of aspen shake, the sound of rain before the rain. Scored spruce, the notched rings in the bark still fresh and bright with sap weeping from the wound, are dead where they stand. Wisps of her hair fly loose. Clouds roll in, dark and gray. Every blade and leaf and needle thrashes and thunder calls over the mountains. Chair rocks and she sits and waits for her heels to dig the ground, her arms to unfold, feet to stand. Storm comes, and she has no reckoning for the cold, every drop on her face and skin is a reminder of something moving beyond this heavy nothing pinning her down. And Lawrence is fine, dare she say more carefree, with Joseph here, and she should have stayed with Sheila, but she let them bring her here. The bus so small, and where it happened, and they walk on that floor every day, walk across the spot, and she knows they do not care as she does. And she would prefer if Lawrence never said another word, the rattling sound of his voice pains her, of him getting on. Something dark has taken root in her heart, she can feel the weight, and so she will sit in the rain, and let it grow.

Soaked and shivering, and Lawrence and Joseph rush to her side in the downpour. "Don't make a fuss," she says, and they lift her and carry her inside to the couch, peel away the blanket, stoke the stove, the rain a hail on the metal roof of the bus.

Joseph towels her hair. "You'll be all right, if I can help it, and tomorrow we can borrow a loader and tractor from the sawmill, thanks to me and the bottles of cherry wine I brought." He places the towel on her shoulders. "You'll keep saving for a tractor, you're mighty close, but we need to clear the land."

"Saving?" says Marie.

"For a tractor," says Lawrence.

And with those words, a strength returns, and Marie stands. "I said I wanted a hospital and you talked about the expense," she says. Her eyes narrow and take aim. "You killed him."

Lawrence's mouth falls open, stricken.

"Was your doing," she says.

"Marie, you're tired," he says, and steps near. "You're not well."

Marie swings her fists and he holds them both. "You killed our son," she says into his jaw. She struggles and kicks and he braces, arms tensed against her.

"That's enough," says Joseph.

Lawrence loosens his hold and surrenders.

"I wish it had been you," says Marie. The truth that was waiting these months.

"You don't mean that," says Lawrence.

"Promise her," says Joseph. "The hospital if—"

"There will be no need," says Marie.

Lawrence blazes to the door, a slam.

"He'll be a while," says Joseph. "Damn fool."

Anger she can live with, and if Lawrence is the mark, so be it. He has his father, the work outside, and what does she have? Anything but grieving, the waiting for, and not knowing how long, the days passing all the same.

Lawrence misses supper. Joseph and she sit at the table and he says, "I know I don't know you, but you're my daughter-in-law, you're family, and I know you're suffering. Can't say I understand, only the fear of losing a child." He clasps his hands. "I know Lawrence is a hard one to know, and a hard man at times."

Marie taps her fork on the table. "He's so different from you," she says.

"I think about what he lived through," says Joseph. "A small boy in the fields with me picking potatoes, our German name a curse in the air, and him driving a team of horses around to sell cords of wood in the winters. Nothing was ever enough. The drought had lasted years. And he was the only one taken out of school to work on the farm, and then the army at eighteen, sending his money to me and his mother."

"He told me only a little," says Marie. She stares at her plate.

"He doesn't talk much," says Joseph. "Though sometimes he lets you know what he wants you to know, storing up for years and years and pouring out the well."

"I'll believe you when it happens," says Marie.

"I blame myself," says Joseph. "For how he is. How poor we were." He dabs the corners of his eyes with his napkin. "Lois says I have a crying nature."

"So, does he take after Lois?"

"At times." He stands. "I have something to show you," he says. "Been waiting." He sets down his suitcase and rummages through his clothes. He brings her an envelope, and inside are photographs. One is of two boys in a field, their hats too big over their eyes, their thin frames drowning in their coats. "The taller one is Lawrence," he says. Another is Lawrence sitting behind the wheel of their first car, a front tooth missing. "We don't have many pictures," he says. "But I thought you should have a few." At the end Marie stops: Here are the wedding photos that Joseph had promised, he had brought the same camera with him. She recognizes the dress, but not herself, or the moment, the slight smile on her face, and Lawrence is wide-eyed and serious, his arm at her waist.

"Was a beautiful ceremony," says Joseph.

She nods, but has nothing to say. The couple in the photograph are not joyous, or radiant, but caught, as if forced together. Marie gently slides the photographs back into the envelope and puts them inside the old hatbox, under the papers, the marriage certificate, which states her maiden name and then her married name, Beringer, and she feels neither one belongs to her.

And she and Joseph eat their supper and then turn in, the dishes left to soak. She knows she is not moved as he had hoped. The pictures showed their failings, even then. And did Lawrence ever ponder her life as she does his? Brood over her, try for understanding? Her own life had hardship, though she finished high school and did not serve in the war. She hears him at last, late into the night when the darkness finally arrives, and he lies down on the floor and she swears on her life, no matter what Joseph has said, there will not be another child.

———

THE BLIZZARD, THE CORD wrapped around the neck, and was there nothing to be done? Ain't a truth in the saying? If Marie believed it was so? His own strength, as he held her back, his father his witness. Was she knowing her own mind? Seen this before, in himself, in a fellow soldier, no longer willing, lying down as they lined up to jump out of the plane. If she wants to fight him, let her, at least she is standing. Rain trickles down the window of the army rig. He will sleep here if he must.

When he went with Sheila and Sly to the hospital, Marie woke and would not calm until the nurse wrapped a sheet into a bundle and placed this in her arms. And when he smoothed her brow she shook her head, he was a stranger to her. This pained him, her face turning from him, as did the thought of losing her, which meant that he could no longer be alone.

He thought he could if he must. But now he was beyond his own reserve, and he had allowed this to happen.

And will there be a settling? Who to blame and fault? His sense that the world was coming alongside him has been taken away. The burial was a turn to say *enough,* to find a way back into the days and the use of his time, farewell to what could have been. He had thought of what he wanted to teach his son about the land, as his father had done. But he still has so much to learn, maybe that is why, for he is a son again with Joseph here, and there are moments when he is burdened, and his father places a hand on his shoulder, and he is so grateful tears well in his eyes, but only for a moment, and he wills them away. And as Joseph says, what is faith untested? The worn pages of his father's *Saint Andrew Missal,* prayers edged in gold. So count not his sins and transgressions, the glass bleary as he opens the door, the late summer light breaking through the mist, and every drop touched by sun.

———

JOSEPH SHAKES MARIE AWAKE, the heaviness of sleep around her eyes. "You slept through breakfast," he says. "We have a day ahead." Outside, Lawrence drives the loader toward the base of a cut tree and uproots a stump. "Sawmill came through," says Joseph. He offers her a mug of coffee. She sips and winces and her lips burn. He laughs. "A touch of whiskey in the morning will get you going." He hands her a plate of hash and sits down beside her. "We're going to drive the tractor today," he says, "you and me." She shakes her head. "I'll teach you, something you should know, living out here. And we don't have enough time to build this cabin to be wasting the hands God gave us. But before all his work—" He takes a deep breath. "I was worried when Lawrence told me he was leaving to homestead in Alaska. But I told him to go, make a life for yourself, sonny boy, land is what you know. Then he wrote me a letter about how you had trouble with the baby being born, and a sadness I ain't ever heard before, had set his hopes too high he said, should have known better. In some ways, that he had wanted a child was a comfort, as was him marrying you, as I can't recall my son asking or wanting for anything, that's the truth. But I tell you this not to make excuses on his behalf. I'm here to help any way I can." He places a hand on her shoulder. "You're young but you're strong. Stronger than him, I suspect."

His words on her mind, and Lawrence, but there is work. And so this is the gas lever, this is how to feather the choke to warm up the engine, and this is the shift and clutch and brake. The tractor lurches forward, a new line over the land Lawrence cleared with the loader, and Joseph follows her on foot to gather turned rocks in a burlap sack. She, in blaming Lawrence, had meant the harm, and every word, but then here is Joseph, trying to make her feel sorry for him, and how do you reckon that? She rounds a corner and sets for another, and with the teeth of the till breaking the ground, the roar of the engine, the hum and jostle, she sights the path ahead and the steering wheel trembles in her grip. *For idle hands are the devil's work,* says Sheila with her crochet hook and knitting needles, the stitches and mending, and Marie never took to those lessons, she did not have the patience, but these rows and the order of rows, scratched dirt neat and plain—are a mark of her own making on the land.

———+———

LAWRENCE PUSHES A TREE stump to the edge of the clearing and turns the loader around. He shades his eyes. Tractor tills a line and someone—he squints, his father—rakes and picks the rocks. He eases his foot off the gas and slows. He'll be damned if Marie is driving the tractor, as that was his father's way, he could be sure, *Oh, that man thinks he has the world fooled,* his mother says. But even he could not convince Lois to come here, watching the farm and the diner, a long way to travel, *you know your mother,* though the farm is little more than a small cabin and twenty acres for Joseph to fret and mind, and Joseph switching from job to job, scheme to scheme, the diner his latest, a disaster from the start, says his mother, but give the man a hammer and a few nails and everything is right again. But he envied his father, his ease, and his way with people, with Marie. And with Joseph here, he has not woken in the night, shaking, doubting his whereabouts, has not walked in circles waiting for the hours to pass.

Staked eight acres, and when they are cleared they will stake more. He aims the loader at another stump. What can he do but wait on Marie? Not that he did not think of the boy, but the summer light meant his mind was on the land, the clearing, the plans for the cabin. Then he will plant crops this coming spring, potatoes and alfalfa, what his father always grew, said you need to feed your family and the animals, though Lawrence will not have livestock. And to see potatoes in his own fields—after all the fields he had dragged his hands through as a child, farms in Minnesota and the Dakotas and Idaho, pieces of raw potatoes in his pocket for when hunger struck, that bitter taste of dirt in his mouth, Joseph and Lois bent over and picking a row, filling baskets and sacks, and all the times he heard, *Come on, sonny, time to wake up,* the voice of his father calling him in the darkness before sunrise—that day will be right as rain.

⁓

NOT A SURPRISE WHEN Sheila comes to visit, but no one knew she was coming. Drove herself for the first time. "I know you're checking on me," says Marie on the steps of the bus.

"Had to," says Sheila, bringing in a few bags. "You got two useless men looking after you." With her free hand, Sheila moves Marie's hair out of her face. "Is that a smile?"

Marie shrugs.

"Looks like you're behind on laundry," says Sheila, noting the pile in the bus. "And the cleaning," she says at the dishes.

"Joseph has been doing most of the cooking," says Marie.

"I can see that," says Sheila, unpacking. "That's why I've been baking. Cookies, biscuits."

"Punch bars," and Marie grabs one and takes a bite.

"But this can wait. I'm of a mind to go swimming," says Sheila.

"Haven't been," says Marie. "Not since—haven't wanted to."

"You have a perfectly good lake all to yourself," says Sheila. "This won't stand."

Towels in hand, they pass by the men at work in the field, Lawrence still driving the loader. Sheila waves and Joseph, who is raking a brush pile, runs up to them. "Company," he says. "Cause for celebration."

"Looks like it's coming along," says Sheila.

"Wish I could go where you're going," says Joseph. "My boss isn't as nice as you, I guarantee."

Sheila laughs. "You take care of him. I got this one," she says. And she puts her arm on Marie's shoulder and they head toward the lake.

"You don't smell so good," says Sheila.

"Drove the tractor the other day," says Marie.

"Then we're going to swim this stink off you."

"Bathed last week," says Marie. "Joseph heated the water."

"You just sit there like a lump?" says Sheila. "Or was there soap and washing?"

Marie stops walking on the trail. "I'm doing my best."

"I know you are," says Sheila. "And I'm here to help you."

"You helping or judging?" says Marie.

"I'll always worry about you," says Sheila. "And what happened was one of the worst things."

"I don't feel nothing," says Marie. "And it scares me."

Sheila takes in a deep breath. "Right to be."

At the clearing, Sheila throws down her towel and begins to undress.

"We forgot the pistol," says Marie.

"What is a bear going to do? Come in the water for us?" says Sheila.

Woods surrounding and the sun high. Marie unlaces her boots. Then hesitates. She did not want Sheila, or the trees and sky, for that matter, to see her, what had brought a death, a failure, how many times had she not been sure, questions of being a mother, had come to the lake and eaten mud? And she must have asked Sheila when she was staying in Anchorage, though what she remembered came and went.

"I will throw you in the water myself if you don't get a move on," yells Sheila.

"I'm coming," says Marie. And she peels off her dungarees and the rest and runs into the water.

"We're swimming five laps," says Sheila. "Then you can do what you want."

They frog-kick side by side, as they used to do as kids, heads bobbing above the surface. And then they float on their backs under the bright afternoon. Sheila takes a hold of Marie's hand, tightens her grip, and lets go.

Joseph is cooking supper and he will not let Sheila help. "You made the biscuits," he says. Hash with fried eggs—because Sheila always brings a few dozen.

They wait for Lawrence but then Joseph says, "I told him, but he gets it in his mind he has to finish something." So they eat at the counter, the three of them, Joseph sopping up the yolk with a biscuit.

"What was Lawrence like as a child?" says Sheila. "Have any stories you can tell us while he's not here?"

"Hard to say if he ever was one," says Joseph. "Always working then. Like now." He helps himself to another biscuit. "Eats like a horse, works like a mule. Not much has changed."

"Speak of the devil," says Sheila, when the bus door opens. Lawrence walks in, nods hello, and Joseph stands and gives him the stool. He dishes a heaping plate and fries three eggs.

"How's it going out there?" says Sheila.

Lawrence chews slowly, and there is a long pause before he says, "Good, when I have help."

Joseph is the only one who laughs. "We all got to eat."

"And Marie and I will get to the laundry tomorrow," says Sheila.

"What laundry?" says Lawrence, deadpan, and looks over his left shoulder and then his right. Everyone laughs then, even Marie.

Joseph heads outside and brings in a bottle of cherry wine. "And we got four, so we can play spades," he says. He turns to Lawrence. "Don't you dare say you're going to bed." Joseph opens the bottle and brings out a deck of cards. "You ever played?"

"Give us the rules," says Sheila.

"Sheila, you're with Lawrence. I got Marie," says Joseph, and he tells them how to play. They pass the bottle around, but Lawrence refuses. Joseph pours him some whiskey. "I know you're not one for cherry wine," he says, "but don't ruin our fun." They stay up late, and forget themselves, and the time, and Marie drinks her share, rowdy with Sheila, Joseph slapping his knee, until Lawrence throws his losing cards down with a yawn and calls the night.

CHAPTER 14

SKIN OVER BONE

JULY

SCORED SPRUCE, WITH ASHEN sap and runs of resin, marked for the cabin as straight and strong, are felled. Cut posts soak for two days in barrels of coal-tar creosote to seal the ends. Holes, three feet deep and narrow, are dug with a long-handled posthole digger and the sealed post is placed into the hole and the sides are filled with dirt. A string line measures the mark from the first post, so every piling is sunk to the level, four feet underground and two feet above, and water is poured to pack the dirt. Lawrence keeps a pencil behind his ear, has a sketch on the back of the co-op instructions on how to build a cabin. He has never built one, has helped neighbors with theirs, made a shed, but could not say, *From the pilings to the roof, this is my doing.* Though Joseph could. By the sketch, the cabin measuring thirty-by-thirty feet will have twenty-four pilings on the perimeter, five feet in between, and twenty-five pilings inside for the floor. Forty-nine pilings in all.

"If you make an eight-foot span, then you won't have to cut the four-by-eight plywood," says Joseph.

"I want a perfect square of pilings," says Lawrence, "seven-by-seven."

"Luck-by-luck?" Joseph says.

Lawrence shakes his head. "Work-by-work."

"Want as few cuts on the wood as possible," says Joseph. "Three pilings across is what you need."

He could argue the point, his plan. But he says, "Three it is." Thirty-by-thirty will be a large cabin, unwise in the race against winter.

And there it is, a hope and prospect, and with Marie, he can admit, though building a cabin seems more possible than being alone with her. Of habit, he lets his father carry on talking, to fill their unspoken days. He decides at supper he will try, for what are pilings without a floor, a floor without a roof, a cabin without a wife or child?

The three of them sit down at the counter, and he sits in the middle, by Marie, where Joseph has been sitting these months. And his father understands and eats quickly, which is not his way, and says he will take in the evening air and leaves. He has Marie alone, and this weighs in the air.

He pushes hash to the side of his plate with his fork. "You see the pilings we placed?" he says.

"No," she says, startled. Her hair falls forward over her face.

"I can show you," he says. And he sits on his hands, when was the last time he touched her hair, and he wants to tuck it behind her ear, look into her eyes.

She opens her mouth to answer, then closes it, and the moment passes. She pushes herself away from the counter. "Think I'll go on a walk," she says.

He does not offer to accompany her, she would not want him there, and he sinks into his seat as the door of the bus shuts. Her dark hair is streaked red from the sun, the summer, darker skin on the bridge of her nose, and she will be back before the clouds of mosquitoes come alive in the shade. This is what he knows. He can give her time, for what he could not give. And even with the light, and the longer days, his father says, this is her winter.

—+—

MARIE WAKES BEFORE THE men, many a care on her mind. And can scarce recall when she rose without dread for the day ahead. But her thoughts are of what is yet to pass, for Joseph will be leaving before long, with the cabin on the way. She had not known her father, and her grandfather was a thorn to Valera, of what she knew, and Joseph is a blessing to her and Lawrence, a godsend. She has never had someone, besides Sheila, who showed her how she should be. She quietly puts coffee on the stove, warmth in the belly should help. She pours her cup and sits at the counter, but is restless. Times such as these, her steps lead her outside, to where the cabin is being built.

Find a wrong, and move heaven and earth to find another, and she is tired, not for the same reasons as before, but for the strength to remain as she was, with no need to pardon Lawrence, though he had never asked, and her resolve of who to blame, because she did not want to blame God in the end, enough sermons in her life to know where that led, and easier to blame Lawrence because he was there, and is here now, in the flesh. When she spoke to Sheila of what she had said, that she told Lawrence she wished for his death, Sheila stopped knitting. She closed her eyes. "You're my sister, and you've had a terrible loss," she said. "But I have never known you to be cruel." She looked at Marie and reached over and grabbed her by the shoulders. "Must be the hurt talking. You have to know that. I suspect he does."

And he is building a cabin, for them, there are holes for the posts, piles of dirt. Land moved and shaped every day by shovels and hands and tools. In one pile, she spots a strange white stone and rubs it clean with the end of her shawl. Carved, not rock or wood, but of bone, the length of a finger, a hole on one end, three fine notches, two jagged teeth toward the sharp point. A hook or a spear. Old. Ancient. For hunting, or fishing. People were here a long time ago. Athabascan? She should show her find to Lawrence and Joseph, but this is a history not her own, and what was she here for, and something fierce rises up in her, and she opens her hand over a dug hole, but this is too close. If this is to be her home, if she and Lawrence will make their life, she does not want this reminder, and she would know that under one post was a crushed mark of the past. So she walks into the woods and buries the hook in the shade of moss and ferns. She will not remember, a secret she gives to the ground, and wipes the dirt from her hands.

Marie turns around, her stride long, her mouth open to the air. Out of the trees, and the sun and moon in the sky at the same time in the early morning, as if one were not enough, sharing or fighting for their place, who could tell? Morning and night, the light and the dark, everything at once, stars, and clouds, she wanted it all, and no one could tell her otherwise.

———

LAWRENCE STIRS, AND HEARS himself shouting, and his father is shaking him. "You're home, my son, you've been home a long time." He pours Lawrence a glass of water and they sit on the couch—Marie is not there. But the smell of coffee on the stove means she will be. "Those come back?" Joseph says, and Lawrence nods. But this one, a field of paratroopers, guns at the ready, and he tripped and fell, and there was a small body, covered in blood and blackflies, so many he could not see the face, but he knew that this was his dead son.

"You should talk about it," says Joseph.

"You know enough," says Lawrence. "How about some coffee?"

"Marie see you like this?"

Lawrence shrugs. "Few times. Comes and goes. Thought it would be going."

"I have my rosary," Joseph says.

Lawrence puts his head in his hands.

Marie walks in the door of the bus. "Morning, boys."

"Morning," the reply.

"We're just scheming," says Joseph. "Have plans to make you something today."

She glances at Lawrence. "Maybe you should get some more sleep before you do that."

"We're fine," says Joseph. "As fit as can be. We'll be headed to Walt's General."

"I'll pick up the mail," says Lawrence, following Joseph's lead. Be good to take a drive, roll down the window, feel the wind on his face.

———

A HAUL OF WATER from the lake, and Marie remembers repellent, and has plans to swim. There are two eagles, she has not seen them here before, standing on the bank, heads bent down, basking in the sunlight. They walk away from her, side by side, and she tries not to be a bother, but they flap their wings and fly away. She fills and carries the jerry cans, and after a few steps sets them down. There are what must be bear tracks along the shore, fresh in the dark mud. And she scolds herself because she has grown accustomed to going where she pleases, no thought to danger for some time. But she has the pistol, a habit, and holds a can in one hand and the gun in the other. A rustle, a dark form in the trees beyond, and she heads back to the cabin, looking over her shoulder. A reminder, with every step, of the safety of the bus, and she has shot a few birds and animals, been deer hunting a handful of times when she and Sheila were living with Rosalie and Carver Calhoun, but no creature the size of a bear. Out here one has to remain sharp, alert. After a while she assures herself she is not being followed.

At the bus she waits and plays the Victrola to calm her nerves. When Joseph and Lawrence arrive she tells them of the bear tracks, of the jerry can she left behind. Lawrence's brow furrows in concern, he says she should not go to the lake without one of them. Joseph says they will haul in pairs, and in due time search for a spring, a closer source. But Lawrence claims to be an unbeliever in his father's tall tales and water witching. "Made me dig three wells before the fourth hit," said Lawrence. "You didn't tell her that, did you?"

"But if we found a spring," says Marie.

"First tries are rarely fruitful," says Joseph. "Words to live by."

Marie knows he is speaking to them both.

—+—

LAWRENCE KNOWS HIS FATHER is watching over him, worried if he is alone out here he will be lost to the woods, a boy who grew old beyond his years, and then shined the boots of his army uniform, and went to war, and grew older still. And Joseph trying for them all, as he nails an old door to the top of two old barrels laid out on their sides and anchored to a beam of wood. "What do you think? A table for the wash. No more kneeling over tubs on the ground," he says. "And this wringer, a find, bigger and better."

Marie runs her hands over the wood of the door. "Be nicer if you did the wash for me," she says, and Joseph laughs.

"Was Lawrence's notion," he says.

Lawrence wishes this were true, that he knew the fixing. Smell of tar and sweat and smoke, their pants and shirts and the whole stinking mound of laundry ridden with creosote. He and Joseph fetch water, and Marie heats a big pot over the stove. Then Lawrence fills the tubs for her. She adds soap to one, runs a shirt over the washboard. Mosquito lands on her arm and she slaps in time, before the sting of poison that brings the welt. Cold in May should have kept them away, as Joseph says, and it snowed then, and they were still a bother.

Up to her elbows in suds, and Joseph and Lawrence drink coffee. "You just gonna watch me work?" she says. "Don't know about you, but I could eat."

"Was just about to ask," says Joseph. And he beckons Lawrence into the bus. "Stop acting like an old crow full of piss and vinegar," he says. He places a pot on the stove. "You're my son and I know how you are but you're a married man and you've got to learn."

Lawrence brings out a bowl of hash and beans to Marie. "Here," he offers.

"Have to hang these on the line," she says.

He picks up a rinsed shirt. "Sit in your rocking chair," he says. "I can get these on."

She wipes her hands dry on her apron. "Never seen you near the laundry," she says.

"Near all my life on the farm," he says. "Thought maybe I'd done my share."

"You thought wrong," she says, almost teasing.

Pin by pin on the line and she inspects his work.

"I dare you to tell me you can do better," he says.

"Try as I might," she says, "can't fault your hanging."

He gasps and clutches his heart.

She laughs, and then stifles, as if caught, and this is the crack of the first tree falling.

MARIE FOLDS THE LAUNDRY, warm and dry from the sun, the creases neat. Valera used to say, *And who feeds you and puts clothes on your back?* And once Sheila said, *Well, are you going to let us starve and run around naked as the wind?* Valera said the point was that she could, and that was what mattered. To be in someone's charge, Marie knew then and there she was a beggar in that house.

She knew what a home was because of Carver Calhoun, who owned a mill and a fine house, the only one of Rosalie's suitors who wanted to be a husband and a father. Rosalie told everyone they were married and wore the ring, and took her and Sheila along, for once. That was the time Marie could not quite believe they were happy, and when Rosalie ran off he tried his best, but she and Sheila would find him weeping into his boots, and they stopped attending school, ran wild in the woods chasing armadillos, and Carver hunted doves and deer and squirrels, no way to eat so many, and she and Sheila would have been fine as ever to live that way, but his sister came to town in her white gloves, looked the girls up and down, and when Carver admitted he and Rosalie were never married, the sister packed their things and he drove them back to Valera, tears in his eyes, *You were like my own.*

She could have a home here, the cabin being built, the new wringer and table for the basins that meant someone thought of her and her comfort. And as Sheila says, a good turn doesn't mean it wasn't earned in the first place. But with all her might she will make sure this work, this trying, is not in vain. No amount of soap can fix what is ruined and tattered, and so she would take care from the beginning, and in doing so would be cared for.

———+———

AS A NEW BATCH of posts soak, they fell scored spruce, saw the branches, leave the bark to save time. Every two days they sink six pilings. At the Knik Sawmill, they bring the logs and pay for time—rough-cut two-by-sixes, one log cut in half for the start of the walls. When the pilings are set, Lawrence wipes a tar-ranked handkerchief over his brow and surveys the buried logs that will carry the weight of his cabin.

"That's a foundation," says Joseph.

Lawrence stands on a piling and holds his balance, arms open, sun on his face.

"That's a smile," says Joseph.

Half logs are positioned on the sides, flat down, two feet hanging out at the ends, and holes bored with an auger, and the half logs are spiked to the pilings. Side up is notched with an axe and chisel and mallet, and that notch is scribed, Joseph holding the log still as Lawrence notches to match, and then the log is fitted. With the base logs down, rough cuts are nailed to pilings along the edge. Two-by-sixes are nailed to the center piling and the joists are crossed with saddle brackets, the bones in place. Four-by-eight plywood is cut as needed, and staggered and flanked, and then nailed down, skin over the bones.

"That's a floor," says Joseph.

Lawrence walks the length and the sound is solid.

CHAPTER 15

YONDER SPIRITS

AUGUST

RAILROAD SPIKES STAKED ON a rising cabin wall, and Joseph and Lawrence pulley a rope around them, and trundle a log to the top along the leaning ramps made from other logs, a doorway cut in the middle. Tie off the ropes to spikes in the ground. Then Lawrence climbs the ladder, axe through his belt loop, throws his leg over, and measures for the notch. Joseph does the same on the other side. Rotate the log so the measuring faces them and axe a rough notch and then chisel. "Ready," Lawrence shouts, and Joseph shouts back, and they turn and set it in place. Axe another notch on the upside, slip the rope off, and come down.

"Looks good," Marie says. Leather work gloves shade her eyes.

Joseph smiles. "You here to help?"

"If you need," she says.

"But wood won't chop itself," says Lawrence, arms crossed. He is sure she will slow them down. They do not have time to waste.

"Pay my son no mind," says Joseph. "You can tie and pulley the logs. Save an old man's back."

Lawrence stares ahead at the rising-up cabin and holds the rope in his hands.

"Pull 'em up," says Joseph.

Lawrence threads one, two, three lengths in the time she takes one. Log on her side slides out of the loop and falls to the ground.

"Watch her," says Joseph. "Follow her so you're even."

"I'm going as fast as I can," she says.

"Don't have time for this," says Lawrence. "Have a cabin to build."

"Our cabin," she says.

He tilts his head toward a decision. "Our cabin," he says.

They set the log and the loops and the rope.

"Marie's in charge," says Joseph. "She makes the call now."

"Pull 'em up," she says.

Log rises on the ramps, even, as Lawrence matches her pace. They reach the top of the wall and tie off to a spike.

"Mark my words and scratch the dirt," says Joseph. "That there's the secret to a long marriage."

How long? Lawrence wanted to know. And when the cabin is finished his father will leave. He is building this for his children and his children's children—a notion that steadies him, but what of Marie, the everyday of living here with each other, together? How would the days turn into years?

———+———

SORE AND ACHING, MARIE washes the dishes after breakfast.

"It's Sunday," says Joseph. "I'm taking it easy. I'm old and tired."

"We have work to do," says Lawrence. He tightens his bootlaces.

"Go on ahead without us," says Joseph. "We have the Lord's work."

Lawrence turns to Marie. "You coming?"

"How about we rest this once?" says Marie, though he has never asked before.

"Rain's coming," says Lawrence. "Ain't a day to rest."

"For me it is," she says.

Lawrence avoids her eyes. "I'll be going, then," he says.

The low is purple with fireweed, the fields teeming with flowers, and did Lawrence remember the promises they held? From here, as he walked, he could be Joseph, lean and quick, but for the black hair. This was one of the times she could not figure the line. How the father could have raised the son.

Joseph turns to her. "We're going water witching."

"We are?"

"We'll find us a spring so we don't have to haul all our water from the lake." He holds up a bottle of cherry wine. "Drink and the spirit will move you."

Joseph, at the table, takes a share, and Marie swigs and coughs and shakes her head.

"We're not leaving til this is gone," says Joseph. "The spirits command."

Closes her eyes and drinks, then stoops and pounds her fist. "Lordamercy," she gasps.

"And mercyalord," says Joseph.

Back and forth, the bottle, and she finishes the last, the heat in the throat.

"We'll know if we're drunk with the spirit when we stand," he says.

He stumbles out the door and she rushes to catch him. She passes Lawrence, who is pulling a log up by the rope on one side, tying off, and then working the other side, and she has her doubts about letting him work alone, but is barely standing on her own two feet.

Joseph up at the branches of a birch. "Need one branch splitting off into two," he says. "Don't have the feeling, but keep your eyes open. Found one on the farm right under my feet. How I knew where to dig the well."

The third birch tree, she points to a branch and he whistles, that's the one, and not too high. He has a small, thin rope and measures across the tree, then ties a cinch over his left boot and the right, with rope spanning the middle. He shuffles to the tree, widens his stance so the line becomes taut, grabs hold with his hands, and jumps and the line holds him in place, and he scales the trunk til he reaches the lowest branch, and pulls himself over. Carves at a twig with a pocketknife. "Timber," he calls.

He saws the arms so each point is the same length, a wishbone. "Hold the two sides," he says. "Close your eyes. Let your mind be water."

Water, water, water, she mouths. Her whisper echoes back and her hands shake and her knees give and she stumbles and the rod slips out of one hand.

"You've been touched," he says. "Go on."

She stands straight, claps both hands and the whispers are louder, *Water, water,* and she points, and leads the way. They walk left, and make a wide turn into the dewed green of ferns and fiddleheads, and then the whispers are at her back, and she turns around, through the same woods, and silence. She stops in her tracks, lowers in defeat.

"Just wait," he says. "Listen in the yonder."

A rustle in the trees, a mosquito, her own breathing, and he follows her to the edge of the woods, and up the ridge, a steep hike, Joseph at her elbow to keep steady, sweat an itch at the back of her neck, and at reaching the crest, they both lean on either side of a spruce. She peers over the cut with the rod, the tops of trees, and the sigh comes from below, over from where they came. "There," she says.

They wind a trail down the long arm of the ridge, and walk back through a canopy, green and mossy, shaded from the sun, the smell of mud and earth, a narrow of stone and rocks, before the land sinks into marsh. Joseph inspects the branches of a shrub. "Looks like you've got wild blueberries here," he says. "We'll have to come back for those when they're ready." Marie suddenly turns around, a voice at her back, and turns again.

"Should be close," says Joseph, and casts his eyes on the facing of stone.

She walks around a large, speckled rock, and finds a dark vein of moss, wet, a trickle.

"Here," she shouts. A crack in a stone and a gush of water, cold.

"Look at that," says Joseph.

They kneel and draw handfuls, water sweet and fresh and pure, no more hauling from the lake to fill the pots to boil. Joseph douses his white hair and hollers. When she can drink no more and her teeth ache, they collect smooth stones and pile them to keep moss from growing, so the spring will be found.

———⊢———

LORD'S WORK, AND WHAT does his father, pray tell, think he is doing, while he raises the logs of the cabin alone? They should be helping, not banding together against him, Joseph and Marie, his wife. *His wife.* All these years, Lois a scowl and Joseph a fool in the corner, making the children laugh, and he had sided with his father, a hardness to Lois he did not understand, though when he was born she said she was sure they would both starve, the drought and the choking dust, and what he remembers is the scraping by in the years that followed. With this knowing and the pressing of work to be done, he sees why she lost her patience. And Marie, did she want to live in a bus any longer than she had to, the cramped quarters, sleeping on a couch, cooking on a small stove? So be it, he would carry each log over to the pulley, finish what he started. And shame on them.

—+—

BEEN COMING BACK TO herself, these months, the thinning of her blood. Good to know her own strength again. Joseph leaves to fill the jerry cans and she could walk over and let Lawrence know his father was right, the whispers in the woods, and what they revealed. He would have to believe her. He has the cleared land and the felled logs, is certain of his purpose. And she could point to those rocks and that water, at the least. He had no hand. She knows he is of one mind about the cabin, determined, will work himself into the ground to build those walls. So long since she wanted to tell him anything, even as she thought about their son, who would have had his black hair, and God forbid, his stubborn nature.

—+—

WHEN LAWRENCE COMES IN for dinner, late, sweat soaking his shirt, Joseph and Marie are sitting outside on tree stumps, pleased with themselves. They found a spring, here, drink, water witching led her to the place.

"We'll show you," says Joseph. And he stands, and wavers, drunk, and sits. "Tomorrow," he says.

"We're in trouble," says Marie, and she slaps Joseph's arm.

"Son," says Joseph, "we're in earnest. We found one."

"Where's the bottle?" says Lawrence.

Joseph reaches behind a stump. "A fine batch, if I say so myself."

Lois, how she loathed his cherry wine. And Marie and Joseph drinking like they were the ones raising logs for hours. He shakes his head and places the wine he took on the counter of the kitchen. Those two will certainly be of no use to him now. Of a mind to take the bottles and smash them. But liquor so red and bright his mouth waters. He takes a drink, certain they cannot see him. Working on the cabin all day, and the burn in his mouth creeps down his throat. Thirst begets thirst, and he cannot stop himself, and reaches the bottom and the warmth takes over, loosens and spreads over him, and he is swimming, a stream, and his steps are heavy and a trail and another, and he knows his failings and the errors of his ways, the child he held in his hands, a father to no one, and if the words will find him, his mouth opens, if he could tell her everything he held inside, the god-awful truth, how he came back from the war when so many died, those who were more deserving, Wilson and the others, and what if he needs her, he knows he cannot live by that need. And he does not want to be alone with his rambling thoughts, and he has something to tell them. The door of the bus, the steps, and the ground, and he does not fall, and he straightens his stance. What has he said, he is lost, and where should he start, and he tries again. "Speak up, son," says Joseph. They cannot understand him. "I'm cursed," he says. "Do you hear me? Cursed."

And Marie stands, tears in her eyes. "If you are, then I am," she says, and he forgets himself and goes to her, and holds her, and steadies himself, and her cries come, deep and wailing, from some other place, and she buries her face into his neck, and her sorrow is his sorrow.

CHAPTER 16

CLOSE HOLLER

SEPTEMBER

A YEAR SINCE THE window cracked from the falling tree, and how had it not shattered that day? But this was when she had known, more than the plainspoken vows by the priest, the first pinned-down truth of what it is to be married—the close holler, the almost-to-the-quick hitch in your side when your lungs swell and you come to, and the light is a clean, stark white and you don't know how your feet carried you so far into the woods, the taste of blood in your mouth, and the silence breaks with a flap of a sheet on the line, and then you turn back.

More alive, then, for taking the chance, and cheating the old man in the shadows, and that's life, she knew that much, can say, *There but for the grace of God go I,* but you have to eat. She packs dinner for Lawrence and Joseph in a burlap sack, stew in a thermos, beans and hash and the last spruce hen. Working on the roof, they stopped coming in, a fever to finish the cabin, so close, and the lessening hours of daylight, no time to think of moose hunting, though as she turns from the bus there are far-off shots of hunters after their winter stash of meat, a reminder of others out there, which had happened only a few times this season, and the sound, miles away, is a shock. Somewhere a cow or bull is shot, bleeding from a wound, and nothing the animal can do to save its skin. She would have rather died than the baby, or so she believed, and how Lawrence would have raised a child alone brings a crooked smile. Then, as Lawrence held her that day and she clutched to him, she was not herself, the shaking loose of nails hammered tight, and the crying and the pouring out, and she was beholden to it, would not stop or let her stop, the ache of all she could lose, the losing never came alone, and not having the baby knocked her clean out of her senses, and the years of moving and moving along, the sending for and the sending away, a floor or bed if lucky, and Sheila telling her *there now,* so much water to sweep into the corner, and the heave and heaviness in her chest, could have been an hour or so passed, but she could have sworn she stood there weeping for days, for years, and in this they returned to some unspoken, softer way, of what could be, in time. And here, the roofline of the cabin, a place to live, and a twinge in knowing she is alive, and would rather be so, well, ain't that something.

A roof over her head, and not living in the bus come winter. Joseph stands on the attic level, above the ceiling, and inspects a beam. Lawrence walks, slow and balancing, up a skinny log pole, a long slope from the ground to the corner of the cabin, one boot to the fore and then the other, lean and careful, higher and higher in the air, his head bent to watch over his steps, elbows at his sides and arms driving the front, ready to bring his body in line, or to catch his fall as the pole bends in the middle under his weight, bows and trembles, and she holds her breath, but, still and calm and climbing, he does not falter.

She is counting on this man, the one who reaches the attic, who is building this cabin. She holds up the sack and he nods and she leaves the supper. Rain, a soft patter, and she runs back to the bus, which seems smaller than before, Lawrence still sleeping on the floor, night after night. That first on the land, the paper mail bags, the soot, and who was she then, and the other first, the bridge and the river and becoming his wife, in name and blood, and would she want him in that way again, the starting, the try, the long winter waiting ahead, that chill in the mornings, as the trees turn, leaf by leaf, showing what has been kept hidden.

———+———

TIRED AND SHIVERING, AND his feet carry him up and down the log to the attic, in the rain, the wind, as long as there is daylight and his boots track. They have the build, the fire they keep burning to warm their hands and coffee, as weather allows, and soon a trip to Fort Rich for supplies, and he has a list running of what they will need after the roof is in place, and he is thinking on the woodstove, how to heat a cabin this big to his standard, and after picking potatoes and driving a horse to sell wood in the winters he swears he will never be that cold again, not another day in his life, and then he thinks on Marie, the two of them alone.

"Where you gone to?" says Joseph.

He brings himself back to the task, the haul of the logs, but work is no longer the cure. His thoughts turned and turning over, and no matter where the start, the hang is on Marie. Her bringing supper and wild blueberries. Her humming a song from the Victrola. Her freshly washed hair. But there is, in his make, the need for evenness, for the keel, too little is better than too much, too little can be handled. How sudden the autumn came, as the aspen and birch leaves flash bright and golden, a catch of the eye before the falling. But something to be said for the spruce trees, unchanged, steadfast in their evergreen.

———+———

HAD SHE AND LAWRENCE changed in this year? Marie rifles through her hatbox and finds the wedding photos. The one of her and Lawrence, staring straight ahead, and she decides the picture will need a frame, for when they have furniture and a cabin, a rightful place, and there are others she wants to put under glass, the next trip to salvage, one of her and Sheila and Rosalie, there were none of her father that she had, though she remembers one of him and her mother that Rosalie must have kept, and then she comes across the pamphlets on statehood she was given at the Moose Lodge: *Let us end AMERICAN COLONIALISM! by Ernest Gruening, Governor of Alaska, 1939–1953, ALASKA THE UNITED STATES COLONY, Keynote Address.* She recalls learning about the thirteen colonies in school and looks over the twenty or so pages and pauses at what catches her eye. There is so much she does not know about the history here, and nothing would have convinced her not to move, as Alaska was far away from Texas and Valera's notions of who she should marry. But having no say on the matter, she knows what that means. She has lived the lack of radio and roads, heard how there should be more jobs, and jobs to build what is necessary. She should be able to vote for the President, for the governor. And why, for over eighty years, was this a question? A fight? She should be treated the same as other citizens of the United States. And of course Alaska should be one of those states.

———

JOSEPH AND LAWRENCE COME in for supper. Marie serves beans and hash and turns off the Victrola.

A long day, a pain in his shoulder. But tucked into the windowsill near the counter, a photograph. He leans in closer, him and Marie, their wedding day.

"Where'd this come from?" he says.

"Your father gave it to me for keeping, but I thought it was time to bring it out."

He takes a step back and crosses his arms. "I was worried Mother would ask about the veil," he says.

Marie nods.

"I told her later," says Joseph. "She was fine in the end."

"If I know anything, I know that isn't true," says Lawrence.

"No worse for wear," says Joseph. "And she'll always have a reminder of that important day."

"I admit I don't remember much," Lawrence says.

"No one does, son," says Joseph. "But what do you remember?"

"Only that I wanted to get married." He turns to Marie. "And that the bride was beautiful."

Marie blushes as she sets the silverware down.

"That's all that matters," says Joseph.

They settle into their seats. Marie asks about the cabin, and what they did that day, and Lawrence predicts they are a few weeks out.

"Was reading about statehood today," says Marie. "Seems we, as Alaskans, are getting a bad deal."

"Alaskans, I like the sound of that," says Lawrence. "But I heard you have to live here ten years before you can go calling yourself one."

"We've got acres, and we'll soon have a cabin," says Marie.

"Living out here on a bus for over a year—can call yourself anything you want in my book," says Joseph.

"I'll say." Marie dishes him another plate.

"Ain't right," says Lawrence. "Why did the government buy Alaska if it's not going to be a state? Just as good as the others, better."

"Seems to me," says Marie. "That's taking without giving."

"Can do what they want," says Joseph. "In no-man's-land."

Here they are, and the government said he had to clear trees and plant crops and he did not question the proving up, because this is what was asked. And he was ordered to jump out of a plane, and he fell from the sky with a parachute. And he returned home at his father's request, which was a relief, though he is ashamed, and grateful to be alive. Nothing good can come from this line of thinking, he knows, but he did not need to have felled so many trees, pulled those roots, for one cabin and perhaps a garden. But this bare patch is his doing, will be where he grows potatoes and alfalfa, the dirt a testament that those years in the fields were not in vain.

—+—

WHEN THEY PULL IN, Sheila is driving and Sly is in the passenger seat, eyes closed, with the window rolled down. He always drives if they are together. Sheila slams the door and he does not rouse.

"He can sleep it off in the truck," Sheila tells Marie, shaking her head. "Maybe he'll be of some help to Lawrence and Joseph tomorrow."

Sheila brings her things into the bus. "You would not believe how much money he wasted last night," she says. She taps her fingers on the counter. "There," she says. "Said my piece. Where are these berries we're picking?"

Marie lines the rucksack with burlap and packs the canteen and pistol. No one has seen tracks since the ones by the lake. They cover themselves in repellent. "Should we put some on Sly?" says Marie, looking out at him and the rolled-down window.

"Let him get eaten alive," says Sheila. "Though they'll probably keep away, with him smelling of whiskey. Like he bathed in it."

They pass the men working on the roof. "Almost finished," says Sheila. "Would you look at that?" She waves and Joseph waves back.

They walk into the woods and Marie knows there are ripe bushes near the spring.

"You ever think about having another baby?" says Sheila suddenly. Then she covers her mouth. "I'm sorry. It's too soon. I've just had something on my mind."

"I don't know my feelings," says Marie. "About that. About Lawrence." Marie did sometimes think of the boy she lost, how old he would be, but had avoided his grave since the burial.

"I would never want to hurt you," says Sheila.

"Can't be hurt any more than—" Marie throws up her hands.

"All he's been talking about lately is wanting a baby. And everything's come to naught." Her shoulders sag. "And yesterday I'd had it. I kicked him out of the trailer. And you know the rest."

"You two never stay mad at each other for long," says Marie.

They reach the spring and the blueberries are ripe. Marie holds the canteen under the water. They pick a handful to eat, their fingers turning purple with the juice. And they keep eating, even though Marie insists they fill the rucksack. She places one berry in the sack. "You're going to show me how to make hand pies," she says.

So they pick and pull and fill the burlap. Then Sheila takes a mound of berries in her hand, opens her mouth wide, and shoves them in. She chews with her cheeks bulging. Then she chokes and spits them out, coughing.

"Sheila, what in the world?"

She wipes her mouth on her sleeve. "I don't know if I'm going to get through this," she says, head bent down.

Marie, with tenderness, smooths the hair that has fallen over Sheila's face. "I know that you will," she says. She hands Sheila the canteen.

"What if you and I hadn't got married?" says Sheila, after taking a drink. "What if we somehow instead moved to Houston and got jobs? Pawned Valera's jewelry she was always accusing us of stealing."

"We'd have ended up nuns at the boarding school we went to, hated by all the girls."

"And I ain't a nun," Sheila admits. "But I could have been a nurse."

"You think anything could have convinced you not to marry Sly?" Marie picks more berries and Sheila sits down on the ground in a patch of sun. She pours water over her juice-stained hands.

"Money," says Sheila.

"I know you better than that," says Marie.

"I don't think you do," says Sheila. "But that's neither here nor there."

"I bet there's land near here," says Marie. "Why don't you homestead?"

"Sly keeps not saving enough," says Sheila. "And work isn't steady because he isn't."

"You moved up here," says Marie. "That's something."

"About as much as he could muster," says Sheila.

"Or live out here on this land," says Marie, and her voice fades away, unsure.

"Lawrence would never," says Sheila. "That man and his one hundred and fifty acres."

Marie holds up the heavy rucksack. "This enough?"

"You always need more," says Sheila. "But as many as that will make is good by me."

Sly is waiting for them at the bus, lounging on the couch. His hair is wet. He went and took a dip in the lake. "To punish myself," he says. He shivers at the thought of the water.

"You think I'll forgive you now," says Sheila, "because you went swimming?"

Marie heads out to give them a moment. She leans against the side of the army ambulance, but this never takes long. Soon Sheila will be sitting on Sly's lap and laughing, his arms around her, the quarrel forgotten. Marie toes the dirt with her boot, the sound of hammering in the distance, of driven nails meant to last.

CHAPTER 17

EYE IN THE GRAIN

OCTOBER

THE FINAL NAIL, AND the cabin stands, finished with the sweat and ache and bruise of work. Thirty-by-thirty feet, rows of felled and cut spruce logs eight inches in diameter, the bark black and brown with a reddish scrape, the dark rust of the corrugated steel roof painted with zinc, rafters with a pitch steep enough to slough snow in winter. The front porch with steps and gravel hauled in for low spots. And windows on all sides to let in the light, found at army surplus at Fort Rich, the ones in the front and back of the cabin do not open and have eight square panes, those on the sides open and lock with small brass keys. What he could buy there was respectable for the amount he saved. Hard-pressed to say what did not come from surplus or salvage, for most everything did, the kitchen table with two leaves, the chairs, not one alike, the dressing screen made from old skis, the lantern hanging on a hook above, the white enamel cooking stove and oven, the gray military-grade lead paint on the floor, the insulation in the attic and crammed into cracks between the logs, the woodstove for heating, and this is his handiwork, the promise to himself that there would not be a draft in a cabin this size, a large sixty-gallon military barrel outfitted as the stove and a thirty-gallon barrel connected as a chamber above so wood burns and hot smoke rises in the pipe and holds in the top barrel and radiates another round of warmth, and the brick hearth is the work of Joseph and Marie, the couch from the bus brought in and placed under a window, the two cabinets and the dishes stacked inside, and, of course, the frame Marie found for their wedding photograph. The bed is of carved oak, stored in the bus and passed down from his grandparents to Joseph and then to Lawrence, the headboard with shined crests of wood, carved posts, an heirloom, an eye in the grain.

Dared not sleep inside the cabin before finishing the work, an unspoken oath, and supper on the table proper, and Joseph tells Lawrence to sit at the head, and no, Lawrence sits on the side, and so Joseph takes the end and makes the sign of the cross, and Marie and Lawrence follow, and they fold their hands to recite the prayer. But this time Joseph reaches out, on his left he grasps her hand and on his right he grasps Lawrence's hand, and he waits, *go on,* and nods, a willing on them both. Lawrence has a fist on the table and his hand opens flat and she slides her hand across and he slides his hand toward her fingertips, not touching, and this is the divide, as far as they dare reach. Joseph leans forward, brings their hands together in front of him, the clasped and unclasped, and he begins, as he does before every meal, "Bless us, oh Lord," and together they say, "and these Thy gifts, which we are about to receive, from Thy bounty, through Christ, Our Lord, Amen." Joseph keeps hold, and says, "And bless this cabin and this land and those that dwell here. Safe passage as I leave tomorrow."

"Tomorrow?" says Marie, and pulls her hand free.

"Yes," says Joseph. "Work's done."

"You knew?" she says to Lawrence.

"Knew it would be soon," says Lawrence, he can barely speak. "Not tomorrow."

"I won't let you," she says.

"About time," says Joseph. "This is your home. I'll sleep in the bus tonight."

"No," says Marie. "You'll sleep here—we have the couch."

"Then it's settled," says Lawrence, and he fetches more firewood. Has to be out of that room, why didn't his father tell him, give him more of a warning?

—+—

MARIE WASHES AND RINSES the dishes in the two basins and Joseph dries them. Without him here, how will they be? There have been moments, but what of the long, dark days of winter?

"It's not goodbye," says Joseph. "I'll be back someday."

Marie shakes her head.

"You'll be fine," he says. "Just fine."

He hands her a red handkerchief from his pocket and she dabs her eyes.

"You here alone, I'd worry. Him here alone, I'd worry. But together? You'll find your way."

She folds and unfolds the handkerchief.

"I'm an old cuss of a man," he says. "I know what I'm talking about." He places a hand on her shoulder. "A smoke and a drink, that's what we need." He holds up three cigars. "Been saving these."

"Your stash," she says.

"Yours now," he says.

They stand on the porch and Joseph passes the wine.

She would have stayed up all night, playing cards and burning oil to avoid thinking of his leaving. But they turn in. Marie changes behind the dressing screen and climbs into bed and pulls the covers over her shoulders. Cabin is quiet, and on the couch Joseph breathes with the heaviness of sleep, and she waits for Lawrence to decide. Will he sleep on the floor as he has these many months? But oh, to sleep in a bed, the soft pillow, the legs stretching out, the clean sheets, the patchwork quilt Sheila made for this very day, wood burning in the stove.

His footsteps approach the other side. A tug on the covers and the weight on the mattress, and her back faces his, inches away.

"Good night," she whispers to the stillness in the air, to the stove and the walls and the roof.

THE CABIN FINISHED BEFORE the full of winter. And when his father leaves, who will be a help to them? What will be left? What will be the hold? A homestead, and the acres? Lawrence drives toward Anchorage, Joseph's truck is parked in Sly's yard. But in Wasilla, Lawrence ignores the turn for Anchorage and heads for Palmer and the Glenn Highway.

"You miss something there?" says Joseph.

"You'll see," says Lawrence.

When his parents bought their first car, his father would tell them they were going on a trip, and he sat in the front seat as the oldest, as Lois often stayed behind fretting about the expense, the destination a secret. Mendota Bridge is one place that stands out in his memory and where he took Marie after the wedding, and also to the statues of Paul Bunyan the lumberjack and Babe, his blue ox, and Mount Rushmore on a longer trip, the stone carving, though Joseph said, *A mountain should be a mountain,* and crossing rivers around the state, to see what men could build. *But nothing,* he said, *compared to what God had made.*

The Matanuska Glacier is a bridge of ice in a valley of snowcapped mountains. Years and years, time frozen before them, a radiant blue and green marbled with dark veins. A little stream pools in the flats and they walk the edge to reach the wall.

"In all my life I ain't seen anything so beautiful," says Joseph. There are tears in his eyes.

"Who can say they have touched a glacier?" says Lawrence.

"Who can say they have such a son?"

Lawrence shakes his head.

"You will be well," says Joseph, a hand on his shoulder. "You and Marie."

Lawrence hears the voices of children echo from the ice, but no one else is around. And then the sound of his steps following his father. Joseph will leave, as he must. And then what will be his life with Marie, and what will be in the asking? Lawrence knew this day was coming, but all the knowing had not prepared him. One winter alone in a bus, and he and Marie survived, this in their favor. And the cabin now standing. And so.

He drives and rain breaks over the road. The windshield fogs and Joseph sleeps with his head against the window, a long turn.

"Tell me what to do," says Lawrence, and Joseph startles awake, and nods, thinking on the words.

"I can tell you one thing," he says. "I learned a long time ago that an ornery man is a hurt to himself and those in his charge. And we had so little as it was. You hear me?"

"I hear you," says Lawrence.

But his father could find blessing and bounty in every lack, a poor man's trust in providence, *even the sparrow hath*. Lawrence knew this to be false, would not make peace with a miserable plight as Joseph had done. Though his father had years on him, his own strife. And others had talked of the bruising fear of their fathers, and in the barn Joseph would tell Lawrence to rub trough water in his eyes and cry out as he belted the post, to make Lois think the punishment had been dealt. But he wonders if he had needed that fear, though he would never tell Joseph this, who has fallen back asleep, the rain a fog on the highway.

Lawrence parks in front of the trailer. Sheila rushes out in a hooded coat and Joseph says, "My son, please remember what I said," before opening the door. Sheila, a sadness behind her smile, hands Joseph his keys, and there is a waiting in her eyes. Safe travels, and Joseph waves farewell, and his truck disappears down the road. Then Sheila turns to Lawrence and speaks her burden at last.

———

MARIE SWEEPS THE PAINTED floor, the first time, the first chore in the cabin. She adds wood to the cookstove and heats water for a bath. Alone, when was she last left to herself, left to do as she pleased? She soaks in the tub and washes her hair. Her belly, no one could know she had been with child by that flatness, not a scar or mark. What will they be? She knows more about Joseph than she knows about Lawrence. Joseph talks to her. No need to dirty more dishes and she eats saltines and lies down on the couch, her hair wrapped in a towel. She startles awake after a long, restful nap. Lawrence could be back soon. She combs her tangles and hums a song she remembers from the Victrola. Buckets the bathwater, and then tilts the tub and swishes out the suds. With Joseph here, had she ever thought that this was not hers? "It is," she says aloud. A thirst. Water, water, and each step toward the spring the trees are a blur of shaded green. There she drinks her fill, and what is empty will no longer be empty. But there was a child. And that child is no more. What can she claim? Not the sky, and not the crackling leaves and the white peel of birch bark. Maybe the spring of fresh water, and she cups her hands and drinks til she is sick, but not the rocks, not the clothes on her back, not a stitch.

These acres, the grave of her son. She is having a spell, her skin hot to the touch, a pain in her chest, and at the cabin she changes out of her pants and slips the white nightgown over her head. Maybe she should drive after Joseph, or visit Sheila. Anything to avoid Lawrence and the silence, and what if she tries and he does not, they depended so much on Joseph.

She collects what she might need. The army ambulance is here. But where are the keys? They are not on the hook, not on the counter. She opens a cabinet and slams it shut. And cannot forget the hatbox and documents and pictures and the claim. This lot, this land, and there must be a way for her to belong here. Then the engine of the truck, tires on gravel, and Lawrence has returned. Her hands clench at her sides. Steps on the porch, a stop, and then Lawrence opens the door, a question. So there he is, the man she married. What is to be done? What are they to each other? A cabin, a scratch to kill, a deed?

He holds out a letter. "Sheila sent this along," he says. "Some bad news."

"Tell me."

"Your mother has died."

She covers her mouth with both hands.

"I'm sorry," he says, and offers the proof.

She reads the thin pages and slides the letter under her pillow and covers herself with the quilt and lies there until evening. He promised Sheila he would bring her to Anchorage in the morning. But before the morning there are these hours, shuffling and carrying, and wood from the stack. *My mother is dead,* she says to herself. *My mother.* He fetches water from the spring. Oats cook in a boil. She is not hungry. She is not. A spoon clangs on the table and falls to the floor. He lights the lantern. Then his steps are near and he sits on the bed beside her, and she holds her breath. *Marie?* He draws the quilt from her tearless face, her eyes closed, and he whispers into her ear, *Marie, Marie,* mouths the hollow of her neck, the strap of the nightgown. Her hands reach for him, and this is how they go on, in the staying, in the salt.

CHAPTER 18

ONE DOES WITH WARNING

NOVEMBER

A BRACING FOR WINTER, wake and wait for morning. Lawrence rises to feed the stove and fill the cabin with the heat of new logs, and in these early hours, her thoughts are of her mother, Rosalie. Lawrence drove her to see Sheila, and a shock to them both, Rosalie dying this young, and neither had money to go to the funeral, and besides, that letter meant the burial had been held. Valera had Sheila's address and the wits to write, she could have very well not and that she did was more generosity they had wrangled from her their whole lives, and the letter said Rosalie had taken up with a well-to-do man who brought her down to Houston to see a doctor who said he could try to fix her heart damaged from the typhoid fever she had as a child, why she was frail and sick all her days, but she died before he had that chance, and Valera, in her swerving script, said Rosalie had been laid to rest in Conroe. The last time Marie saw her was at the chapel when Sheila married Sly, and then she met Lawrence and stayed, so she never said goodbye to her mother, not in the way one does with warning of dying, though Rosalie had been saying farewell to her daughters their whole lives, and ain't that a shame, to live your whole life leaving a place only to have your bones set there for the everlasting, but maybe that is what she would have wanted, a headstone inscribed with her one married name, Rosalie Ann Kubala, and the inscription BELOVED DAUGHTER, which declared her rightful place in the family.

"You dreaming?" says Lawrence in bed beside her. "Who you talking to?"

Marie stirs and her body aches with tenderness. "Don't feel right," she says.

"You sick?"

"My mother," says Marie.

"That's a story," he says.

"Thought it was behind me," says Marie. She sets her feet to rise and stands and sits down.

"The matter?" says Lawrence.

"Under the weather, I suspect," says Marie.

"I'll make the coffee," says Lawrence.

The smell of the brew fills up the cabin. And when the cast-iron warms the hash, she shakes her head at the air of cooking.

"I won't be eating this," she says. "No coffee neither."

She shuffles to a kitchen chair and sits down.

"You want anything?" says Lawrence, with concern. "You always have coffee."

"Pilot bread," says Marie, and with the words out of her mouth, she knows this feeling. She knows. And the night she received news of her mother's passing, how she and Lawrence returned to each other. Could wait to be sure, no need making a bother over an inkling, and the losing of the last one, the burying of her first, and she is not mistaken, both sick and hungry, and, "I think I might be in that way," she says.

"Now I've got to sit down," says Lawrence, and he crosses his arms, one side of his mouth stretching into a grin, his foot tapping the wooden floor.

"The hospital," she says.

His face reddens and the tapping rests. "I promise," he says.

"Then it's settled," says Marie.

But to be settled, Marie is still waiting, that hold, and thinking on this child, the coming months, the promissory title. Folks used to say in the later years that Valera could, even as a woman, have made a claim on the acres, prove her husband reckless, but she was wedded to her woes. Would rather be wronged, go on about her slights and sorrows by his hand than talk some sense in the eyes of the law. From the troubles of Valera and Rosalie she knew that documents made a path in the world. And in August, she and Lawrence will have lived this time in the cabin he built, and with the crops he will file and sign the proof. And what is to stop her from adding her name?

Lawrence heads out for more firewood and she rushes after, without a coat or boots, the snow cold on her feet. She paces the porch, *Got every right, this land, having his child,* and burns through her reasons, she will wait and ask when there is a chance, and the sun rises in the late morning, shadows of mountains beyond the dark line of the low and unseen water, and a stretch of dusky sky, a pale yellow and lavender, and a thick stir of clouds with sweeps of fire and fireweed, and who could say this was not meant for her?

"I'll never understand how you're not cold," says Lawrence, with a laugh. "You coming in?"

She shakes her head. "Look at the sky."

They stand on the porch, Lawrence holding a stack of firewood. "That is a vision," he says, and then heads inside, and the last of the clouds steel to gray.

She returns to her pacing, her arms crossed. What made her a married woman, not a wedding, or a wedding band, and her ring finger still bare, for there had been lumber and nails and furniture to buy. And not a child, or how many there will be, but the license, signed and dated. And what she has learned, with the note that said, *150 ACRES,* is that one scrap of paper, scratched and folded, could lead to another that would be recognized by the powers that be. Her name on it would not be deemed official, not by any law besides her own, but that would be enough.

——+——

HE CANNOT SEE HER walking on the porch and he opens the door and she is sitting against the wall, knees tucked. "Come in," he says. "Out of the cold."

She stares ahead.

"Please," he says. He knows she will stubborn herself to frostbite. "What is the matter?"

"I know I don't have a ring," she says. "And this child on the way."

"We'll get rings," he says. "When we can."

"That's not my worry," says Marie.

"That we could lose—"

"I was thinking of next year," says Marie. "If everything goes to plan."

"God willing," says Lawrence. Then smiles. "That's something my father would say."

"I want to ask you something," says Marie. "And there's no right time."

"Ask me," says Lawrence. He opens the door wider. "In here."

She follows him into the cabin.

"This seems important," he says, "which calls for this," and he pours whiskey from the bottle. They sit down at the kitchen table.

"August you will have twenty acres of crops," she says.

"Yes, I will," says Lawrence.

"I want my name on the land," she says, with sudden force.

"That's not how things are done," says Lawrence, measured.

"I want to write my name on the papers, in ink," says Marie. "I want to be there at the bureau."

"Won't mean anything," says Lawrence, and he shakes his head in disbelief.

"If it don't mean anything, then why not? You'll know and I'll know, and God is our witness."

"It's not a woman's place, for good reason," he says, the anger rising in his voice.

"You didn't seem to mind for the wedding, how we both signed." Her hands grip the seat of the kitchen chair.

"Are you trying to make a fool out of me?" and he slams a hand on the table.

"Make you a fool?" she says. She jumps up and the chair falls back and hits the floor. "You take that back."

"Let me think," he says. "Just sit down."

"Not until I can sign my name," she says.

He drinks the whiskey, the kill in his throat. His father had warned him against this orneriness, and he knows what his father would advise.

"You can sign," he says, against his own conviction.

"You swear on your life? On this child's?"

He will have to convince her, and himself. "I swear."

"No shame in that," she says, as the words she will hold him to pass over, what is sworn is sworn, is done, the coming weight.

He hands her the bottle, watches her drink, and then takes his, and they are, in this, together. Where was the line and who made the line, and would they know what crossing had happened? The whiskey in his mouth, *if you burn I will burn,* on this land, in this very place.

What did this child mean, for her, for him? A bond that could not be broken no matter their foolishness. What has he done, and yet, he did not know her, Marie, his wife, who would ask this of him, and she did not know him, and he could not have foreseen all that had happened, in a matter of minutes, the tie to her, in another child, and then the promise of everything he had worked for and wanted for his life, and the taking.

He has chores, he says. And he staggers away from the cabin, away from her. The land belongs to him. This he holds. And Marie? If he willed. But her eyes when she asked, as if she had known, and he is forsaken, her in the nightgown out in the snow, the waves of light surrounding them, and again, with the news of her mother, that wanting. Married, for children, for this life here, which he could have made it alone, plenty had, and was there more burden in sharing what he had found with a compass and a mistaken map? So there is Marie, and the child she carries, and he is helpless beside her. She could not know, and he will not confess, how his hands betray him when they reach for her in the night, and so he will better his judgment, he will retreat.

CHAPTER 19

A LOG CABIN, A LIFE

DECEMBER

CHRISTMAS, THEY ARE AGREED, one gift for each other, the same allowance, and when the time is right, Marie is to tell Sheila about the baby. She has not been sick in the mornings for a few days, and her belly is easily hidden, or the truth would be revealed. Lawrence and Sly have cigars on the porch and Marie has her chance, and she wrings her hands and trades her telling for how Lawrence agreed to let her sign her name on the deed, for her own keeping.

"Didn't think you had it in you to ask," says Sheila. "I never would."

Marie ties her apron strings.

"What gave you such a notion?" says Sheila.

"Thinking about Mama, and maybe Valera taught us something useful in the end," says Marie.

Sheila places a bowl on the table. "Thought you and Lawrence were dancing around each other," she says, and stirs in the cornmeal. "First year is the hardest. So much you don't know. Sly and me had our share of rows. You remember."

"I remember a few," says Marie.

"When I'd come see you at Valera's. Stay the night."

"Sly wasn't working out of town?" Marie heats the cast-iron pan on the stove.

Sheila peers into the bowl. "Drinking out of town is more like. I put my foot down."

"How'd he take that?"

"We're here, ain't we? Moved all this way. We'll have a family, someday."

"You will," says Marie, and she moves to grab the hot pan handle, and Sheila yells, as she could have burned her bare hand. And that was her way, always looking out for her. Marie does not know what kind of mother she will be, but has no doubt that Sheila would be a natural. And cannot bring herself to tell her, not yet, and will have to warn Lawrence not to give her away.

———————

SLY TAKES THE FLASK from Lawrence and drinks the rest on his first turn. Family, brother-in-law, but if not for the sisters, Lawrence would not choose to smoke cigars with Sly, here or anywhere, as Sly throws his hands, a slosh on the porch. Sly had tried to join the military but had a heart murmur, and just as well, Lawrence can reason why he would not have lasted long, the lack of discipline, the loose firing of his mouth.

"We're hoping for children soon," Sly says, and Lawrence nods. "Figure one of these would be for that," and the cigar embers. "You ever think of how you'll be as a father? Your old man is a good man. Mine, well, he was a bruiser."

"Want more?" says Lawrence.

"I'm still standing," says Sly. "But trying to be good. That's what I like about you. You don't have to try."

"We all do," says Lawrence.

"What she deserves," says Sly, as he watches Sheila in the window. "That woman is the best thing that ever happened to me."

Snow in the air, waiting, but what did Lawrence know with such certainty? Some days he forgets what Marie had asked, and the hours fly by, in good weather and good spirits, and she falls asleep in the crook of his arm, and then he remembers and lies there, wide awake. And others, he wants more than anything to be alone, his breathing shallow, a flutter in his chest, and he has to catch himself and wait for it to pass. But he is trying. Sly had found a Christmas gift for Marie and Sheila, something he would have never thought of on his own, to be sure, and so he went along, hoping this would cover his feeling of having two minds, his restlessness.

—+—

A TRADITION IN LAWRENCE'S family, a German custom, kept even after the war and German towns changed their names—after the pump and lighting of the kerosene lantern, after sitting down to supper, sweeping the floor, and washing and drying the dishes, after a dessert of condensed milk and vanilla over icy snow, a pouring of cherry wine, and the stoke and approval of the fire in the stove—to gather around the small spruce tree decorated with a red garland of painted wooden beads and open presents on Christmas Eve. He hands a ribbon-tied box to Marie, and Sly hands one to Sheila.

Sheila and Marie untie the gifts and lift the lids to find ice skates in smooth cream leather, blades sharp and new. "They're beautiful," says Sheila.

Marie runs her fingers over the leather.

"For the lake," says Lawrence. "We can go there tomorrow."

"Marie, say something, for goodness' sake," says Sheila.

Marie chews her lip and her teary eyes catch the light. "Of course," she says, a soft nod, and wipes her eyes. She stands and thanks Lawrence with a kiss on the cheek. She suspects he is over the allowance, and her gift is clearly not. She hands him hers, wrapped in old newspaper and twine, and prays he is not disappointed.

He unfolds the wool mackinaw coat in red and black plaid—secondhand, and Sheila mended a few tears and rethreaded the buttons—and tries it on for size, and Marie worries the shoulders are large for his thin frame, but the coat is enough of a fit. "A keeper," says Lawrence, and his smile is a relief.

Sly's gift from Sheila is a fur-trapper hat, and he bounds over to her, the flaps hanging around his chin, and nuzzles her neck, and her laughter fills the cabin, and she has knitted scarves for them in teal yarn, and another pouring of cherry wine, and Sly sings a carol in his booming voice, and Marie steps out the back door for the outhouse, swaying and humming along. On her return, the cabin windows shine from the lantern, the gentle falling of fresh snow, and one voice singing has become three, and she walks around to the porch, and away, to take in the light seen for miles and miles, the tip of the powder-covered roof, the deep tracks of her trail that leads to a life, a homestead.

————

PRISTINE, THE MORNING, WHITE mountains in their pearl, every bare branch laden, abundance over what is scarce, before the rousing, the rustle, the others asleep, remembering the times with his father, whittling figurines, a loon, a rabbit, a dove, the only gifts, there was always a tree even if supper was broth, and his father would say, *This beauty of a winter morn is more than we deserve.* Lawrence did not know his meaning then, but he could now, as he leans against the kitchen table. He has this cabin, and in the new year he will be a father, and a crop of twenty acres will fulfill the deed to the land. Which brings him to Marie, and he knows what he swore, he cannot go back on his word, but he is changed, since that day, an unknowing. He had woken up fearing he had disturbed the others. But no one stirred. Sly and Sheila, sleeping so close on the couch, old to each other, and she turns and he turns, of the same, and would that ever be him and Marie, and did they have that once, when this living was a dream?

————

SPRUCE TREES FLOCKED WITH snow, and Sheila and Marie walk with skates over their shoulders, the snow clean and bright.

"Someday this will all be yours," says Sheila.

"Ours," says Marie. "After we have farmed twenty acres."

"You still have no wedding rings," says Sheila.

"The money," says Marie. "Or rather, the money Lawrence decides to spend."

"Thought Christmas was the time," says Sheila. She shakes a branch and the snow rains down on Marie, and Sheila tilts back her head and crows.

Marie loosens the snow from her scarf and shivers and opens her mouth to tell Sheila that she is having a child, but why ruin her laughter, her lightness?

Lawrence and Sly are at the lake, camped with a bonfire started, the shovel and broom they used for clearing, flasks in hand, Lawrence in his red mackinaw, a thermos of coffee waiting. Marie promises herself one turn around the lake, with care not to fall, and laces the skates, Sheila at her side stands in the snow and holds out her hands, as is her way since they were girls, and together their blades carve the untouched ice, and Lawrence and Sly wave as they pass by, how Sheila remembers too well, balance and glide even as Marie stumbles and Sheila holds her, and they carry on, close a lap, and Marie, on a swing of the turn, releases Sheila's hand and sails to the drift and bank, safe. "Go on," she says.

Sheila follows her. "You're not quitting."

"I need to rest," she says.

Sheila stands over her. "Tell me," she says.

Marie shakes her head.

"What did Lawrence—?" and Sheila's eyes narrow.

"No, sit down," says Marie.

Sheila sits close, concern in her face.

"This," says Marie, and she lifts her sweater and places her palms on her belly.

Sheila draws a breath, and does not look at her. "I'm over the moon for you," she says. "I really am."

"Sheila, wait," says Marie, as she leaves. Her sister more a mother to her, even as a girl, and what could she say or give her, as Sheila turns again and again, blade over blade, the scrapes and lines, the ice another face to be washed clean.

CHAPTER 20

THIS OLE HOUSE

JANUARY 1958

A FAINT BEACON IN the blue of the frost, and the Knik Bar is in full swing, though Pete is dancing alone to the jukebox. Jones pours the beers, and *down the hatch,* and Lawrence raises his glass to Marie, and the music stops. "I'm trying to write to my wife," says a man with a scraggly beard that makes him look older than he is, and he holds up the electrical cord and huffs back to his table in the corner.

Jones shakes his head. "If he touches my jukebox again, he's done."

"He's lonesome. Can you blame him?" says Pete.

"This is my fine establishment. I can blame whoever I want," says Jones, and he nods to a man who comes through the door. "Like Henry here, you should meet Lawrence and Marie, their property might be just miles from you." Henry Mor, clean-shaven, short, and stocky, lives near Point MacKenzie and is moving his wife to Alaska in the summer.

"You hear they might build a causeway out here?" says Henry. "Why I picked my spot. Rumors are we're going to be a state and the capital will be close to Anchorage. So they'll want to build a bridge across the water and our land is prime."

"First I'm hearing," says Lawrence.

"Juneau won't give up being the capital," says Jones.

"A capital you can only reach by air or water," says Henry. "That make sense?"

"They'll say it worked all this time for the territory," says Jones.

"State could change things," says Henry.

"And then maybe we'll finally win this Cold War," says Pete, and he leans on the bar for support. "What have we got these missiles in Alaska for?"

"I don't want to hear anything more about Sputnik or the Russians today," says Jones. "A few men from the Nike site came by the other day, said they've been on alert ever since that satellite launched."

Pete turns to Lawrence. "No hard feelings from the last time, I hope," and he salutes. Though Lawrence has never told him or anyone at the bar about his time in the service.

"Knock that off," says Jones. "I don't mind you wasting your pay here, but have some manners."

"I'm just having a good time," says Pete, and he finishes his beer. The music starts again. "So," he says, "can I give the lady a whirl?"

"I'll dance with my wife," says Lawrence, who has no more patience for Pete's mischief. He holds out his hand to Marie and Pete backs away.

Marie obliges. "And I'll dance with my husband."

Lawrence is careful at first, she is with child, though she hides this in a cardigan, but then he spins her around and around to the blare of "This Ole House" like he's known the song his whole life, a knee-slapper with a woman's belled voice, and everyone chimes in at the chorus. When the song ends, she is a fluster, face shining.

"Where'd you learn to dance like that?" says Marie.

"Army," he says, and grins.

"Have to catch my breath," says Marie.

Pete turns down the music and the man writing to his wife orders a whiskey from Jones.

"Told you beer only," says Jones.

"Fine," says the man. "And I want to know. What does 'Knik' mean anyway?"

"Heard different things," says Jones. "Some say it means fire, or fire on the water, seen overlooking the bay. This area used to be a trading outpost.

But then I was told it was from the name of the Alaska Native people that lived in the area, or what they called this place."

"Saw some Natives in town," says the man. "So they're out here?"

"Not so much," says Jones, with caution.

"Good to keep to your own," says the man, with a solemn nod. "Heard all the Negroes in Anchorage live in Eastchester Flats. They have their places. We have ours."

"So tell me," says Jones, "why'd you come all this way north from the Lower Forty-eight?"

"Government in my business. And too many of those kinds, if you ask me. And now they will let anybody in our schools. And let anybody vote. Nothing civil about what Eisenhower did. He'll get what's coming to him."

"Was that what I was asking?" says Jones. "And in this bar we respect the President."

"Where you from?" says the man.

"So many places it doesn't matter anymore," says Jones. "But here, mostly."

"Where you from?" says Henry to the man.

"I claim allegiance to no state or union," says the man, arms crossed.

Henry points at himself. "Pennsylvania." He points at Lawrence.

"Minnesota," says Lawrence.

Then Marie. "Texas," she says.

"Here we are," says Henry, and he raises his beer. "The United States of Alaska."

Jones and Lawrence and Marie raise their beers, but the man refuses. When he leaves, Henry says, "He lost me on that last bit. Could be cabin fever. Hope his wife is here soon. Mine's taking care of her sister who's ill, and I know I've worried about myself, staring at the walls."

"Seen it plenty. Thinks he can come up here and make his own rules," says Jones.

"I have one neighbor close," says Henry. "Charles and his family, and we built our places together. Keeps me in the right mind. And a welcome to know you two now."

"I know what else will help," says Jones, and he hands Henry a newspaper, the *Anchorage Daily Times.*

"Good man," Henry says. "We become a state, and you think we'll get radio towers and telephone poles out here?"

"Took me years just to get electricity and that jukebox," says Jones.

"Only one for miles," says Henry.

"I'm a businessman," says Jones. "Beer and bellyaching and a little music, what else is there?"

"Heard you have a sourdough started in the Gold Rush," says Henry.

"Listen, you cheechakos need to live here ten years before I would let you near my stash. I'll give you sourdough when you're a Sourdough."

"What about me?" says Marie.

"For you, darling," says Jones, "five years."

"I'll remember," says Marie. She turns to Lawrence, and he has forgotten how many beers they have been served. "What about you, darling?"

"Time to go home," he says. "Before it's too dark."

"I'm here Thursdays, if you ever need," says Henry.

Marie stands and veers, leans on Lawrence. "This ole man," she says to the bar, "is mine."

The patrons whistle and congratulate Lawrence. Because he can, he makes a show, and carries Marie over his shoulder, and walks out the door. He steadies her against the army rig, and remembers he should be careful with her because of the baby. He is a little drunk, and helps her inside.

"Take me home," she says, and laughs. He drives slowly, rolls down the window so the cold air will keep him awake. Back at the cabin, he helps her up the steps of the porch. She winds the Victrola and plays a record. He tends to the fire in the stove.

"We didn't dance at our wedding," she says. "Not proper."

He shakes his head.

"For me?" she says.

A calm this winter night, and they sway and the song is unknown to him, the words are a wash, but the meaning is plain, and her head rests against his shoulder, one step and another step, and neither of them leads, and he follows and she follows. They find themselves at the bed. They find each other, in that dying, and tearing down, hollow and given. But while Marie sleeps, her hands cradling her belly, he is troubled by his willingness, his yielding. He stands at a nearby window, a few stars as sharp as he is dulled, loose, and spent, and there is the dipping spoon in the sky, the long handle, the measure for a hunger that cannot be.

———+———

SHE WAKES TO THE sound of shoveling snow in the dark morning, and she rubs her eyes. This again, and she is not going to pretend as she did before. She lights the lantern and stands in the doorway.

"What is the matter?" she says.

"Just an early start," he says, looking down.

"I know you did this before," she says.

"Can't sleep," he says. And lifts and piles.

"Should I worry?"

"Comes but always goes," he says.

She crosses her arms. "You can talk to me."

"It's the doing that helps," he says.

There is no convincing him. "Just don't stay out too long," she says.

She returns to bed and leaves the lantern burning. Sharp scrapes of the shovel, over and over, and what could it be? He seems to regret her, and she wonders why, his pulling away, just as she starts to believe she knows a thing or two about him. In his letters to his father, he must tell Joseph the truth of what he is feeling, and she is tempted to try and read one, but how would she take him reading her letters to Sheila, and she has her answer. When he is finished she will make him talk, this cannot go on. Another winter of him escaping outside when he can, the long silences.

She wakes to bright lights, a chopping of air, and falls out of the covers in a scramble to stand. Cowers on the floor as she finds her bearings, and Lawrence runs to the door and the shotgun, and they realize a helicopter has arrived. Something drops from above and lands on the snow with a thud and Lawrence gives a wave, and she swears she hears a voice yell down, *Happy New Year.* She wraps a blanket around her shoulders as Lawrence walks up the porch carrying a boot. The helicopter leaves and the sun has just begun to rise, but not enough, and she brings out the lantern again. Lawrence is in a daze, and he unpacks the newspaper in the boot, and brings out a brown bottle labeled VANILLA and a note that says that starting next Sunday the battalion chaplain will be coming every Sunday to hold a church service at the Nike site, homesteaders welcome.

"That's what they woke us up for?"

"Scared me half to death," says Lawrence. "I think they had a laugh."

Marie opens the bottle and takes in the warm scent. "Strong," she says. "Looks like someone made it themselves."

"Should we put some in our coffee this morning?"

"We should," she says.

"You don't want to go on Sunday, do you?" he says.

She can tell he does not want to, and the last time he went there was to ask a favor, send a letter to Joseph to ask him to come to Anchorage. "Only if we think we need the company," she says.

And he is not one for company. And here he is, carrying on as if the night did not happen.

"Lawrence," she says, "are you worried about the baby?"

"I'm happy," he says.

And without thinking she says, "Are you happy with me?"

He runs his hands through his ruffled hair. "Of course."

"Something is bothering you," she says.

"If I knew what it was, I would tell you."

"Are you at least trying to tell your father?"

He nods slowly. Chews on the question. "In so many words."

She laughs, and he is taken aback. "I'd say few, not many."

"Right about that," he says.

So she lets him be, and they drink their coffee with vanilla and powdered creamer.

"So that causeway," he says. "And if we're a state and Anchorage the state capital. This land would be worth a mint."

"As if you knew," she says, thinking of how he chose the acres, becoming lost, the helicopter lifting him into the sky.

"Been thinking," he says. "Soon as the ground is thawed and dry, I'm going to go to the bureau and demand a proper map. Stake the land. Not the wooden ones, metal ones with my last name, so there will no question this is Beringer property. Who knows what could change?"

"A good plan," she says, for all that could come to pass this coming year, after waiting, after one winter living in the bus, and another in the cabin.

———+———

HE HAD WOKEN UP to crawling on his skin, nothing there but a sheet and quilt, and waited for his bearings, and the trembling to ease, and while he shoveled snow he found comfort in the weight of a load being moved, in the path uncovered. But there is a pain and guilt, a voice that says that he should not be here, his father made a petition and he returned home a son. And there were so many sons who were lost. At least his misery was a penance back when he had nothing on the farm, before he moved north. So having a cabin, a wife, is a burden, even if for so long he was without. And his father did not know everything, he could not bring himself to admit that he was a coward, in the war, marching on foreign soil. Dirt, he knows, and it knows him.

He has not replied to his father's last letter. So he sits down to write, and maybe reveal what he has kept to himself since the war, but his hand hovers over the paper after *I have something to tell you.* He imagines his father's face, the pained furrow of his brow, and he writes instead that they are going to have a child. And he does not tell him what Marie asked of him, in a way he does not believe it himself.

Marie turns from the stove and peers over his shoulder. He covers his words as if he has written what he was thinking.

"I thought you would've told him by now," she says.

"Got behind," says Lawrence.

"Tell him we miss him," she says.

"I'll write that from you," says Lawrence.

"Let me write it," says Marie. "He'd like that."

Because Marie told him that Sheila had a hard time hearing the news about her being with child, and suspected she would not visit or write back for a while, Lawrence gives her the pen. She sits down and takes the last page. When she is done, he, without looking at her note, folds and tucks the letter away in the envelope.

CHAPTER 21

THROUGH THE FLARE

FEBRUARY

FREEZING AIR THICK WITH fog, white as death, hovering and sitting low, black tips of spruce poking through, and Lawrence walks through the snow without aim. A child on the way is good news, and building the cabin had filled his mind with nails and hauling and measurements, and then Joseph leaving when it was finished, and Marie's mother dying, and he lost the days, and missed October 20, did not give the attention as he did every year. But then the spells of not sleeping and that helicopter from the Nike site came, and now he cannot stop thinking of this error in the wait of winter, the hours of darkness. His only official jump as a paratrooper seven years ago, the plane, the flying boxcar, and the engine is loud, the sweat and shaking, no room, crammed in and sitting on the floor with his knees bent, the command, *Stand up,* and how he stood when no one else could, the gear front-loaded and heavy, rucksack, water, reserve, rations, rifle, and he grabs the straps of the soldier to his left and lifts him up, every soldier helps another to their feet, waiting for the signal, and then the green light, and the rush of cold and thin air, the relief of being weightless, and he pulls the release cord, and the tilt of the chute as it fills, and the bloom of white parachutes all around him, and how brown and dry the mountains and the shorn rice fields below, their borders a loose sprawl, *who made them, who decided,* and he prays for the snipers to miss as he pilots the canopy, elbows in, knees bent, chin tucked, feetfirst on contact, then on his back, through the flare, through the shock.

He knows he must be worrying Marie, in the cabin behind him. Ice fog sets in the light, yellows in the distance, and he moves slowly, careful not to disturb the air. He remembers they landed north of Pyongyang, and the next day walking along a railway line, then through a valley, and this was where the enemy battalion appeared in an ambush, with mortars and cannons, blast after blast, thunder shaking in his ears, the plumes of smoke, calls for the medic, the order to withdraw west, and he does not look at the blood or he will be sick, and useless. Wilson the medic bringing a soldier to safety, but he presses forward, scrapping to higher ground, the ringing in his ears when the firing stops, and not a scratch, not a wound on his body. Another night waiting for an attack, bayonet on his rifle, and he does not move, the scream and flap of helicopters coming for the injured, so many are missing, and Wilson is missing, and a patrol finds him, shot, his body shielding the body of another soldier—he had gone back, had heard there was a man down. And Lawrence has to live knowing Wilson saved those men, and he only saved himself. If his father and family knew, what would they say? How could he explain, his confusion, how his feet trudged onward and then gave out, and he promised he would be a better soldier, for Wilson and the others, and suddenly the discharge papers, and the return to the farm.

And here, all the training, the orders, were words he learned and could no longer speak, and the haze of battle, the dust of debris and dirt, and the dead, and as he sinks into unmarked powder, this soft landing, the snow beneath him as he crawls and waits for each beat and pulse to be heard, and earned.

—+—

A NIGHT OF TURNING, of pacing, loading the stove, and when he finally sleeps, the morning light edges through the windows. Then the quilt falls on the floor and he stands, hair mussed, groggy to her questions. Lawrence throws on his coat and hat and pants over his long johns, and the heavy clobber of boots as he heads out the back door toward the outhouse, but then walks through the cabin to the front porch, and down the steps, and maybe a bit of fresh air will do him some good, though it is cold as ever, and he had best take a quick turn. Time ticks with the stove, and she boils oatmeal and cleans the pot. She walks a circle around the cabin. He should be back. But he is not himself, and what if he is lost in the fog, setting lower and lower, and she hollers his name from the porch, and her voice does not carry, sound swallowed by the air, his gloves were in his coat, at least. The mountains beyond the marsh and the bay have moved closer, and there are more of them in number, another row, crests and broken teeth, white snow and dark ridges stretched and mirrored along the horizon, as an old sermon once said, *the mountains trembled,* and Pioneer Peak towers over them, unmoved.

Marie covers her eyes, the strange sight in the winter cold, she must be ill or faint. She calls out for Lawrence and there is no answer. She calls again. She should drive the army ambulance into the fog and search for him. Finds the keys and near the door is the loaded pistol, a sound that can be heard for miles. She stands on the porch, sures her stance, and aims for the sky and shoots, a hollow pitch, one bullet down, the echo, and stillness, and she readies another, how could he not heed the signal, how could he leave her here for so long, and then the red of his mackinaw coat, the wave of his arms, *Marie, I'm here,* and she lowers the gun to her side.

He trudges up the porch and she brings him in and makes him sit down near the stove. Unlaces his boots. And then she places both of her hands on his knees and fixes her eyes on his. "You're telling me what this is all about," she says.

And in his weariness, what he had not told his own father, or another soul, he tells her. He was not a good soldier, not honorable, or brave. And a hero's welcome at home, the pride in Joseph and Lois as they said he served his country and was home now to help them, a son's duty. Though his brother once said that Lawrence stole from him by coming back, that he could have taken care of the farm himself, had one good leg and two good arms, and then they never spoke again of any matter, only business and fixing the barn, and rightfully so.

"No one would blame you if they knew," she says. "Not your family." She holds his face in her hands. "Not me."

And these are the words he has wanted to hear from her, but not for this.

———+———

MARK THE DAYS AND lose the days. Marie keeps him up late with cribbage, shuffling the cards and pegging points. A pile of butterscotch wrappers on the floor. He is waiting for her to look at him with pity, or the pain of knowing. But they both squint under the light of the lantern. And here they are again, counting fifteen two and fifteen four, and they are waiting for winter to tell them when, and they are waiting for a child. The hospital, her asking, and how he could not explain his fear, better for him to be wounded than him to see the wounds of others, better still to not have either. Could he explain now, with her knowing, but he is worn of talking, and it is enough to lay down a hand, and *a pair for two and a pair for four.*

Her face, her long, dark hair, those golden eyes that change color in the light, green with her concern, and tears she might have hid from him in the outhouse. He thought he was back there, in the war, as real to him as the snow, as Marie's smile, as he cuts the deck for a starter and turns over a jack and she pegs past him on the board, *two for his heels.* He yawns, he is finally tired, not the kind after a day of felling, but a deeper kind, a ratted knot undone, thin and frayed.

"Time for bed," says Marie, the game unfinished.

And he knows she means their bed, and not the couch he has taken to more and more with these fits, with Marie dying of the stove's heat, sweat along her brow. She gives him all of the quilt and lies beside him, and he is warm and his mind is quiet, blank.

———+———

AND THE MOUNTAINS TREMBLED, she saw them with her own eyes, and would not concern Lawrence. Had they heard her pleas, her searching for him, the mountains so close, as if she had beckoned them with her calling? Above the fog, the view clear, not a cloud, and Pioneer Peak reaching past the heavens. And she was not feverish, as she is now, the pillow soaking beneath her hair. This is the same as the last, though her belly is bigger. Worry, but worry not, will not happen a second time. What is luck but a willing, they say, and then a nod from God above. And she envies Lawrence because he can point to a war, to something out there, that he survived, and she—her very own flesh and blood a failing. So she understands Sheila and will give her time. And she knows what Lawrence told her is between them, and she will tell her sister only a little, enough to be honest. Snow taps at the glass, a web of frost across the corners of the windows, and she leaves the bed to open one, the little brass key, the thrill of the cold on her skin. *Dear Sheila,* she begins. *This winter night.*

CHAPTER 22

WHAT COULD BE LOST

MARCH

ON THIS DAY, ANOTHER life ago, there was a child, and there is a heaviness to the morning. Lawrence breathes in the dark, and they are lying back to-back, Marie stretched on her side, a folded blanket to rest her heavy belly, sweat and damp beneath her head. They are both awake but in agreement, not yet. The cabin is stoked with heat, stifling air, and Lawrence has the quilt tucked around him, lean as he is, a shiver of a man, and she is a spilling over, stretching and growing, her bones loose, her patience thin.

She sits on the edge of the mattress, sick and shaky, and the sound again, a sudden calling scream, the flash of the stove on the windows, and a deep sigh as she rises, tips to the door, and undoes the latch. She leans against the doorway, and beyond the porch, where the woods and wilds end, a fox stands at the tip of the clearing, black nose and eyes, black stockings on his front legs, still, and listening. And then his head turns, another fox comes threading through the trees, and they run together, their rust-blown fur a blaze against the snow and spruce.

———+———

COLD WAKES HIM, A sense that the fire could be out, though he knows he filled the stove an hour ago when the day could not begin, so he willed every muscle to fall, through the floor and the snow and the dirt, down to the end of the pilings. Empty hours in the dark, until this draft, and he opens his eyes to the morning, the cabin door swung open. He places his feet on the floor and waits, he will dress, he will hold himself upright, for her, for the child they buried. How time could soften some of the blow, Marie blaming him—that which threatened to ruin them both. What had they granted to each other, but another beginning, this date on the calendar noted with a small cross.

—+—

STIRRINGS INSIDE, AND LAWRENCE asks her to close the door. He is clothed, and waiting. She dresses, and they set out, as planned, the first task, so the day can go on, and Lawrence brings the candle and matches, the pistol in the leather holster, not the shotgun, for the bears are in hibernation. Snow is packed under their boots, a somber trail toward a vigil. Neither speaks, the deeper woods hushed around them, the bluster of the air softening with rays of sunlight. Marie drags her feet, thinking on the hours of pain, the waiting, the blizzard that held them, the wrap of the baby in her arms, there is a bitterness there, a spring from a stone, that comes in the darkness, or with a kick inside her belly, a sense of what could be lost, how one might say the will of God almighty, not for her, no comfort in God taking a child, in the fate of a blizzard, even in blaming Lawrence, or herself, but a regret in carving into the tree the date of that death, the deep scar that will outlive her in the end.

—+—

THROUGH THE WOODS THEY walk, and with each step, Lawrence has the feeling he is watching himself from above, a moving speck on a map that is white and unlined, and he knows where he is going, but on the map he reaches the edge of the white and turns around, and he knows they should do the same, but what reason could he give? So he staggers forward.

He had almost lost Marie after, he sensed that much. And then on that day her mother died, when he drove back to the cabin, he could see it in her eyes that she had made a decision, was set against him. And then he told her, and in that waiting for her to take in this other loss, he began to understand she was where she should be. A giving, a taking. Nothing in his life, not even the war, had gutted him so deep, and then waiting for the ground to thaw to bury the ashes of his son. And they are coming to the place, but they are not alone.

—

MARIE WALKS SLOWLY BEHIND Lawrence, and he stands to close the distance and waves a hand as she approaches, he must hear the foxes, but he pulls the pistol from the holster. Beyond him, at the marked spruce tree, is an animal digging with large paws, a small bear but an ungodly making of one with a bushy tail, hunched low to the ground, clawing the snow at their son's grave. Marie shouts and covers her mouth, and the animal raises its head and bares teeth, and sniffs the air, a patch of white on the neck, and hisses, a devil if she ever saw one. Lawrence fires a shot, and misses, and the animal charges, bounds toward them, and he fires again, and Marie buries her face against his back, and another shot, and he steps away from her, and shoots, and unloads the chamber, the tap of the trigger and then the unmoving silence of death. Lawrence kneels in the snow, sunk, the pistol loose in his hand. Marie touches his shoulder. This is not an animal they can name, with long fangs, and claws, a black snout, that found what was laid to rest, and she rakes snow to cover the hole that had reached the frozen ground. She traces the numbers on the bark of the tree and Lawrence says they must go, the danger of the kill, of blood, and he was foolish to waste bullets.

Lawrence does not know this animal. And what other nameless dangers are out there waiting for them. This is not how she wanted to honor her son, with the hollow ring of bullets in her ears. She walks heavy steps, the snow trampled beneath her feet, and the woods are not as they were before—no care for what they meant to remember and leave behind.

—

IF HE NEVER SAW blood again, if men could be made without blood, if animals, how clean the cut or injury, as with the deer he hunted with his father, the hanging up of them, the relief when they were drained, entrails and the rest, and the skinning and the peeling back, the sharp lines. He has no stomach for this animal, no use, so let the bullet-ridden body be dragged away. If not now, then in the spring, in the thaw, when the bears are awake.

So why a thief, when he begged for one moment—to turn to Marie as they paid their respects, to look at her and know that they had grieved, and have another chance? And why the snow, the beauty of it, only to be stained?

—+—

DOOR SHUTS BEHIND THEM, the sound of their return. Marie lights the candle on the sill of a front window, her hands trembling, the flame for the child they had buried. Lawrence was a witness besides her, the echo of each shot, one after the other, too many bullets for a kill, but for what it had taken from them. And that creature, that animal, why this day, the cruelty? A sudden turn, and they were in danger. She shields her belly with both of her hands—and he kept them safe.

How she and Lawrence move around each other, careful, watchful, and they drink coffee, hot, and then cold, and make more, but nothing to eat, their hunger is a giving in, to what they cannot say, a surrender. And the candle burns into the hours, their only light, burning low and lower, and wax drips onto the sill, and they sit in chairs at the ends of the kitchen table. Their dark forms are cast on the wall, their shadows old and thin and stooped, and his head turns and his arms rise, but in his weariness they fall, and then his shadowed hand reaches toward her, stretching across the table, and if she reaches out the shadows will twine, and she does, and for a time these other selves are one, and then the candle flickers, and they are as they were.

CHAPTER 23

OF THE DAYS

APRIL

THAW AND MELT, AND the cold trickle beneath the snow, the dripping from the eaves of the roof, and at night, the setting of the freeze, the mornings of ice and slick, a wound that heals in the night and breaks your neck. Marie, her belly growing, her swollen feet still in her sight, and the sickness has become hunger, and she eats wet cornmeal, flour in spoonfuls, pilot bread, the crumbs in the sheets, under her pillow, and Lawrence shakes them out, and the dustpan fills with a fine sand. The last of the winter stash, waiting for breakup to clear to drive to Anchorage for supplies and canned goods, but until then, stay, wait, and Lawrence chops firewood, at least he has this, but her, with her belly, the slow walk, the fear of slipping on the ice, what can she do? They have gone through the rolling papers and she tears out pages from a dime novel and her cigarettes are long and thin, covered in words that disappear with the burn, and one day the tobacco tin is empty and she folds a page into her mouth, and she winds the Victrola and a woman's voice sings opera, and she misses Sheila, and what should be, and should have been, and she heeds the swell of sorrow, and in feeding herself she is feeding the child, and with these tears she is making a way for the child, and the Lord giveth and he taketh away, and he has taken more than his share, he has received his portion.

Drag of hunger, the heaviness around her eyes, ache in her back, tenderness, a bruise without a bruise, and she will sleep away the months, and there comes a morning when she wakes early, before Lawrence, in the first hushed hours, the broom a swish on the floor, and she empties the cupboards and wipes the shelves. Lawrence turns away from the light of the lantern, and she heats a basin of water and scrubs the floor with rags, every corner, under the couch, wrings them, and washes the windows, the sills, and then she goes outside, and he sits up, searches the room, finds her in the frame of glass, shakes his head. And she shovels the snow on the porch, she cannot stop herself, she must, she polishes the kitchen table, the chairs, and collects the soiled clothes in a heap and she stoops to rest, and this is how Lawrence finds her, in the pile of laundry, slack-jawed and snoring, and lets her be, and when she opens her eyes he is sitting at the kitchen table, says, *You've pert'nere gone done all the chores, though there's wood to stack,* and she nods and stifles a yawn.

And he suggests they take a walk, the warming of the air, the slush on the trail, and he matches her slow steps, the sun strong and blinding, and the warmth of her parka, and she loosens her scarf. She takes his arm to steady herself, the trail rutted with thinning snow and bare patches of dirt, on watch for grizzlies though early for the season, and the path to the lake appears, the old habit, hauling water back and forth with the jerry cans. The lake is breaking out of a frozen skin, the glass of the ice is clear, the skating lines erased by time and weather, and they walk around the edge, a thread they will have to find again, the lift of the pall, and with the cabin in sight, two eagles swoop overhead, black wings cutting the gray, they have returned, one with a twig in its talons, and fly over the bus and land somewhere beyond. "These must be the pair I saw," says Lawrence, "when you were staying with Sheila and I knew it was time to bring you back here. As if you sent them." Marie and Lawrence follow through the woods toward the ridge, to a large nest in the crook of a bare cottonwood, built scrap by scrap and hidden from them, bleached bones of branches and twigs stacked and twined, the tree overtaken and burdened with the weight. So much hoping, of making this theirs, of gathering what was broken. One eagle chirps, a high note, the eye of winter is closing, and bless the feathers and blessed be the air, blessed are they that wander, and they that want.

Dishes stacked after supper, the heat of the cabin a drowse, and he will feed the stove less, he says, the soak of her nightgown, and she splashes water on her face and neck, and sprawls on the stripped bed, the covers rolled to the bottom edge, a rest and she will finish the dishes, early yet. Her eyes closed and her mind spilling, and she hears the cabin door close, and the old doubts, what of Lawrence, what feeling, she thought she knew the temper of his weather, and this child their bond, but without, what is knowing, his flat-footed tread on the porch, why the army almost did not enlist him, told him he was slapping God's face with every step, how his eyes are the tell before the rest, his thumb sliding along the table edge while he listens, and the low timbre of his voice, the strength of his callused hands, and is this enough, and will it be. But there is a difference, his agreeing to her having her name on the land, that day he told her about the war, and he did not hold her to her bitterness after losing the first. And this one coming, a new start, but she is filled with worry. She could not bear that loss again, and her hands rest on her stomach, and she breathes, slow and steady. And when she wakes, the soft light of a lantern approaches, Lawrence and the quilt on the couch, a kindness to let her sleep, but who has come in the night to their cabin? And no one is there, the dull shining brightens, every window aglow, more gold than green, and bursts of violet, a blue she has not seen before—the northern lights, she can name them, that slow and wavering kindling in the sky.

CHAPTER 24

WINTERKILL

MAY

A 1946 JOHN DEERE Lindeman Crawler, a tractor with metal tank track instead of tires, bright green paint. Sold for a bargain, though he worries if he should have made the purchase. But a front dozer blade for snow, brush rake for branches, disc harrow for plowing. He would not have to barter or borrow one as his father did. And for planting alfalfa, a rented grain seeder hitched behind, set to till the soil half an inch with lime and seed, and Lawrence tests the break and sink with his boot. Strange to think all farms are the same in the end. He could be standing in any one of the fields he had worked in his life. What did it matter to the government that wild land here in Alaska should be cleared, marked by the till, tamed into rows? A measure of the willing? So here he is. Alfalfa for their terms, and then potatoes for himself. And he has plans, once this is finished, to finally ask the bureau for the correct map and stake his property lines. He had the metal stakes made, Sly knew someone, had a good feeling when he ran his hands over them and the etchings of his last name, drove one in the ground at the bottom step of the porch just to see, and made Marie come out to show her how it shone.

And maybe he got ahead of himself at Teeland's Country Store. He asked about Grimm alfalfa, and a man knew that it was from a farmer in Minnesota who brought the everlasting clover seed with him from Germany, planted only what survived winterkill, and over the years, a hardy crop. The man was a pioneer farmer, testing what would grow in this frontier back in the day, and Grimm was a success, though the one weakness was wilt, and in years since better seed came to the fore, though he said Lawrence would need a warm and dry summer, which was uncommon. Plenty had tried and failed, had better luck with Timothy grass or rye. But Lawrence was set on alfalfa, and for twenty acres he bought eight sixty-pound bags of seed on the man's good word, twenty pounds for each acre, and a remainder, and after the spread the furrows stand, and for a firm bed he pulls a cultipacker, also rented, a ridged roller to press and flatten the field, creak of metal tread as the tractor caterpillars down a line.

—+—

MARIE MAKES SUPPER AND sets the table, and this tires her, her breathing heavy. The floor is unswept, the dirty stack of dishes. What can she say she has done, though she has not slept the last two nights, her belly stretching. But Lawrence has, and soundly, and she hears him, back from the field and whistling on the porch, *oh when the saints, oh when the saints come marching in.* She has sharp pains, though it is not time, a little bleeding, and just as she is about to tell Lawrence to drive her in to Anchorage, that something is wrong, they go away. But she is watchful.

And the baby kicking is a comfort and stops her from thinking the worst, because not moving was the first warning she remembers from the last. When the whistling ends and Lawrence shuts the door, the baby gives her a rest. She has a hunch and tells him to keep with the song, and he does, and the kicking and jabs start, and she laughs, and tells Lawrence to go on and touch the side of her stomach. He marvels, the strength of the little one. And then Marie puts a record on the Victrola, and, "Wouldn't you know? This baby likes music," she says. So she knows something for sure.

—+—

A DAY'S WORK AT the day's end, and he leans on a tree at the edge of the woods, the last acres finished after supper. A shriek sounds from behind, and he turns, and a bear cub is watching him, two little ears and a blond face, and he backs away, on alert for the mother, the sow, no gun because he was in the clearing on the tractor, but he can start the engine, and then a grizzly bear charges at him, and he knows not to run, so he braces himself, and the sow bites into his leg, her jaw locked on his thigh, and thrashes and tosses him to the ground, *play dead* is what he remembered Bernie said, and he clamps down his mouth to temper a scream, and he lies still through the pulse of pain, eyes closed, the smell of rotting and the steps of the cub, sniffing near him, and another cub, there are two, and sweat drips from his forehead, the sow growls, she will attack if he is a threat, and he wills the cubs to move on, and then a pressing on his back, a claw, chomping teeth on his arm, a release, and he gasps for air, a sign he is alive, and the sow bites his shoulder with force, and breathtaking might, and he tenses to stifle a cry. He waits for another strike, a burning cold on his skin, and he is dying a slow death. Marie is sure to find his body, the blood, and there is the child he will never see, the years before him on this land, so it is this, or the bear will return, and what will be the end?

And then the quiet, the thud of his own heart, and he realizes the sow is gone. And could come back, and he will die if he stays. Or she will attack if he tries, or he will reach the tractor. He raises himself to his knees and limps in agony, and then turns the choke, throttle, and cranks the wheel starter, the pop of the engine, and steps up on his good leg and throws the bloodied one over the seat, dizzy and sick, and drives toward the cabin as fast as he can hauling the roller, and he looks over, and the bears have disappeared, but that does not mean the sow is not stalking him. He takes the handkerchief out of his back pocket and ties a tourniquet above the bite, there should be more blood from the deep gashes, but he cannot stomach the sight of even this. When he reaches the cabin he yells for Marie, for the keys to the truck, and she bawls at first seeing him, then hurries from the porch, and helps him. Her belly behind the wheel, and sobs and panic, and he has her pull in to the Knik Bar to find Jones, who takes over and hands him a bottle of whiskey, and he pours the alcohol on the wounds, and drinks himself into a haze.

He wakes to vomit, fear, and whiskey in his blood, and stitches and bandages, and the doctors say he is lucky, none of the punctures hit an artery, or he would have bled out, one deep bite nearly to the bone, but he was not clawed as others had been, a man before came in with half his scalp lifted off his skull, and now Lawrence could say he survived a mauling. And he is left-handed, even after his schooling had tried to correct this, tied this one behind his back to a chair, but it never took, and this is the side uninjured. His right wrist is sprained, but he is fortunate to have his hands and face spared. And when Lawrence says they have black bears in Minnesota, the doctor says these are a different breed, been known to kill a man.

———+———

THIS IS WHAT SHE did know, that she had said, "I'm his wife, let me see him," without a thought, as if this had always been so, and that she should be by his side, her large belly covering for not having a wedding ring, and after that day she borrowed Sheila's. She had not thought to worry about the baby, her condition, until a nurse said she should sit down and remain calm, and Sheila stayed and wrapped her arms around her, as if the months apart had not happened. Lawrence had been so happy that day, that is what she remembers, and this seemed a punishment but for what she cannot say. They were doing well, for once, the two of them, and how would he be after, he barely spoke to the nurses, or to her.

Sheila stays with her and knits, the clack of the needles a comforting sound. Marie remembers little from being in the hospital the last time— soft voices, white walls, that this is where they took her son from her. Which had not crossed her mind in the rush of wanting to know that Lawrence would recover, only now, and so the past hurts are making room for new ones.

Sheila is making a blanket for her neighbor, who wants to pay her. "Sly said I was knitting us out of house and home," she says. "I didn't send them but I made some things for your—"

"How would I know that?" says Marie.

"I tried to write about twenty letters," says Sheila. She places a hand on Marie's knee. "And that animal you told me about, god-awful. And now this grizzly."

"Don't you ever do that to me again," says Marie.

Sheila gives her knee a pat and resumes her knitting.

They overhear a conversation in the hallway about statehood, a bill has been presented for a vote in the House, been shot down twice before, "But third time's the charm."

Sly turns the corner to drop off sandwiches, his day off. "How is he?"

"Nurses are worried he isn't talking much," says Sheila. "We tried telling them that's his way."

The doctors allow the three of them to go into his room, which smells of bleach and sweat and there is a curtain separating him from another patient. Lawrence grimaces when Sly walks in.

"Hey, buddy," says Sly, with good cheer.

"I'm not your buddy," says Lawrence, through a groan.

They laugh at this, even though Lawrence is serious.

"Well, you must be feeling better," says Sheila.

"Or more yourself," says Marie.

"How much money?" says Lawrence.

"Don't worry about that," says Marie. "Worry about getting better."

"We took up a collection at the Moose Lodge," says Sly.

Sheila and Marie glare at him. Lawrence was never to know.

"No charity," says Lawrence.

"They don't know it's you," says Sly.

"Sylvester, get out," says Sheila. "You're not helping."

Sly, defeated, shoves his cap over his blond hair and leaves the room.

"Promise me," Lawrence says. "No help. We can sell the tractor or the army rig, the ambulance."

"Too late and no need. Already been taken care of," says Marie. "I don't know how much we have. All I know is what you tell me, which isn't much."

"I didn't plan on this," says Lawrence, and he turns his head away from her.

"She's doing her best," says Sheila. "And you're in pain."

They leave the room and Sheila whispers, "Such a baby, that man of yours," and Marie cannot help but laugh with her in the hospital.

———

NURSES WAKE HIM UP to change the dressings, the peeling away, the seeping, that thick smell of ointment, which he is grateful for since he does not want to smell old blood, or the bedpan, or the other patient in the room who talks in his sleep, and keeps him from sleeping, and he did not want Marie and Sheila and Sly to see him, but he was not given a choice. And if he was, he would not stay in the hospital a moment longer. There were so many times in his life when he should have been injured, or died, and did not, and this was senseless, he had been doing what he was supposed to do, as instructed, tilling the acreage to plant a crop. He could blame the government for the rules that he was following to prove the land, take his anger to the man at the bureau, who would smirk, and pretend to listen. But maybe this was owed by him, all those misses and byes, for being unscathed. Perhaps fate had caught him in the jaws of a grizzly.

What he hears sometimes, besides his own pulse, is the small and strange noises of the two cubs coming closer. If they had stayed away, had not been curious, had not needed protection. An attack for each of them, if he looks for reason. He will try to forget the collection from the Moose Lodge ever happened after he has Marie write a note of thanks on his behalf, which he will sign. No use in hiding. News travels fast, and Sly cannot keep his mouth shut. And he will have Marie send a letter to his father, tell Joseph he is well enough, could have been worse in the end, and they will be back at the homestead soon.

—+—

AFTER TWELVE DAYS, THE doctors say the wounds are healing, and Marie can tend the two deepest ones, the shoulder and thigh, and wrap them with fresh bandages. When they remove the stitches, Sheila and Marie return with Lawrence to the cabin. They prop pillows behind his back on the bed and decide to draw water from the spring, wary, Sheila carrying the jerry cans and Marie with a pistol in hand. A short distance, but a risk, and she had done this so many times alone, without care.

Lawrence sits on the porch with the shotgun, waiting for the bear, watching over the alfalfa. The green shoots, tender and sprouted, and he worries the moose will graze on them, and he has her and Sheila post scarecrows made from the seed sacks. For a while he needs them both to help him walk, and then just her, the crutches ready for him in the corner.

Marie had found the spots of his blood in the tilled dirt, and turned them with a rake, the woods in her sights, could not imagine this life without him. His wounds tender, and soft, the healing begun, and how weak he had been, and bitter that he needed the crutches, and help to bathe at first, though he could feed himself, his left arm unhurt. But it is his silences that are bothersome, his hours in the sun, the burn on the tip of his nose, as he keeps an eye on the field.

She waits for him to speak of what happened and will not ask for the risk of him withdrawing. What could he be thinking all this time, and then he talks of someday planting potatoes, a vegetable garden, after long stretches of the quiet on the porch if the weather is right, her in the rocking chair, her belly growing, him with his leg propped on a wooden Blazo box, how he will find a mower to cut the alfalfa in July, but what was in his mind, his life in danger, did he think of her, and of what has passed in these two years? She is bursting to ask, and holds her tongue, until finally, one afternoon, eyes on the rows of sprouted green, he says, "I did not want to leave this place," as if a solemn truth has been told, but to her, with what has happened, this is a scrap, a splinter.

Still, each morning she unwraps his bandage and cleans the weep on the wounds, dabs disinfectant, her touch one of tenderness, a bowl of warm water and a rag, and she washes behind his neck and ears, his chest and his hands, there are parts he insists she leave, but he needs her, he refuses to take the full dose of the aspirin the doctor prescribed, and sweats through the pain at night, his face turned away, but she hums a song so he knows she is taking care.

—+—

A COW MOOSE APPEARS on the edge of the field and lowers her head over the tender leaves of the alfalfa. He aims, not to kill, but to scare, and shoots a shell. The moose does not scamper away, but looks around, and when she has decided the danger has passed, bends down to eat. Lawrence fires another and she is unmoved, and he readies the trigger, and then she walks into the trees.

So he waits, and watches, and the reasons come to him, for what happened that day in the field changed his mind, about how Marie, against his better judgment, had made him lose sight of what was rightfully his.

No woman, or animal, in the eyes of God, could take that away from him. He found this parcel and signed for the right. Felled the trees. Cleared the acres. Built the cabin. Why should it not be, or was this the orneriness his father warned him of, but with a wife a man halved himself, and with a child is halved again, and no telling with a child that has died, and the war, and so on, and soon what would be left of him, of who he was when he placed a claim on the lot, the black ink dry and final, the holding already in his grasp, the lake that pointed him here, and he could not lose sight of the path he had set himself on, a clear purpose, one aim, owning this land. He would mend, and when that happened, when the wincing and the aches and the last of the stitches were faint or gone, when he did not have to brace against his weight, or a crutch, or anyone else, and he was whole again, upright, on his own two feet, without weakness, then he wanted the homestead, and every last speck of dirt, to be his. He knows what he promised Marie, but this could not stand.

And what of his father's warning? His father with a scratch of land, a few acres, the diner, a farmer with the smallest of hopes, and so many of them—he could not see beyond a single day's work, the morning milk, the provision of daily bread, could not bear Lois's anger more than an evening, could not stomach the unhappiness of his children, as, so he believed, *the meek shall inherit the earth.* But his father would not, and had little to bestow. And words of wisdom were surely not enough. And what could Lawrence give his own children if he became a man who had given everything to his wife? He had slipped so far beyond what he thought possible, how quick the injury, and how slow to recover.

CHAPTER 25

IN THE TERRITORY

JUNE

WHEREVER SHE IS, HE is there, a shadow. The crutches follow her, to the spring, to wash the outside windows, because he cannot fell trees for firewood with his lack of balance. And she wants to swim at the lake, because it could be her last time for a while, and he trudges along with the shotgun, covered in repellent, and this long walk is good for him, which is why she tries not to mind. Both of them short-winded on this path through the woods.

At the lake she pulls the housedress over her head. She would never wear this outside of the cabin, but who will see her? She leans over, a lower ache, a towel around her, and she waves him off. At the edge she bares her body, and wonders if Lawrence averts his eyes, and she would not need to be modest out here in her woods if she were alone, but she has filled out even beyond what she remembered. He will not come swimming and she wonders if he finally will when his leg heals. In the water she floats on her back, her belly up, and kicks her legs, a new heaviness, and circles the lake, and above two eagles soar, black wings crossing the sky, as if signaling that they are well, as so she will be, and it is time.

—+—

LAWRENCE SLAPS A MOSQUITO on his neck. He was never a good swimmer, but could manage. But if he lets his guard down, as he has before, no telling, and what matters is Marie and this child, and leaving for Anchorage when she says. Even if they have to stay awhile with Sheila and Sly, though he will be back to check on the cabin and the alfalfa. He has other reasons besides his scars, his view sitting on the bank, for one. Marie's belly above the water, more naked than the moon, as she swims on her back, without a care, her eyes closed to the bright sun. And then when Marie is tired, she comes out of the water, her dark hair wet, her large breasts in the stark light of day.

"Tomorrow," she says, and he nods. This is their last night at the cabin, just the two of them, could be weeks before the baby comes. Only after will they buy things for the baby, because she wanted to wait and he knows why. Fortunate to not have much before, no room in the bus. And she packs her belongings, but he will be back and forth, has tested his injured leg for driving. He loads the truck, and she leans over on the porch, and she beckons him over, and lifts her blouse, and her belly is moving, and he kneels and presses his ear to her skin and hears his own flesh and blood.

———

AT SUPPER LAWRENCE MAKES the sign of the cross and recites the prayer, *Bless us, O Lord,* the first time since Joseph leaving, and Marie recites with him.

"We should say grace before every meal," he says.

"Because the baby can hear us," she says.

"Good to give thanks," he says. "Just in case."

"Always good," she says.

To cover them, and what would be the harm, and Lawrence has received a letter from Joseph, and she wonders what he said. Lawrence heads outside for firewood, has the rucksack to fill and help carry, and she has a chance to find the letter, but stamps this out of her mind. She washes the dishes and leans against the counter. What did she know for certain, about raising this child? Only what Sheila had taught her, as her sister, a few steps ahead. Valera around too much, and Rosalie around too little. What will be enough, so her child is not looking back on the years and wondering as she does?

Through the kitchen window, Lawrence stands on the porch, his back to her, stooped over his crutches. Something in him has changed, and she is wary. Preparing to be a father, she supposes, in his own way, for this child, *which we are about to receive.*

———+———

THE ACCOUNT OF THE grizzly reached his father, and so Joseph's letter contains gratitude for guardian angels, a little money, and wishes from Lois and his siblings that he will soon be in full health. And there is an account of the family and the diner, and a declaration, *A child is a blessing from the Lord.* What is all this for, the acres, the cabin, the alfalfa with buds growing in the field, if not for a child? He has Marie walk the field with him, her holding the shotgun as he surveys the perimeter, the scarecrows, but still, moose and rabbits have grazed in the few dark hours of the summer nights. He will leave a message at the Knik Bar and ask Henry to check on his crop from time to time. There was nothing he could build, due to his crutches, and the only fences he knew were for corralling animals on the farm. What scale would he need, and this would be in vain. No way of knowing if the alfalfa will keep, or if he will ever plant again.

One crop, one name, one deed. Twenty acres of alfalfa is all he needs. There are moments he falters on the decision to break his promise to Marie, which should not have been asked of him. Even then, his words false to his feeling, and who else would hold him to it? His father, but he did not know. And Marie would turn her attention when the child came, or so he hoped. And that is all the reason to say grace.

He locks the latch on the cabin door after the Mercury is packed, and places a board spiked with nails at the threshold, and at the base of the porch steps, to ward off bears. Marie offers to drive, but the Mercury is easier on his leg than the truck. Not seen a grizzly since, though there was that creature at the grave, and he has wondered what if he did, would he shoot the sow, and then what of her two cubs? Enough of death, and perhaps a bargain has been struck, to stay out of sight, and live.

Marie fills the glove box with saltines and pilot bread, a burning in her chest after breakfast, but she says these are the remedy. He honks the horn three times, for luck, and a spruce hen startles out of hiding, which means he has been heard.

—+—

WALKING AND PACING, A sharp tightness, and Marie tires with each breath, but an ache of nerves moves her around Sheila's yard. She had sent Lawrence, and his crutches, with Sly for the day, to give herself a moment's peace. Marie's belly is sitting lower, she is sure of it, a pressing on her hips. She waves at the neighbor, who has two children and gives her a look of understanding.

Sheila calls from the trailer, "Let's go to town," and why not, she is as uncomfortable as she can be. Sheila says she can borrow a skirt and nylons, get out of those dungarees, for once, and Marie is surprised she can fit into anything.

Paved streets of downtown Anchorage, the concrete sidewalk, and the click of Sheila's one pair of heels that Marie envies as she shuffles in boots and swollen ankles, a smock top over her big belly, a dab of sweat behind her ears where the mosquitoes hover, even here, in this city, in Alaska, or the *territory of Alaska,* as the news reports on Sheila's radio say. They have been listening in anticipation as the House passed the statehood bill and now the Senate is debating and has not voted, even though it has been days. Each morning they think there will be a decision, only to be disappointed. And she has not forgotten, if Alaska becomes a state and the capital is moved near Anchorage, and a bridge is built over the water, then their land becomes all the more valuable. Though that would mean more people, when they have miles between neighbors right now. But she is close, close to having this baby, and close to having that deed and title squared away.

She and Sheila stroll down the blocks, Sears and Northern Commercial and Wolfe's Department Store, and Marie follows Sheila's turns, she knows where she is going, turns left at the post office, more stores and the sounds of engines.

Two women pass them, their long black hair down their backs, their loose and long-waisted dresses in a bright blue and purple floral calico, white trim at the gathered skirt that falls past the knee, an elderly mother with her daughter.

"Kuspuks," says Sheila, before she asks. "That's what the Native women are wearing."

A man whistles, and shouts for everyone to hear, "Wait for me, Eskimo gal. All I want is an Eskimo kiss. Come on."

They turn and the women are huddled together and walking faster, as the man, in his military jacket and tie, stumbles across the road.

"I'm talking," he says, drunk. "To you." He trips over his feet. The women are gone. And his buddies appear, also military, and usher him back inside. Those who have stopped and watched in silence return to their day. She had known the feeling, the threat from one of Valera's sons, and still had just stood there and stared. And could that have been Lawrence in the war, so far from home? She would not ask. He would not tell her and, if she was honest with herself, she did not want to know. Other questions about him were on her mind, him as a father, their life on the homestead when they returned. "Let's sit down," she tells Sheila, and they turn to look at each other when they reach a cloud of grease coming from the Lucky Wishbone. The time they sat at a booth with Sly and Lawrence and ate themselves sick on that pan-fried chicken.

"End of the month," says Sheila, and reaches into her purse. "We can maybe split a dinner or order malts."

Marie, through her hunger, says, "Malts will do."

Inside the diner the booths are filled, but two seats open at the counter with a glance at Marie. A man with a long, bristled beard is seated at the counter beside them, a carved cane propped on his stool, the handle the head of an eagle.

"Coffee?" asks the waitress.

"None for us," and Marie orders two chocolate malts.

"You're missing out," says the bearded man. Picked bones on his plate.

"We know," says Marie. Waitress brings two tall fountain glasses and steel cups and Marie spoons the malt into her mouth, cold, creamy, and thick. Sheila sips two spoonfuls, then stirs with the straw and slides her malt over to Marie.

"Sheila, you drink that right now," says Marie.

Sheila shakes her head. "You ate nothing at breakfast."

Was true, not even saltines. She could not eat then. A shout sounds in the kitchen. The waitress runs out behind the counter with the radio, and static and then a voice says, "We're in. Senate passes vote. Welcome to Alaska, the forty-ninth state of the United States of America," and the diner cheers and whistles around them, and they laugh along, and Sheila starts drumming on the counter, and Marie joins in.

"Those bastards couldn't keep us out," says a man, who raises his pistol and runs outside and fires a bullet into the air. Gunshots and sirens answer in celebration, and Marie covers her ears.

Then George and Peggy, the owners, bring out fresh and piping-hot baskets of chicken, on the house. Marie and Sheila help themselves. A bearded man seated at the counter is the only one not enjoying himself, a scowl on his face, and he says, "Damn government's going to tax us for all we're worth. Didn't want us to vote, wild men and Natives, but sure as hell wanted our money and our land."

"Leave it alone, old man," someone says. "Take your cane and go back to the bush."

"Fight in two world wars, then tell me what to think."

"This is good news. Let us have our good news."

"Patriotism is for the young," says the man. He reaches for his cane.

Marie stands to give him room and holds out her arm.

"No need, darling, but I thank you."

"We thank you for your service," says George. He leads the man through the crowd to the door as a woman rushes in, teary-eyed, with a bundle of forget-me-nots, and she hands out the small blue delicate flowers. Marie and Sheila each place one sprig in the sweeps of their dark hair.

—+—

LAWRENCE SITS ON A stool at the shop, radio on in case there is news of a vote, and Sly takes his crutches, without permission, and tries them out. "Careful," Lawrence says. "I need those."

He only agreed to come here when Sly said he would take him to the Moose Lodge on his break. Marie had sent in letters to thank them for the charity, and turns out Bernie was the one who organized the collection. If Lawrence went this early and showed his face, it would not be crowded.

Until then, he will suffer Sly. And the other mechanics are not his wife's brother-in-law. Not sure what that makes Sly to him, but he already had three brothers back home and he was quite all right that they were so far away in Minnesota. He had worried, his first year here, that his father would send one to live with him, without warning, and he would be obligated. Sly laughs at every little thing, gives Lawrence the feeling at any moment he could fall on his big, soft face and find it funny. Untroubled, slaphappy, what one might say, how either you joined in or wanted to punch him. And just as Lawrence has reached his limit of politeness, Sly says they are heading out.

"One beer for me," he says to Lawrence when they walk into the lodge. They sit at the bar and of course the bartender has a radio tuned in, everyone in Alaska must be listening. They order, then someone puts his hands on Lawrence's shoulders and he turns to find Bernie.

"This what happens to married men?" he says. "They disappear and come back injured?"

He takes a seat next to Lawrence. Tells them about this new kid he has on the carpenter crew, has one arm, from the war of course, but you would never know, as fast and skilled as the rest of them. Sly is constantly greeting people because there is no one he doesn't know, and Lawrence turns his back. Any one of them could have donated money to his hospital fees. Sly orders another beer and Lawrence lets him, without jawing, as he is staying at the man's trailer. When Sly finishes he says he has to get back to work, and Bernie says he can give Lawrence a ride.

"He means well," says Bernie, when Sly leaves.

"Cut from a different cloth," says Lawrence.

"And what are you? Cut from stone?" says Bernie.

"If I was," says Lawrence, "this bear wouldn't have done a number on me."

"Five out of ten," says Bernie. "You still got your pretty face."

"I wanted to thank you—" says Lawrence.

"No need," says Bernie. "Was nothing."

"And thanks for not coming to the hospital."

"You kidding?" says Bernie. "Last thing you would have wanted."

"You should come to the homestead," says Lawrence. "Can show you what I've been up to."

Bernie shakes his head. "I got enough. And if I see your land I'm going to want what you have. Besides, got my eye on a woman around here."

"Bring her, too," says Lawrence.

Bernie glances over his shoulder and then leans in and whispers, "She doesn't mind my old self. Going to ask her to marry me soon."

"How soon?" says Lawrence. And before Bernie can answer, the bartender and the two men next to the radio give a shout, and the volume is raised, *passed the Senate with a sixty-four to twenty vote, on this momentous day, the thirtieth of June.* Sly runs back through the door out of breath. And then another man follows and shouts, "Pour me a beer and call me a fool. Alaska's going to be a state."

—+—

DOWNTOWN SWARMS AND TRAFFIC halts. Marie and Sheila pass the post office and the grandest American flag hangs over the entire side of the old federal building, a big white glittering star fishing-lined down to the third row, a new star, a forty-ninth star, for Alaska. Alaska the free, the brave, the last frontier, the mountains, the eagles, the bears, the rivers teeming with fish, the snow, the ice, the woods, the forests, the timber, the gold, a wilderness, a territory, and, as of today, the state that will border no other state. A span larger than Texas, largest in the union. Cameras and flashes, shouting, cheering, a carnival. *Bring wood to spare,* someone says, *a bonfire tonight, so bright we will burn the midnight sun.*

Marie and Sheila drive back to the trailer, slow and idling, cars backed on every street, and decide to bring the old chair that wobbles. Sly and Lawrence home early from work. Boss let everyone leave—this is once-in-a-lifetime. So they will dress in their best and head to town.

"Hurry and shower, we're missing it all," Sheila tells them. She clips on green earrings that match her cardigan, applies red lipstick. "Wish we had pearls." She dabs lipstick on Marie. "If we're going to make history, we might as well look the part."

"I still can't believe it," says Marie.

"Something we'll remember for the rest of our lives," says Sheila.

Lawrence says he will drive and they cram into the truck with the chair in the back and the windows rolled down because the men smell of beer. Cars pack the avenues. They find a place to park after circling twice and Sly carries the chair over his shoulder. He is not the only one with an offering. Others carry tires, scrap beams, boards, pieces of fences. Everyone is headed in one direction—swing coats and plaid Pendleton shirts and suits and bow ties and clean-shaven jaws—a respectable lot, these newly minted Americans. Marie has an eye out for the two Native women, but does not see them, or anyone else wearing kuspuks. A parade blocks the road, waves and pennants, and a marching band with major-ettes plays music, drums and brass, and a taxidermy bull moose with wide antlers rolls down the avenue, should be in a museum, someone says. After, the crowd convenes at city park, and in the middle of the open field Boy Scouts collect the bonfire donations and stack them in a heap, and Sly hands over the chair.

———

WAIT FOR THE DARK, what little will come, summer solstice still alight. With the news, his care is of the homestead, to be a landowner before this becomes official, and before his land jumps in value. Too much change is worrisome. And Bernie, he could see it in his eyes, a lovesick fool. A cannon blasts and Lawrence ducks his head for cover, a nod he sees in other men, veterans. He swallows and braces for another blast, and another, the thunder, and two men walk, hands over their ears, away from the crowd, stricken. The crowd counts, ten, eleven, twelve. He shifts with his crutch and reaches for Marie's shoulder and startles her. Twenty-two. Twenty-three. Twenty-four. *Should we leave?* she mouths. But he does not want to call attention to himself. Twenty-nine. He is sick, a throbbing in his head. And he leans on Marie for support. Shouting and raised hands. Forty-three. Forty-four. Voices loud and louder. Friendly fire. He holds on. Forty-eight. Screams for forty-nine. And then a Boy Scout with a torch sets fire to the towering pile of forty-nine tons, and a blaze kicks up, ignites cherry bombs and firecrackers, pops and sparks, and he sways with the crowd, and one last cannon blast for a salute to Hawaii, and the state it hopes to be. Cowboys run their horses around the flare, a wide circle, the Wild West in the Far North. But wild no more.

———+———

IN EVERY EYE, A flame. All around them, a surge, a pressing to hear, and Marie links her arm with Lawrence's. Someday she will have this to tell her daughter. A daughter, she has decided, she has her way of knowing, and has told not a soul. And a man stands on a wooden crate in front of the raging bonfire, and he shouts, *Ninety-one years of waiting,* and lifts his arms to lift their voices, and the crowd responds, *Ninety-one years.* Tears run down his face. *A territory no longer,* shouts the man. And the crowd is his echo. *A territory no longer. We have been heard. This is Alaska, the great land. This is our land. We are standing on hallowed ground. We are standing, equal and united, on American soil.* And the crowd claps and stomps their feet, and the man stands down, and hurls the crate into the fire. And coins and what can be thrown follow, and Marie has borrowed Sheila's purse, and this she holds tightly to her chest, and Lawrence shifts his weight to her, and she turns her head, and Sly has his crutch and heaves it into the air, and the crutch flies high and falls into the scorching pile, for what are they burning—if not the territory of the territory, and everything that was before?

———+———

COULD KILL HIM, RIGHT here in front of this crowd, Sly grinning and drinking, beers and flasks passed down. A group of men appear with a large cut tree, dragging it across the street to the park, and they roll it into the fire, and the crowd roars. The air force band joins the Shriners, and the dancing begins with drums and brass. Lines of held hands form and snake through, and others join. Sheila grabs Sly before he is carried away so they can leave. He wants to stay but she insists.

Lawrence leans on Marie and his remaining crutch on the way back to the truck. At a street corner is a gathering watching the fire and the revelry from a safe distance, all Negroes, dressed fine. One woman in a tweed coat with fur cuffs stands at the front, frets with the gloves in her hand, and steps back as they pass. Lawrence turns his head—the rowdy dancing, the flames licking higher and higher, horses galloping, the screams of a firecracker—and, witnessing it here, there is no way to know if this is a tribute or the beginning of trouble.

They turn down Second Avenue to offers of help, a ride, and Lawrence will take none. At Sheila's prompting, Sly tries to apologize, says he got caught up in the moment, will replace the crutch he threw. And Lawrence says, "If you buy me a new one I will break it over your head." Will bide his time to pay Sly back for this. Did the man not think?

"But what a story to tell your kid," says Sly.

"Anytime now," says Marie, and she smiles at Lawrence. But he is not consoled.

There is still some light, and when they arrive at the trailer he is certain. He will drive back to the homestead right this minute, he is tired but wide awake. Says to check on the alfalfa.

"But I could be close," says Marie. Though she knows he will not go to the hospital.

"A day or so, I'll be back," says Lawrence. He needs to be away from Sly, wait out the shakiness in his hands. Road will calm him. So he heads out as soon as he can in the Mercury, away from the city and the crowd, from what Sly had done, and those pitying glances of strangers, and the shouts and the noise, into a darkening sky that hangs low but does not give in, and then the hours tilt to morning, and he reaches the cabin, the porch, as the sunrise breaks over all that will be his.

CHAPTER 26

A GIVEN NAME

JULY

MOSQUITOES CHOKE THE AIR, a thick cloud hovers over the field, the oil of repellent on his skin. Buzz drowns the turn of the tractor from where Lawrence stands, one crutch still needed, the deep wound on his thigh the last to heal, but he drove the truck here.

A warm taste in the wind on harvest—sweet, grass, dust—the bloom of a fresh cutting. Alfalfa in the field, purple blooms and the green stalks with slender leaves fall as Henry Mor, with a rifle ready, pulls a sickle mower, the jagged teeth cobbing through each cut. When the alfalfa dries, Henry has his neighbor, Charles, and some men coming to bale, men who are impressed his crop survived, and will buy at a price less their trouble, as he has no use for alfalfa besides the proving.

Marie is still in Anchorage waiting for the baby to come and Lawrence tracks his leave, back and forth to tend the land, the dates written for record and filing on the homestead in August. And with statehood, Henry says homesteading is under the federal government, and withstands, has precedent over what the state decides, but Lawrence wants his claim in the clear beforehand, so there will not be any doubt.

A few days of sun will let the cuts dry for the balers. No rain, no rain. Sky will hold. Or will it? Seems ages ago, the picking, and the scythes in hand on the fields of poor farmers, scrape and by, scrape and by, and press on. Even the poor farmers owned land and tools, and the hired hands working the dirt owned nothing, not the black under their nails—stolen dirt, you could say, but earned if there was a way to hold stock. He is going to own this land. And he has Marie and he will be a father, made a cradle and is painting the stain. But what will be required of him? When he signed for the army, he did not know the meaning, your life is not yours, for duty to your country, and the wake up to carry, to march, to a breaking to build a soldier, to *yes, sir*. But he knew, back then, what they wanted him to be.

He parks the truck in front of the porch. Hum in the distance catches his ear, a flash of silver, a small plane flying, close and low. Too close. Too low. Something ain't right. Plane has to turn or lift. Line of flight is a dive. In the middle of nowhere, in the middle of a hundred and fifty acres, claimed, and a plane is coming to crash into the cabin he built, tree by tree, log by log. Waves his arms and shouts. Shotgun is in reach, the cold metal, the trigger, shoot a pilot down? Can the pilot see him? The cabin? Out of the plane, an unspooling in the sky. Pink tissue paper, streaming and unfurling and flitting in the light. Pink rolls down the roof of the cabin, bounces and lands at his feet. Pink. A baby girl. First of the twelve, and with this number, chances were there would be daughters, he knew that. But he thought the first would be a son. He chastises himself, the first was a son who did not live to see a day. And he cannot be greedy after such a loss. But a boy on a homestead makes sense. A boy to trap and hunt. He planned for a son to take his name, take over the land for his sake, to step into his place. He kicks at the pink paper on the porch with his crutch. And then the helicopter, the one he knows from the Nike site, flies over, to make sure the mission is complete, no doubt. *Sly, you bastard.* He would do something like this. Lawrence would tell him, *Buzzing my cabin in a bird plane, don't think I wouldn't shoot. You think that's funny?*

A girl. He should have been able to choose, to have what he wanted. But a girl he will take, count your blessings—a daughter, and she is alive and well.

———+———

LAWRENCE DRIVES THEM HOME along the Knik Arm in the early morning, the water high and slick with light at the river crossing and

Marie holds her newborn, Colleen, the mountains on her side, sharp peaks laced in white and shadowed in green and blue. Lawrence is quiet and unsure, as if he is meeting them both for the first time, Marie and his daughter. And now that she is a mother, she wonders how Rosalie could have left her and Sheila in that clapboard house, stink of dirt and rotting wood, and rats dying in the walls and the heat drying out their deaths. And Valera waking them up in the middle of the night, telling them they could not sleep on the bed, and the three of them with their ears to the floor, listening, *Do you hear?* They nodded, *Yes, we hear them,* rats chewing through the house, even if they heard nothing, learned the first time when asked and told the truth, *No,* and Valera slapped both their faces for their lies, and Marie and Sheila would rise in the morning, necks cricked, from sleeping the night on the hard floor.

Her daughter will never have to sleep on the floor a night in her life. Colleen Marie, named after her, was Sheila who first called her Marie and it took. But this one will be Colleen. Lawrence said the firstborn son is named after the father, so she followed the line, firstborn is a firstborn, a given name is given for. She had waited to see the dark line on her stomach as before, and it never showed, had known this one would be a girl. What would Lawrence think? she wondered, and he could have surprised her, but she did not tell him, could not risk his disappointment. And had thought of Sheila for the middle name, but suppose Sheila is saving the name for hers, when the time comes, though that time is a worry and bruise in the soft middle of waiting. But she could tell her how it was, of what she remembered, Sheila waiting in another room, as she was alone for hours, and then the nurses gave her a shot for the pain, and she woke up with straps around her wrists, her mouth dry, and her voice hoarse as if she had been screaming, but could not remember the birth. A swaddled baby in her arms, a sick feeling in her stomach, the nurse showing her the glass bottles and canned milk. Nothing was as Sheila had described, from those stories from their old neighbor, the midwife. No one to see her through or hold her hand. As if she had been asleep and this happened without her. And how could she know that this baby was hers, the one she carried?

But it was the smell, warm and baked, sweet, the scent on the top of the head, no bread she could name, that told her, and tells her now. *Leave her, let her sleep,* as Sheila says, and she does, and she will, but after a time, the doubt, and she jostles the baby's arm, and the yawn, the flutter of eyelids, a cry or wail, and Marie is content until the ache returns. As Lawrence has his eyes on the road, she lifts the baby and sets her ear near the nose and mouth, listens and feels for breath. The baby wakes, then, with a whimper, and Marie holds a bottle to her mouth, and it is the latch and the draw that tell her, for certain, that this baby is here, she is safe.

In a drowse the drive ends. Lawrence unloads and Marie stands on the porch with Colleen. The fields are low, the alfalfa has been cut and baled and carried away.

"I have something for the little one," says Lawrence, summer in his voice.

The cradle he made, polished to a gleam, stands at the foot of the bed.

Marie runs her hand along the rail and with a bye, the rockers tilt back and forth.

"Let's see," he says.

In the newness between them he has not held their child yet. "Here," says Marie, and nods toward the baby.

"I don't know," he says.

Marie steps toward him and he mirrors the crook of her arms and she places the child there.

"A sack of potatoes," he says, and laughs. "Let me look at you," and she is so small he can hold her out with one hand.

Marie bites her tongue, concern in her throat.

"There you are, little one. Do you know who I am?" he says. Lowers her onto her back, and a gentle nudge rocks the cradle.

Both hover and peer over the baby as she sleeps and suckles the air.

"We having her baptized?" says Lawrence. "Something we should do?"

"We don't belong," says Marie.

"We belong here," he says.

—+—

A CHILD, THIS DAUGHTER who would one day walk across the floor he built. Henry Mor had whistled at the sight, the biggest place he had seen around Point MacKenzie. Asked why a cabin this size, so much to heat in winter. Part of his pride, he has to admit.

But there is, he cannot say, a hollow in his bones, as Marie sleeps, and the baby sleeps in the cradle moved to her side, and what would he give them, and the wanting to give them everything he has, against his reason and good sense, and he should be at an accord, but he gently shuts the door and sits on the porch and lights a cigar, the old tradition after becoming a father. And when he signed the birth certificate, he thought he would change his mind, that these months he would have found a way out of his decision, that having a healthy child home at last would overcome his unease. His promise to Marie will come to pass, and he gave her his word, and what is his word worth, these acres claimed before he knew her? But he has to consider what he will leave behind. His father had done what he could, had surpassed his own father who came to this country, and with these acres he will do the same, and then, who could surpass him? And if he is to be taken, over and over, he could keep the land from being divided, could he not, first with Marie, and then with a will. Perhaps one of his sons, to give and to trust, and then all that he has done would not diminish. He has the crop. He has the witnesses, Henry and Charles. What is required will be fulfilled come August. Knows what he must do—his name on the land will be the only name.

———+———

BABY WAKES IN THE afternoon. So many diapers, flat cloths that have to soak in a lidded pail until washing. Pins are sharp, and each time Marie holds her breath, careful not to stab or poke the baby's markless skin. She nuzzles the top of the baby's head and then lowers her into the cradle, diaper wrapped. She picks up the two empty jerry cans and stops in the doorway. Leave her? This would be the first time. Settles on his old army rucksack that hangs on the wall on his side of the bed.

The straps are to be worn on the back, but she fronts the rucksack over her chest and folds in towels to line the bottom. She places the baby inside and leaves the flap open so she can look down at her face. She carries the two jerry cans outside and Lawrence, stacking firewood, the crutch set aside, says he will take them. I'll go with you, she says, and he brings the shotgun and watches for bears.

At the spring, Lawrence sits and rests after splashing his neck, the sweat of pain, and she fills the cans and drinks her lot, thirst for that cold taste. She dips her finger and traces the baby's mouth. *Colleen, you will be strong. Here, on this land.* She draws a line across her brow, and the baby cries. *You will be your own.* A silent prayer from a mother to a daughter. *You will be water, water. And Amen.*

CHAPTER 27

HOMESTEAD PROOF

AUGUST

WITNESSES OF THE PLANTED alfalfa, of the cultivated acres, and of the cabin he built—Henry Mor and his neighbor, Charles—they give their statements to the Bureau of Land Management, to the same man that wronged him. Lawrence came here ready to demand an apology, and asks for a map, and the man smirks and searches and then hands him one rolled, and Lawrence makes sure this time, and bites his tongue, for this man has the power to undo everything. And there is a line forming behind him, he has never seen one, new homesteaders, young and too eager. A few look like they have never done a hard day's work in their lives. Was that what the man had thought of him two years before? But surely he is not the same.

He is filing, without Marie. She, thankfully, did not want to come to Anchorage on a supply run, the baby not sleeping. He said he would go to the bureau for the map, and check that everything was in order for the next trip. Though, he already knows what the error will be.

And she could add her name later, he tells himself, and yet, he wants the land in his name, as it should be. Statehood and what that would mean, though the Homestead Act is by law through the federal government and will be untouched, Henry keeps telling him, but this is not enough, he fought for his country and lived, only to have blood spilled on his land, mauled by a bear as he farmed his own field, and he did not rest on these notions. The papers are here in front of him. There will be two sets so he can have a copy for his records, and he reads over them with the man watching him.

DEPARTMENT OF THE INTERIOR
BUREAU OF LAND MANAGEMENT

HOMESTEAD ENTRY FINAL PROOF
TESTIMONY OF CLAIMANT

Note: The officer before whom this proof is made will see that all answers are complete and responsive to the questions, and that the answers bring out the pertinent facts showing the entryman's compliance or noncompliance with the laws under which the land was entered. Neither of the witnesses may be present while the testimony of the claimant is begin given.

He pauses, and reads the line again, *begin given,* a mistake, and *begin given, begin given,* as if there is more to come, and this is the start of everything he has waited for. But he does not want to call attention to wording, the man could say he has to wait for new documents, could null-and-void the one he has written on.

Land Office: **ANCHORAGE**
Serial Number: **041180**

Name (Given first name, middle initial, & last name): **LAWRENCE J. BERINGER**
Full post office address: **P.O. BOX 4—854, SPENARD, ALASKA**

He still has his P.O. Box from when he first moved and lived right outside Anchorage, and he can check this without the risk of Marie being there. He had kept it all this time, and now he knows the reason.

☒ I am a citizen of the United States ☒ Native born ☐ Naturalized

☒ I am married. Date of Marriage: *13 AUGUST 1956*

☐ My husband is or was a ☐ native born citizen

☐ naturalized citizen;

___ date of husband's death

☐ I am a married woman and my husband ☐ did ☐ did not hold an un-perfected homestead during the period of residence claimed by me. He resided on the land with me for a total of ___ months during my period of absence.

If the bear had killed him, a bite to his neck or spine, the hit of an artery with teeth, could Marie have had everything as a married woman? Claim what he has claimed?

My family living with me consists of: *WIFE (COLLEEN MARIE BERINGER),*

DAUGHTER (COLLEEN MARIE BERINGER, JR.)

There could be confusion, as his wife and daughter have the same name, and if a son has the same name as his father, "junior" notes this, and he adds "Jr."

☒ I am NOT entitled to credit for military service (43 CFR, Part 181)

He did not want to ask if he qualified, because somehow that he was sent home due to hardship would have to be revealed, and he did not want the man to question him.

☒ I am the person who made the homestead entry or entries noted above.

☒ The description of the lands included in the entry or entries noted above is as follows: *W 1/2 SW 1/4 SECTION 24*

N 1/2 NW 1/4 SECTION 25

Section **24–25**, Township **15 N**, Range **4 W**, _____ **SEWARD** Meridian

---

The residence I claim was made upon the ☒ original entry.

I first established actual residence on **AUGUST 30, 1956**

☐ I did ☒ I did not own the original entry during the entire period of such residence.

☒ I have ☐ have not a habitable house on the land

The house became habitable on *(Give month, day & year):*

SEPTEMBER 15, 1957

They moved in October because they were waiting for everything to be finished, including painting the floor and building the porch. But he guesses they could have moved in around this day.

The house was built after residence was established ☒ Yes ☐ No

Before the house was built, I resided at: **MY HOMESTEAD (ANCH. 041180)**

Periods of Absences from the land in the homestead and reasons for absences:

Who Was Absent
(specify "claimant,"
"family," or "both")

Who Was Absent	Reason for Absence
FAMILY	PREGNANCY
FAMILY	FAMILY DEATH
CLAIMANT	HOSPITAL STAY, INJURY
CLAIMANT	DISTANT EMPLOYMENT

They lost a child, and Marie lost her mother, and he means either for the family death he listed as a reason, though only one took Marie away. But losing her mother, Rosalie, will cover this absence if he is asked. And he has written *injury,* though the man might have heard of the mauling by the bear, he will not give him the satisfaction. He consults his records and adds the dates of leaving and returning.

CHARACTER OF LAND EMBRACED IN THE HOMESTEAD:

Section 25, *GENTLY ROLLING WITH MARSH AREAS + LAKE + PORTION OF CREEK. APPROX. 3000 BOARD FEET OF SAW TIMBER*

Section 24, *GENTLY ROLLING WITH MARSH AREAS, 20 ACRES NOW CULTIVATED*

ACTUAL AGRICULTURAL USE OF THE LANDS IN THE HOMESTEAD:

Calendar Year *1958, ALFALFA, 20 ACRES*

IMPROVEMENTS PLACED ON THE LANDS IN THE HOMESTEAD:

Section 24, *LOG HOUSE 30X30*
Value of Materials: *$ 2500*
Value Of Labor: *$ 6000*
Total Value: *$ 8500*

Section 24-25, *20 ACRES CLEARED AND CULTIVATED*
Value of Materials: *$ 1450*
Value Of Labor: *$ 1350*
Total Value: *$ 2800*

Section 24, *OUTHOUSE*
Value of Materials: *$ 5*
Value of Labor: *$ 10*
Total Value: *$ 15*

Present Value of Improvements: *$ 11, 315*

My homestead is used for trade or business: □ Yes ☒ No

There are no indications of coal, salines, or minerals on my homestead: *NONE*

I have sold, conveyed, agreed to sell or convey, or optioned, mortgaged, or agreed to option or mortage the land in my homestead, or any part thereof: □ Yes ☒ No

I have made another homestead entry: □ Yes ☒ No

Neither of the witnesses was present while I was giving the above testimony: □ Yes ☒ No

The witnesses □ did ☒ did not inform me of their testimony in connection with this proof.

☒ I do now apply the above-described entry or entries and for the purpose do solemnly affirm that I am a citizen of the United States, that there is a habitable house upon **W 1/2 SW 1/4, SECTION 24, N 1/2 NW 1/4 SECTION 25, TOWNSHIP, 25 NORTH, RANGE WEST, SEWARD MERIDIAN,** that residence and agricultural use of the land has been performed and set forth in my testimony; that no part of said land has been transferred or conveyed to another person, or otherwise aliened except as provided in section 2288 of the Revised Statutes; that I will bear true allegiance to the Government of the United States; and, further, that I have not heretofore perfected or abandoned an entry made under the homestead laws of the United States.

_____   _____
(Date)   (Sign full name)

_____

I HEREBY CERTIFY that the deponent was examined separately and apart from the witnesses in the case; that the foregoing deposition and affidavit were read to or by the deponent and affiant in my presence before he or she affixed signature thereto; that I verily believe deponent and affiant to be a creditable person and the identical person hereinbefore described, and that said deposition and affidavit were duly subscribed and sworn to before me at my office, in _____, within the _____ land district this _____ day of _____, 19___.

_____

_____
Official Designation of Officer

How the man would talk if Lawrence brought Marie in to add her name. Her deeds. His deed. But he chose this land before her, before his life with her. He finalizes the date as 23 August 1958. Wavers, hesitates to sign his name, he has been here before, without his wife, their daughter, and the pen writes _Lawrence_. This is how things have always been. And the pen writes _J. Beringer_. And the document is signed.

—+—

MARIE PINS CLEAN DIAPERS on a clothesline inside the cabin, the rainy season. White flags of another kind of surrender, a hunch in her back. There are not enough hours in the day, even in the summer, chores take twice as long as they used to. Baby cries, and she hurries to add more pins to the line. Then a shriek, and she rushes to the cradle. On the baby's cheek, a large mosquito, which she pinches dead with her fingers, blood from the lazy and full insect, and a trickle of red oozes down the baby's face. Marie had been so careful with the diaper pins and she picks up her daughter, *Don't cry, little one,* and she dabs the corner of a towel in water and washes the bite, and Marie is crying, because how could she have let this happen, the first mark, the first injury?

And is this what being a mother is, watching how a child is hurt, and feeling helpless against the odds that this will happen again? And she should have known better, should be better, she is lucky her daughter is here, and growing every day, but the newness is worn, the waking in the night, never feeling rested, never at peace, time to hush now.

—+—

WHEN LAWRENCE RETURNS, SHE is in the rocking chair, just awake. The homestead proof was in the glove box of the truck and he moved it to the back of the army ambulance, the official acceptance will be mailed to him, the land patent, the deed. Though the man said that could take a while. He swallows the snag in his throat.

"Checked on the filing," he says. "Bad news."

"Can we make the claim yet?"

"Lived on the land, built the cabin, cleared and planted twenty acres."

"Had a child," she says, and nods to the baby sleeping in the cradle.

"We have only one crop," he says. "We need two. I misunderstood."

Her hands tense over the arms of the chair. "You never said anything about two. You said all we needed was alfalfa."

"Was wrong," he says. "I say we plant potatoes in May, harvest in July, then we'll be ready."

"Have to wait that long? You wanted to file before statehood. Had some worry about it."

"Ain't nothing hard work can't cure," he says. The lie biding for more time.

He shows her the map in lieu of the other documents. She will not know, and he, in these months, will sit with the weight of his decision. He cannot undo what he has done, but he could draw new papers after this next harvest. Though the man would have the record, and would ask questions. Here they are, in stillness, a father, a mother, a daughter, and Marie with her eyes closed in the rocking chair, and the baby sleeps, and the summer light in the windows rests on the sill, and the latch secure on the door, and the emptied stove asking for nothing, and the air neither hot nor cold, in this holding, in this dwelling, and it is this balance he has betrayed.

———+———

STAYS BEHIND WITH THE baby. Knows not of his every coming and going and does not need to and he asked on the filing and he told her so himself. They say the boldest lies are the truth. Her name, is what he agreed, and another crop is needed, and how is she to take his word, one she believed? He would not have made this mistake, she knows. There is a guilt, but of what ilk? Not of a woman somewhere, that is not his failing. Something owed, then, but what, and there were so many reasons unspoken.

Signs and wonders, lightning, the first she has seen here, and the crash of thunder, wind whipping the trees. The baby screams in the storm and Marie rocks her in her arms. Lawrence has buried himself in the couch. The bolts crack the darkened sky, branching flashes in the back windows. Far enough away to ward off the fear of a strike on the steel roof, and the patter of rain hardens, and tins, a beating, and Lawrence stands, and on the porch, the pound of hail, marbles of ice, and without speaking, they huddle under the kitchen table, and take shelter.

———+———

IN THE MORNING, THE clouds hover in a gray shroud, the ground wet and green, a few dents in the wooden porch from the hailstorm. Baby wailed through the night, each hour without end, and is sleeping. Never seen such pelting from the sky, but this will not stop him today. He rouses Marie to tell her why he is heading out, her arm over her eyes, and she waves him away. He had worried she would want to come with him but this is something he must do alone. He has the map, the lines and borders of the property, his property, a compass, the metal stakes, and this time he will not be lost.

Not another homestead for some miles, but that could change. And what had the pilot in the helicopter called him that day, a tenderfoot, and those young men at the bureau, that is what they were. He should have shown them his scars from the grizzly, told them beware, that land claimed and cleared and tilled in the midst of a wilderness is still what it was, no matter your striving, and why he has the shotgun in hand. Pistol easier to carry, but he is not taking that chance. His scars have begun to fade, the worst on his thigh, the thrash. The pain, the deep throb, is almost gone, a small ache with all of his weight on the leg.

He drives the first Beringer stake into the ground with the mallet and stands back to admire the shine of the metal. And carries and places the rest, through woods, and the marsh, the open meadows. He had wondered what he would find that he did not know, and there is a little creek, on the far south, and he will have to tell Marie. He splashes water on his face and runs his hands over the edge of the mossy ground. On the map only a bend of the creek dips into the line of his lot, the flowing water has to be shared. So there is no question what is his, he crosses the creek, and soaks his boots, and positions a stake on the other side of the bank. And as he walks on, blisters begin to burn on his feet, and the air comes alive, awake with mosquitoes who yield to no one.

CHAPTER 28

AUTUMN CREEK

SEPTEMBER

FUSSING AND HOLLERING, DEAR Lord, save us all, and Lawrence is in Anchorage looking for work, and what she would give to be in his place, and Sheila not coming til the morning. Cradle rocks and the baby, screw-faced and red, cries. And there was Lawrence with his sudden forthrightness, said his savings would not last forever, went to see Bernie about a job, what is he hiding? She has searched and rummaged, drawers and cabinets, and coat pockets, everything back in its place.

How could a baby cry any more after these past two weeks? Rushed to the doctor after a day or so, colic is the cause, nothing to do but wait. Marie holds and soothes and pats and there is no remedy. Colleen takes milk. Clean diaper. No rash. No fever. *I know,* Marie says, *I know,* the words are a comfort, at least to her, and she lays the baby down in the rucksack. In the doorway she moves the wooden board spiked with sharp nails that Lawrence made to ward off trespass, and trudges out into the woods, pistol in the leather holster. Let all of creation, the sky and the mountains, hear. Sometimes walking will soothe the baby for a short spell. Her back strains but she will tire them both. The trees bristle with a gust of autumn and each birch leaf is a little sun. Every day a bit farther, and she is not afraid, she feels nothing, and she reaches the edge of the marsh, the muskeg, and the cut of a creek. She sits down with the baby and sack on her lap, stretches her legs, leans back on her hands, tilts her face to the clouds. Will ask Sheila tomorrow, should she be worried, should she take the baby back to the doctor? Tears well up in her eyes, there was a time she could leave the cabin and hear the birds and her own footsteps. And then the baby is quiet, and there is the trickle of water, water moving, maybe what they both needed all along.

A cloud passes and the light opens over the creek, flashes of red appear, brighter than blood, and she stands to her feet. Fish, and she has never seen them there before. A splash, and one swims toward her, shoring in the shallows, and she stands and rushes in with her boots on, scaring the fish up toward the bank, supper in the pan, you don't say, and she bends over, careful of the baby, and picks up a heavy rock. Steps on the fish tail with her boot and the head jerks. Baby cries. Will be easier if the fish is on the shore, and she scoots the fish there. Then sets the baby down on the bank, close, keeps the holster on. She aims and hits the cheek of the fish with the rock, and it frenzies with escape, and she traps the flail under her boots. Lifts the rock and brings a hard bash to the top of the head, and another, and a dull thud pulses in her hand. Fish shakes and then stills, mouth open in a gasp. Head and tail are green and black, tar, the eye bright gold, the side and belly an angry red, black speckles on the back and fins, the top of the jaw hooked over the bottom, sharp teeth. She bends to wash the fish and her hands in pockets of the shallow, slime and a splatter of blood and scales, and a swarm of fish cloud the deeper water, finning the surface, a bounty for the taking. And the baby wails. Then the grunt of an animal, and over her shoulder, a bear, a grizzly, nosing the fish blood on the ground, sniffing, which is feet away from the rucksack and the baby and her. The baby's wail pitches and the bear tilts his head and snouts the air. The bear stands on his hind legs, as tall as a tree, his fur thick, a mane of yellow, glint of long sharp claws. Dark glass eyes stare at her. Her hands hang empty at her sides. The fish at her feet. And she remembers the pistol, and slowly undoes the safety strap, her hands wet and slippery. The baby shrieks and the bear lowers to all fours, the rucksack near his front claw, his large head looming over hers. With every muscle, Marie throws the dead fish to the bear, an offering, the gray wide-open mouth aimed to the left, the landing, the red jewel in the dirt. She holds her breath, and her hand, trembling, moves again to the pistol. She knows her baby's cry, the hunger cry. The bear turns to the fish, and when white teeth flash and bite into the skin, she snatches the rucksack, runs for both of their lives, through marsh and woods and leaves and branches, and reaches the steps of the porch, the lock on the cabin door, the cold metal of the pistol on the table, still cocked to safety.

She checks the doors again, the windows, and she gives the baby a bottle of milk. And a bear is out there, knows she is here. She brings the shotgun to the table, the shells. She will wait. She has not slept through the night in how long. Baby screaming in her arms. Lawrence tossing and turning, which was still more than she could muster. But a crying baby is a living baby, she reminds herself. And what would she tell Lawrence, she put her down for a second on the bank? And a grizzly appeared. If he knew he would never forgive her, for how close.

Half-awake, Marie hears the truck. She has spent all night in the kitchen chair. Sheila arrives with glass jars and rings and a large aluminum pot, brand-new lids, a net—one of the drillers and his wife are moving to the Lower 48. She unloads from the passenger side of the truck and sets the large pot on the kitchen table next to the guns. Sheila has the wife's handwritten recipes and instructions, one for canning salmon. "Silvers are running, and we're late so they're spawning, and Knik Arm should have some, I'm told. Someday we'll learn to smoke the fish," she says. She has life in her voice, but Marie knows that there is a weight beneath the can-do and the help, a strain to the edges of her words.

Marie tells her about the fish in the creek, and the grizzly, and sleeping in the kitchen chair, and she doesn't want to tell Lawrence.

"Those are your silvers," Sheila says, "in your creek on your land."

"And the bear?"

"One of god's creatures. You can't run around here afraid."

"Could have killed us," says Marie. "Have you forgotten what happened to Lawrence?"

"Even so," she says, "I wouldn't tell him any of this." Baby fusses and cries as Sheila takes her from Marie. Sheila kisses the baby's cheek, *Don't cry, Aunt Sheila is here,* and turns to a window, her back a shield.

"Colic, no doubt," says Sheila.

"Doctor says there is no medicine for it."

"Whiskey," says Sheila, shoulders square to the window.

"For the baby?" says Marie. "That can't be." She would laugh, but Sheila is not in humor.

"Heard the crying lasts months." Not Sheila's way, to hide her face. She bounces the baby on her hip. "My goodness," she says, as a cry pierces into a wail.

"Nothing good about it," says Marie. "I don't know what's wrong with me. I went walking, who knows how far, and I didn't think."

"We're going to the creek," says Sheila, and hands over the baby.

"We can't," says Marie.

Sheila carries the shotgun out to the porch and pulls the trigger, a blast, an echo in the low. "Nothing's getting in our way," she says.

Marie gathers the knife, the net, the burlap sack, locks the door and places the nailed board in front. Sheila is determined, shoots at will, gives a signal, a booming through the woods and brush, a warning to any man or beast, and Marie follows, the baby held against her chest. Each step is a casting off—here is a wilderness, but one where she belongs, where she will live. And what of her sister? What is proven with a bullet, with the distance? She is making a path for them both, as she has all these years, the world against them. What ghost? What wrongs? *If this is not for us,* says the sounding, *if this is not ours, I will make it ours.*

The gleam in Sheila's eyes, not tears, but a stubborn aim. Marie would not dare take the shotgun from her. There is no telling her, no asking. Trigger and pull. The shells loading. The crack of bark hit by split shot. They could come this way again if they wanted, follow a trail of scratches and breaks, wounds on bark. Reckless, to waste shells shooting air, but she would never say so to Sheila, not here. And if Lawrence asks, she will take the blame.

Silence at the creek as Sheila sets the shotgun aside, minds the baby, and keeps watch, no fresh bear tracks. One minute killing the air, and another tending to a child. Marie wades into the water with the net, aiming for the silver salmon that have bloomed red with spawning, and dart and dodge, but in a half-hearted escape. She flattens the net on the creek bottom and waits, and two silvers swim over the net and she lifts the handle and bags them, and they arch and splash, a catch. They take turns and rack ten, and Sheila slices their bellies with a knife and guts them, some have eggs, the females with the soft-rounded heads. One skein she washes, ruby beads, plump and dark. She picks a strand of three eggs and sucks them into her mouth.

"Here," she says.

"Fish eggs?" says Marie. She plucks two and crushes them between her teeth, salt and sweet. She sways with the baby.

Sheila carves out the meat from the cheeks. "Waste not, want not," she says. "You know how many times we heard Valera say that growing up?"

Marie nods.

"Been on my mind," says Sheila. "Our grandmother and Rosalie." She fills the burlap with the cleaned fillets. "You think they had spite for each other? And us?"

"At times."

"You think we'll be any better?"

Marie glances down at the crying face of her daughter. "We already are. You'll see."

"I thought I was going to have—" says Sheila. Her hand grasps the burlap, tight. "But a week ago—" And she shakes her head.

"I'm sorry."

"Sly doesn't know," she says. "I was just thinking to tell him, but then nothing to tell."

"That ain't nothing," says Marie.

"It's worse," says Sheila. She walks to the water and washes the blade, flicks the knife dry.

What could Marie give her sister, for her hurt, the ache for what she herself held in her arms, and how could she tell her, how heavy the burden of a child, the worry, each day and night, a life in your hands. The baby's cries, and Sheila's voice, fade into the trees, and she turns toward that quieting hush, sun through leaves, the light and dirt. *This is your land,* says the ringing in her ears, despite what Lawrence may keep from her. Every acre, every animal, every fish, every spring and creek.

—+—

BERNIE IS NOT HIMSELF, yelling at the crew, even at the kid with one arm who is more keen than the rest. The job is gutting an old saloon, floor soaked with booze, though the bar is staying, some story about the wood being etched by the same pickaxe that struck a gold nugget back in the day. Lawrence has never seen Bernie in a bad temper and finds out he has taken the spot of a man who had enough and quit. Lawrence says he needs to talk, and Bernie, knowing him, thinks this must be a serious matter.

Lawrence walks Bernie away from the site, toward the surrounding woods and a felled tree on the ground.

"Is it your leg?" says Bernie as he takes a seat. Lawrence is managing without crutches.

"Nothing with me," says Lawrence, who sits beside him. He pours coffee into the lid of his thermos.

"With your wife?" he says.

"I'm asking you," says Lawrence.

"That bad?" says Bernie. He opens his pail.

"Rest of your crew is going to walk before long," says Lawrence.

Bernie sighs. "You know that gal I told you about?" His voice lowers. "I asked her to marry me."

"That's—"

"She turned me down." Bernie leans over his knees and places a hand on the back of his neck, as if in pain.

Lawrence downs his coffee and stares straight ahead as Bernie chokes on his words.

"She lives near Ship Creek. I had a job out there. Just happened." He takes a deep breath.

"Why can't I have what I want? I work hard."

Some of the men are standing and looking over at them. "Break must be over," says Lawrence. "Take another ten," he yells to them.

"I was there when you met Marie," says Bernie. "Saw how easy it was for you."

"Not been easy. I can tell you that much," says Lawrence.

"I drive by her cabin every day," says Bernie. "I'm on my way to work and suddenly I'm there."

"You have to let this be," says Lawrence.

"I want what's mine," says Bernie. "Same as any man."

Lawrence wishes he had a flask, something to offer Bernie. "After work, we'll go out," he says. "Take your mind off things."

"Won't help," says Bernie. "But I'll try."

Lawrence ends up working near the kid with one arm, Jim. Though he cannot be that much younger, his milky face dotted with freckles makes him seem so.

"What did you say to the boss?" says Jim. "He's not yelling at us."

"I just let him talk," says Lawrence.

They are a pair, his limp and Jim's one arm, but they remove the heavy cabinets with the strength of men twice their size. And a day's work passes with good progress, Bernie his old self, one of the guys, and they clean and put away the tools.

"You serve?" Jim asks him.

"Not like you," says Lawrence, which is the most truthful answer he has given. "My leg, it's not what you're thinking," he says.

Then Jim leans in and says, "This arm. Tractor accident."

"I don't have to know," says Lawrence.

"Needed a job. Being a vet is a sure thing." Jim smiles wide.

"You don't think I'd let Bernie know you swindled him?" says Lawrence.

"I know you won't," says Jim. "You've got secrets, I reckon."

"Same as everybody," says Lawrence. He looks around for Bernie.

"You don't know me from Adam," says Jim. "But I can tell you this, a war isn't the only reason to kill a man." He laughs, as if he made a joke.

Where is Bernie? And then Lawrence spots him coming around the other side of his truck. "Have to catch the boss," he says, and hurries away from Jim, trying to shake off what he said.

"That kid is something," says Bernie, with a tilt of his head.

"Something," says Lawrence.

"The Buckaroo?" says Bernie.

Lawrence agrees and tails his truck. He could use the money, or he might have decided not to work the rest of the week. Will keep close to Bernie. These newcomers are of a different ilk, who can say what they are here for, what they left behind? Surviving a grizzly was a story he could tell, if he wanted. And, at least in a war, it was clear who the enemy was. Jim knew how to rattle a man, Lawrence could say that much. You think you know who people are—and Bernie thought he was getting a wife, not very different from him. He was at the Buckaroo lot in the Mercury waiting on Marie, about to drive away after he proposed and she left him without an answer—and then she came running back in the rain.

CHAPTER 29

BIRCH BARK CALL

OCTOBER

LAWRENCE HOLDS THE ROLLED and nailed birch bark to his mouth and bellows, a deep bawl, from the bottom of his lungs, and he knows the sound he is trying for—a moose call—and a pained lonesome hollers out from the porch. Sly, back for a visit, stands beside him. They will do anything to not be inside with a crying baby.

Cabin door opens and Sheila says, "Y'all making that racket and the darnedest thing—the baby stopped her fussing."

They had taken the baby in to Anchorage again to see the doctor, who said the same. Colic. No cure but time. How long, no one could say. To be out, even with Sly, is a breather, the closed door muffling those inside. Best place for spotting is the roof of the cabin, as the moose wander through the low marsh leading the trees miles down to the inlet. Lawrence props a ladder and climbs and stands his shift, plowed rows of clouds cutting the view.

He was so close to all of this being his. Had been waiting on mail and received an official letter from the Department of the Interior that states he is to give a notice for publication to the *Anchorage Daily Times* that names the witnesses and says he has submitted his final proof on his homestead entry. The "very truly yours" at the end of the official letter struck him as a slight acknowledgment, a congratulations, after the many papers he signed and filed. So he sent the notice and asked Jones to save newspapers for him, as the last step is to provide proof of the publication for their records at the bureau.

Baby cries, so much for quiet, Lawrence shouts to Sly to sound the call from the porch. And he has not spotted a moose, come to mind, when year last they were as many in number as the mosquitoes for how often he came across one. Could they hear this tiny thing wailing through the trees, an alarm, set to her own time, each and every afternoon? And then every night. He and Marie have taken to drinking more whiskey, and a ration of cherry wine on Sundays.

The scope has been sighted in with a target on a tree with the rifle Sly brought—making sure his shot will be good is worth a bullet. He has his elbow steady on the line of the roof, and blinks, a dark shadow appears in the crosshairs, a bear, and he pulls the trigger and the shot rings out. Nothing in the scope. Or near the woods. He checks the front of the lens for a smudge.

Sly appears below with a bottle of beer. "You get one?" he asks. A stumble in his voice.

"Need a proper hunting stand and a new spot," he says.

He gives Sly an axe and he handles the chainsaw. Work is the answer to what ails. And he is finally his old self, though his leg is still a bother, a twinge if he walks a long while, if he is honest. This is all Sly's idea, buddy who owes him has an old commercial freezer, says they can store moose meat for the year, and when the weather is cold enough Sly can bring the meat to the cabin, leave it outside somewhere safe, keep for months. Lawrence wonders if this is Sly's way of trying to make amends for throwing his crutch, which was senseless. There is a difference when he thinks of the bear that attacked him, he knows there was a reason, the sow protecting her cubs, the threat in that moment, and in the end, he lived. Even so, he would have taken satisfaction in killing the sow that maimed him.

They walk toward the lake and Sly points out a cottonwood, but Lawrence is not convinced of the location. He finds a tall birch tree in a better viewing spot, with spruce close enough to reach. They build a spruce-pole ladder to scale the birch and nail a base around its trunk and the trunk of two other trees with two-by-fours and other lumber scraps. They cover the base with plywood. High up, the platform is stable and secure and they rest, eyes scanning the woods, watching through binoculars. He would prefer to let the fresh air do the talking, but Lawrence senses the trap, the wanting to pry open, Sly drinking to forget, in a wash, the buried things that trouble a man.

"Sheila's not telling me something," says Sly.

"Know the feeling," says Lawrence. Though he did not tell Marie about the deed.

"I've asked her and asked her," says Sly.

"She'll come around," says Lawrence.

"Does Marie just come around?" says Sly. "They're of the same cloth."

"They tell each other, no doubt," says Lawrence.

"And then get to telling us?" says Sly.

"No saying."

Sly opens another bottle. "Nothing like a warm beer," he says.

"Just make sure you can climb down," says Lawrence.

"I'll be good by then," says Sly. "Hunting is just a lot of waiting."

"Try the call again," Lawrence says.

The first frost, and the Old Cabin Still thermometer says thirty degrees. The morning light warms them as they walk to the hunting stand, the spangled brightness of the thin ice covering the ground. In the night, the turned aspen leaves fell, the heaviness breaking the stems, and the leaves are still falling in a flutter that sounds of water. The fireweed and ferns are dried to a rust, twisted stalks laced with white. And on a morning like this, even Sly knows to hush. Lawrence had tried to come out here alone, but Sly was on watch, and ready before Lawrence could leave.

Alert for every creature, but a spruce hen flits into the air, the wings beating so fast he can feel the flap in his chest, and a shot behind him, and he flinches, ready for his death. He stands and waits for pain or blood or a surge of knowing, but he is not injured. Sly is on his back with the rifle, he stumbled and pulled the trigger, startled by a stupid bird, he says. His face white and pale, the aim high, he believed, no one is hurt, but for a moment he believed he shot Lawrence, his voice and hands shake.

Lawrence stands over Sly. "Give me the rifle," he says. "Carefully." And when he does, Lawrence says, "And stand up, for god's sake."

Sly is leaning over his knees, taking in deep breaths.

"You walk ahead of me," says Lawrence. One rifle on either shoulder. He should send Sly back to the cabin, but wants him to suffer a little longer, and what if Lawrence made one shot into the woods, to scare him, though he is unsteady on his feet, the shock and the needing a drink, one and he could be rid of Sly coming out here and taking for granted they were hunting buddies, brothers, and Lawrence holds the straps of the rifles, restrains, and this is for the crutch, and turns around and shoots just to the left of Sly, through the trees, and there is the sudden cower in Sly's shoulders—and Sly is the lesser man, and that is the lesson, knowing that Lawrence is the superior mark and could have buried a bullet in his back. "I always know where I'm aiming," he says.

Sly, eyes wide, falls back behind Lawrence without a word. Lawrence holds the guns, and he has command of this hunting trip. Knows those steps behind him are those of a wounded animal.

With care not to slip, Lawrence climbs the ladder at the hunting stand. He reaches the platform and Sly is still on the ground, deciding. "Come on," he says. They drink coffee from the thermos, neither talks, and Sly adds whiskey from a flask to his and offers. The flash of silver in arm's reach, and Lawrence hesitates, and then finally takes it, and pours enough for bite. The mist of morning warms, the sun sharp on the dying leaves.

"So that's what we call friendly fire," Lawrence says.

Sly hangs his head, a sheepish grin. Lawrence wonders if he will tell Sheila about the shot in the woods, but then he would have to admit to the accident. So better to leave this behind them in the trees. A silent agreement. They listen for moose and wait for a sighting, and what the hours will bring.

The baby is passed between Sheila and Marie, and then Sly tries a turn, spinning with her in his arms, and as long as he is spinning she is soothed, but he has to stop, unsteady on his feet, and she wails more.

"This will be all night," warns Marie.

"Time for cherry wine," says Lawrence. "But only one bottle. Only have so many."

They will let her cry in her cradle. And they sit at the kitchen table and Sheila has two new decks, time for the boys to learn pinochle, says Valera taught them young so she would have enough in a pinch for the needed four players.

Sly groans. "She already started on me. Made my head hurt."

"Then Marie can have a turn and have you as partner."

The women are ruthless, know how many trump are left, how to outbid each other, and he and Sly are left scratching their heads.

"Takes years," says Sheila. "And we got all the time in the world."

Marie checks on the baby and turns on the Victrola, the music to drown out the cries. Lawrence lights the lantern above the table.

"She will grow out of it," says Sheila. "That's what I heard."

They finish the bottle and Lawrence brings out another, he is feeling generous. "My father says only way to know if you're drunk on cherry wine is to stand up." So they all rise from their chairs.

"Fit as a fiddle," says Sly, "so keep pouring."

The game ends with Marie and Sly winning, the score not even close. Then Sly brings out the whiskey.

"Let's call it a night," says Sheila.

"What else do you call it?" says Marie, and laughs. "I know another game."

"The baby is sleeping," Sheila whispers, and the last record has played its final song.

"We all tell a secret," says Marie. "There are too many at this table."

"Let's turn in," says Lawrence, uneasy.

But Sly and Sheila agree with her.

"I'll begin," says Sly. "I'm ashamed to say I almost—" He pauses. "Accidentally, mind you." He looks at Marie. "And I'm very sorry."

Sheila and Marie are confused. "He almost shot me today," says Lawrence.

Sheila slaps Sly's shoulder. Sly laughs. "That's not funny," she says.

"Don't you feel better?" says Marie.

Sly grins. And pours himself more whiskey. Lawrence has to think of what to say, what he will reveal.

Marie tells the story about going to the creek and finding the silvers. "But what I didn't tell you is that there was a bear. And I ran all the way back to the cabin with the baby."

"Did you have the pistol?" says Lawrence.

"Hands were shaking," says Marie.

"That's something I should know," he says, "living out here."

"And I," says Sheila, "wasted shotgun shells when we went out to the creek to get our fish. Bought some and brought them here so you wouldn't know. But you see a few nicked trees that way." She taps her chest. "I did that."

Lawrence bows his head. He has to take a turn. A lie that sounds like a shameful truth—and then will not have to reveal that he filed the papers. "Sly was covering for me," he begins.

"No," says Sly.

"Listen," says Lawrence. He fixes a stare on Sly, who finally understands he should go along. "It was me who almost shot Sly. Who had the accident."

"I don't believe you," says Marie.

"Was my leg that had the injury—must've tripped. And Sly was ahead of me."

"Is this true?" says Marie to Sly. She grabs his face.

"True," says Sly.

"Well," says Sheila. "Sounds like you boys shouldn't be hunting and we shouldn't be fishing."

"Anything else?" says Marie. She slams her hands down. "Come clean at this table or forever hold your peace."

"You hold your own peace," says Sheila.

"That baby," says Marie, a little too loud, "gives me none."

"Shhh," says Sheila.

"This man," says Marie. She points at Lawrence. "I don't know this man."

"We've gone and tipped the bucket," says Sheila. "Time to turn in." She stumbles to the couch and Sly follows.

Marie slides off her chair and walks slowly to the bed. She lies down on top of the quilt, sprawls across to his side. He gently moves her legs over, her arm, and she is already asleep. He is sure of where he stands with Sly, has another upper hand by taking the blame, can count on the man to be quiet. But not with Marie. Why did she not tell him about the bear at the creek, she did no wrong. Who were they, always around each other, sick of being so near, so tied, and yet apart. He reaches over to touch her hair on the pillow, the curled ends, careful not to wake her, because he cannot tell her that she does know him.

Another day and no luck, and the men trudge back to the cabin, hunters without a kill. An insult to Lawrence, after watching two seasons pass and no means to take the meat. And he sees them now, wounds in the trees from the shells Sheila fired.

"Akin to being married, wouldn't you say?" asks Sly.

"What is?" says Lawrence.

"Hunting. A lot of nothing most of the time," says Sly. "But then a few moments can make all that suffering out in the cold worthwhile." He closes his eyes as if remembering.

Lawrence walks a slow pace, all those hours on the stand, and wonders if he or Marie would agree. They are barely getting through each week, and does she suspect, but who can say with the baby keeping them up at all hours?

"Here they are, empty-handed and empty-headed. While we've had a time," says Sheila. The baby's shrieks fill the cabin. Sheila and Sly pack and leave, and Marie busies herself with quieting the baby. The records played on the Victrola do not soothe the child, neither does Marie's song. Lawrence remembers her singing as they drove to their wedding. Just the two of them. Miles on the road, and no question of where they were headed. A yes and a yes. No warning of their future troubles.

He brings out the birch-bark call and bellows and the baby hiccups in Marie's arms, and before she can wail again, he horns and the bawling becomes a soft whimper. He hangs the call on the nail and then the baby frets.

"Take her," says Marie, and she shoves the baby into his arms. "I'm going."

"Leaving me alone?" says Lawrence.

"I'll be at the bus," says Marie. "I can't be with her."

"You can't just go," says Lawrence.

"You do," says Marie.

"What if she's hungry?" says Lawrence.

"I just fed her," says Marie, and she closes the door.

Lawrence blinks through the shock. Marie has not let the child out of her sight as far as he remembers. "What to do with you?" he says. He walks, with her on his shoulder, pats the baby as Marie has, and she leaves a warm wet spot of drool on his shirt, and he tucks a nap under her chin, surprised his stomach does not turn. He surveys the cabin, the bed, the table. "See what I built," he says, of the double barrels holding the heat of the woodstove. The deed and proof hidden in the army ambulance, a secret, he tells her. Out on the porch, he holds her close and facing away, so she sees what he sees, and the mountains are clear in the cast, Pioneer Peak alone in height and reaching toward the sky. Of every mountain he has seen, Korea and South Dakota and driving through Canada to Minnesota, this is his, this is the one that pierces through and points him homeward. How he felt first seeing St. Michael's—the metal cross on top of the church bell tower the tallest marker for miles, the sheen of the polished pews and wooden rafters, and above the altar and the tabernacle, a wooden carving of Christ, thin and crucified, the cross stained dark, and two arches set high around him, bowed in the shape of praying hands. Years of tithes his father scraped together, and what did they amount to, what price did he pay? There are some sacrifices that should not be made if a man is to prosper. And Lawrence needed the assurance on the land, and surely Marie would understand, in time, that what he had done is what a man does. But as he holds his child, he cannot find the words for what is beyond him, beyond that church, this cabin, this mountain.

CHAPTER 30

LAY A HAND
NOVEMBER

SAWMILL, GRIND OF THE blade, the shearing, the cut to measure, a hire to fill in for a nephew who has pneumonia, all in the family, and every man is his senior and so he sweeps and shovels sawdust near the guy feeding wood to the chipper. Henry Mor put in a word, and they remembered him and Joseph buying rough cuts for the cabin, said he could have shifts. And first day, he is shown the floor and waiting for him is a grizzly bear head and hide draped over a broomstick, the shine of the black eyes, the joke—*We know all the news 'round these parts, son.* He laughs along, for the job's sake. Work when he can before winter. So he keeps his head down and to task, but the asking, how he loathes the asking, the begging, selling cords of wood in winter as a boy, the horse and the cart, freezing, and taking money from those in need, and taking money from those who pitied the sight of him, shivering, the offer of hot coffee, who had all their own wood stacked and readied in plain view, enough burning for years, the charity.

But here he is, tired, as the baby is still not sleeping. When he said he was going to the mill, Marie eyed him, as she had lately, as if waiting for the truth of what he had done or accusing him of being a different man when he walks out the door. But he could not think too hard on this matter, not here. Saw Bernie one last time at the Moose Lodge before he moved to Oregon so can't bother him for work anymore. He is a favor asked, and has to push through the lag, a wife and a new baby depend on him.

The whistle sounds for his late break in the round. He hides a yawn in his sleeve, and one of the older men, Frank Waylon, catches him.

"First one is the hardest," says Frank.

"Doctor says colic," says Lawrence.

"That was my little one a long time ago," says Frank. "Turned our life upside down." He leans in. "And I know you're not having any fun."

Lawrence gives no answer and Frank laughs. "Thought so. But you know what sometimes helped, taking that baby on a long drive."

Come to think of it, Colleen did seem more calm when they drove to Anchorage, the few times they braved a trip.

The men are all part of the Waylon family in some way, Frank explains over a pipe burning sweet tobacco. "My father was stationed in the Aleutians for the First World War," he says. "Then never went back home. Homesteaded a few acres over. Had to figure out a business to stay out here, first the mill in Palmer. And now we have this one, too."

Back to work, and Lawrence picks up his shovel.

"Tommy," yells Frank. "Let Lawrence here have a go at feeding the chipper. His baby has colic."

A few of the other men groan and shake their heads, knowing.

———+———

CRYING AND BAWLING FOR months, and Marie, with Colleen in her arms, walks around the cabin in a tired circle, as the sun slips down through the trees, a faint and sickly yellow. She would rather hear bullets than this, her own heart skittish, run off and don't come back, who's she fooling and how far? And she is uneasy about Sheila. Who said she wanted to be happy. Spent time with Marie and held the baby. And she told Sly and them all about that day with the shotgun and canning the silvers, and talked to her about everything else but why, or how she was doing, Marie did not want to press her, even when it was just the two of them in the kitchen.

Lawrence will be home soon, after his shift, a few he picked up for scant. Devil himself got hold of this child, poking and prodding, if she believed that way, and Sheila says a child cannot cry like this forever, trying her patience and every tenderness, if only she could ask other women, homesteaders miles off. Men at the Knik Bar out here alone, no wives, or waiting on bringing them. Henry's wife still has not moved up, still taking care of her sick sister, Lawrence says. And Lawrence was not keen on knowing too many people, except Henry, but what would be the harm? Maybe now is the time to ask him about going to a Sunday service at the Nike site.

Marie holds the baby and walks to the bus, and inside the stove she lights a fire. Bus warms and she boils a big pot of snow and as soon as Lawrence returns she will bathe. Baby lies on a blanket on the floor, making a god-awful noise, tuned to Marie's last and leaving nerve. Pot boils and placed to cool, and Lawrence is late. She removes the wet diaper and lowers the baby into the tub, shallow inches, and washes the little body with a rag and holds the baby's back, and Marie hears her own voice, *Quiet, be quiet,* and the baby, sitting with clenched fists, ignores the plea, and wails, and the bathwater browns with shit, the baby's eyes scrunched, her mouth a call that more will come, and the voice yells, *Stop,* and a hand covers the baby's mouth with the rag and the other clasps the neck, and the hands tense for a moment, the smallest quickening. One muffled cry, and Marie drops the rag and her hand around the neck loosens, and gentle, gentle, Marie lifts the screaming, shitting baby out of the tub and wraps her in a blanket, the mess be damned, and what happened, a second, a blink, a snap. No ghosts of prints on the baby's neck, as if there were no pressing at all, how hard? A twitch, a pulse, and no more? Rag in the mouth, no accounting, no question, what is the matter, how could she lay a hand on a poor innocent, *You're all right, there, nothing meant by,* and Marie bounces the baby on her hip as her hands strangle a loose fold of blanket.

There, now. Marie is light and feathery and dragging, too awake and too tired, dust of snow and sogged mud. She cleans the baby and readies the diaper. Baby kicks and cries with the cloth underneath. Marie touches the point of the diaper pin to her own fingertip—she could punish herself, prick her finger, bring blood. Pin dents the skin, and she taps, a comfort, the feeling of feeling, and it is enough. If she broke skin, she cannot see. She places two pins between her lips, and the cloth is soiled now but she folds the ends over the baby's hips and secures the sides. Sound of gravel under tires means Lawrence, and she picks up the baby and rushes out, walking as fast as she can carry.

Here, she says, *taking a bath,* and shoves the baby into his arms. Diapers, crying, a blessing, they say, but you can be blessed within an inch of your life and Marie just wants to sleep for a night and not hear one single sound, not one. No one waking, no one breathing, not a creak, no mouths, no scratching, no turning, not a stir in the dark. There was a time when the baby could not be out of her sight, she would not allow, or dare. She rinses the blanket and washes the tub. No witnesses out here, and then the windshield of the bus is cracked. Hauls more snow to melt and heats the pots and pours and fills. Maybe she needs to worry more about herself. She strips her clothes and steps in, her feet redden and the hot water needles her skin, and she swirls and adds snow. Sits and leans back, knees bent, and her head slides down until the water fills her ears, and she holds her breath, and the water is its own sound, the noise of nothing, of everything. She lifts her mouth and takes in air. Every inch of skin that he had touched, too long ago, and the baby has touched and taken, is washed and made hers again.

———

HE DRIVES THE BABY around in the truck, circles the cabin, and she hiccups, and whines, but not a full cry til he brakes. Marie misses supper, so he makes beans, and, after reading the recipe with evaporated milk and Karo syrup, feeds the baby a bottle. He knows Marie has fallen asleep, must have a need beyond most days, to leave him so. Smoke from the stove of the bus, so she is warm. He lays the fussing baby down in her cradle.

In the early morning he walks over and Marie is on the floor, a tarp wrapped around her, and she does not hear him. He nudges her shoulders and she opens her eyes, but they dart past him and she looks around.

"Baby is fine," he says.

She sits up, groggy, her hair mussed.

"I only meant to take a bath," she says.

"And you found a place to rest," he says.

"Will this ever end?" she says.

"Has to," he says. "Some guys at the mill been through it." He helps her stand and picks a dried leaf out of her hair. "Mentioned to try driving. Helped a little bit."

"Saw you going 'round and 'round," says Marie.

"We got ourselves a little spitfire," says Lawrence.

They walk back to the cabin and Marie picks up the baby and cradles her head.

"You have breakfast?" she says.

"We both did," says Lawrence. He has to drive to the mill and closes the door, Marie swaying and patting the baby's back.

Lawrence watches as Tommy, sent by Frank to load heavy boards, struggles, and he offers him his help, and Tommy refuses. Young and green and a barrel of a young man. Tries and fails and has the attention of the crew. So Lawrence, though lean and slight standing beside him, picks up a stack of boards, careful but capable, and tosses the lumber on the truck bed, and with that he knows he has moved up in rank.

Tommy curses under his breath as he is sent back to shoveling sawdust.

"You got some hidden strength," says Frank to Lawrence. "Wouldn't know by the looks of you."

"Heard that before," says Lawrence.

"That Tommy," says Frank. "He already thinks the world is under his feet. And he's not much younger than you."

"You'll set him right," says Lawrence.

"I only got another day or so of work for you," says Frank. "But you should come to our family supper on Friday night. Bring the wife."

"Will do," says Lawrence.

———

WHEN THE BABY WAKES from a nap, Marie is determined. A good day. She bundles her into the rucksack for a walk to the frozen lake. But then an eagle flies overhead, and she follows. Snow as clean as the air. Spruce dusted, the willow, tips of every shrub. And white on the slope of the back of a bull moose, calm beyond the rut, still adorned with a rack of antlers. She reaches in the sack so the baby can see, a moose. Would she remember this? Marie remembered too much, that was what Sheila used to tell her. And now she knows what she meant, how she tried to protect her. How could Marie have done what she did, the baby in the tub and what almost happened, but she is determined to have more patience and care.

She stumbles and catches herself, the baby shielded by her arms, and the cries begin. Not a root or branch, but one of the metal stakes. She is off the path. Marie digs around the top to reveal the full letters of Beringer. "That's your name," she says. "Our name." Still sounds strange to her, Marie Beringer. She would have to practice, the saying and writing. In her mind, and heart, Kubala remained, the name all her life, until these last two years.

Another eagle flies over, a call to her, and she mends her direction. And the nest is larger than before, it must be, the bare cottonwood tree a mere post for the heaviness twined at the center. The two eagles perch at the tallest edge of the nest that is covered in snow, and one begins to chirp, and then the other, and they are singing for each other. Snowflakes fall, light and airy. Marie tilts the rucksack so the baby has the eagles in view. And this is the lesson, not each twig, or branch, or day, but the work in the end, this collecting, the whole. For she is sure they could not recall every scrap and placing on its own. So this is the day that counts, she decides. And she looks down at her daughter's face and says, *Colleen, Colleen,* and each new boot print will be hidden by the hour's end.

———+———

MARIE HAS THE VICTROLA playing, he can hear the music from the porch. When he opens the door, she says they are having vanilla snow for dessert and the baby is asleep, but who knows for how long? She has fried potatoes, grease in the air, and she serves him a plate. He turns off the record and sits down. He lifts his fork.

"Are we going to pray?" she says. And they are united in this. And she silently asks God to make her a better mother. Then she asks Lawrence about his day.

He tells her how he was fighting to stay awake at the sawmill, about

Tommy, the young one who does not have his strength. Then the invitation from Frank.

"Our first," she says. "What should I bring?"

"I'm sure they have everything."

"Would not be proper to show up without a gift," she says. "A bottle of cherry wine?"

"Only three left," says Lawrence.

"Only thing fitting," says Marie.

"Going to have to ask my father to visit again and bring us more," says Lawrence. "Just got a letter."

Marie scoops snow into a bowl and pours condensed milk and the last of the vanilla. "How is he?" she says.

"Same. Is thinking of opening up another diner, but my mother is against it, of course."

The baby begins to fuss and whine and Marie brings her to the table. Marie dabs a finger in the melt of the bowl and gives the baby a taste. But she is not taken by it, and wails.

Lawrence, a slow eater, savors each bite, and then feeds the stove with firewood. He tells her he will come back early morning in time to stock the stove again, needs a good night's rest.

"I don't want to be tired working near a wood chipper and a blade," he says.

"Someday this will be past us," says Marie.

"And let it be soon," he says.

He takes a pillow and blanket to the bus and starts a fire. Even there, he swears he can hear the baby's muffled cries. He lies on the floor, with the same tarp Marie used, and feels close to her, even though they are more apart than before, and he remembers the nights he spent alone in this bus, dreaming of a homestead, and thought there was not anything in all the world that would keep him from sleeping in his own bed in a cabin he built.

———+———

FRANK WAYLON GAVE LAWRENCE a hand-drawn map on his last day of work so he could find the property on the outskirts of Point MacKenzie.

But they are lost and the baby is screaming. Lawrence is freshly shaved and wearing a button-up Pendleton and she debated on her one skirt or dungarees, and went with the pants and a blouse and her parka. And then the baby spits up on her lap. She had anticipated disaster, and brought along another blouse, but had not thought of this. Marie has Lawrence stop and hold the baby so she can clean up best as she can.

They drive and turn around and turn around, and Lawrence curses under his breath. Then Marie points out a wooden sign sticking out of the snow. The cabin is large, but not bigger than theirs, and Frank comes out to greet them with his wife, Sarah, who is also wearing dungarees, and Marie is grateful. Sarah asks about the baby, and Marie says she can hold her. She misses holding a baby, Sarah says, with their kids almost grown. And Colleen cries all the same, which is a comfort to Marie. Not her, not her fault. "Colic," she says. Sarah pats the baby's back. "Oh my goodness," she says. And then she breathes in the top of Colleen's head. "Missed that baby smell," she says.

Marie, to remind herself of it, leans in to wipe the baby's tears.

Lawrence hands Frank the bottle of cherry wine. "My father makes this in Minnesota," he tells him.

"We're drinking homemade brandy as we speak. But we should open this right away," says Frank.

Inside is the rest of the family playing cards and listening to a man playing the fiddle. Sarah passes Colleen to a group of women in one corner who are knitting and who do not seem to mind her fussing, and Marie feels a little guilty. If she knew any of them better, she could ask them if they ever had a moment as a new mother where they lost their sense. On the table are plates and Sarah says to help themselves, sourdough rolls and moose stroganoff and mashed potatoes and blueberry cobbler. Frank stops the music to introduce them and goes around and says everyone's name and their relation to him, his three children and so on. "And I can't forget Tommy, my nephew, and the only musical one," he says. And Tommy, from his chair, gives her a smile.

Frank opens the cherry wine and walks about the room to pour, some gulping down the brandy to make room. When Frank reaches Tommy, who grabs the bottle and downs the rest, and Frank tries to take the bottle back but Tommy finishes the last drop. Frank is embarrassed, and calls

him a "greedy little—" Sarah starts to walk across the room to him, but Lawrence sets down his plate and starts to clap. "My father would be proud," he says. "And he'd tell you the only way to know if you've had enough cherry wine is to stand up." The room laughs, and he raises his arm to beckon Tommy, who does stand, and says, "I can always have another." So Lawrence has saved the night, and he catches Marie's eye and winks at her.

"How about you play another song?" says Frank, and shoves Tommy's shoulders so he has to sit down again. Tommy tilts his head, as if deciding, and then props the fiddle under his chin.

Frank comes and sits down by them as they eat. "I apologize for him," he says. "We try to keep him in line. His father, my brother, died a few years ago."

"That isn't easy," says Marie, as her eyes follow which woman is holding Colleen.

Sarah invites Marie to a game of gin rummy with her sister-in-law. "Should I get Colleen?" she says.

"Take a break," says Sarah. "We know what having a little one is like."

Sarah tells her about her garden, canning vegetables and blueberries, and Marie asks about the sourdough. "Another homesteader gave the starter to me," she says. "Must be sixteen years now." She offers to teach Marie how to make the rolls on a future visit.

Frank and some of the men go outside on the porch to smoke pipes and cigars. One of the knitting women, Bonnie, comes over to join them and play the next game.

Marie asks Bonnie what she is making with the purple yarn. "A sweater. For who, I don't know yet." And Bonnie asks her if she knows how and she says she does not, but her sister does. "You should learn," Bonnie says. "How I get through the winter."

"Though she has a handsome husband," says Sarah, and they all laugh. If they only knew about the past months.

"You have any family near?" says Bonnie. "Or do they live in the Lower Forty-eight like most folks?"

"My sister and her husband are in Anchorage," says Marie.

"That's fortunate," says Bonnie.

"I wish they were closer," she says. "But they're coming for Christmas."

Then the baby cries and Marie goes over and takes her, but Colleen will not be quieted, wailing over the music and the laughter.

Marie does not want to spoil their time. When the men return, she tells Lawrence they should take the baby home. "No one minds her," says Lawrence.

Sarah overhears and says, "She is no bother. Please stay." Marie sits down and the children run up to Colleen and make faces and let her grab at their fingers. Then the music changes and people start clapping. Frank beckons to Sarah, and then other couples join them. A woman leans over to Marie and says, "You should get out there and do some square-dancing. Tommy will call what to do. I'll hold the baby," and she takes Colleen. Marie looks over at Lawrence and he smiles and holds out his hand. They spin, and stomp, and hitch arms, and turn around, until they are out of breath, Marie laughing. The baby has fallen asleep in the woman's arms and Lawrence says they should go and put her to bed. Sarah says to come the second week in December, they will be doing the same. But she tells Marie to arrive in the afternoon, and she will give her what she needs for sourdough.

Marie waves and smiles and heads out the front door. Lawrence gathers the rest of their things and Frank waves on the porch. In the truck Lawrence turns to her. "Those are good people."

Marie nods and wipes away a sudden tear. What would it take for them to have a life such as this? For her to be as wise and assured as Sarah?

"What's the matter?" says Lawrence.

"Wish we had more family here," says Marie.

Snow falls on the windshield, a flurry in the beams of the truck lights. All those women who knew things she should know could share their wisdom on raising a child. Or how to comfort a sister. Ask them about the ways between a husband and a wife. Lawrence sits, straight and severe, his attention to the road, and she knows this was, for him, a pleasant evening of company, but to her could be so much more. *There will be others,* she tells herself, as she holds the baby close, that smell of sweet bread.

CHAPTER 31

SALT AND SMOKE

DECEMBER

A CAMPFIRE NEAR THE frozen lake, and Sly holds the baby, who is wrapped in a blanket with the rag doll that Sheila made her for Christmas. Marie and Sheila are alone on the ice, skating in a wide circle. They are doing so well together, the four of them, which is what Marie wanted. Sly handling his drinking and trying to make Colleen smile with funny faces. Even Lawrence is in high spirits. And she is careful around Sheila, who has been doing most of the talking and asking. Marie tells her how they had now twice been to the Waylon cabin and she had started to learn about sourdough from Sarah. Then Sheila stops in the middle and Marie catches her and holds on to her arms.

"So are you getting any sleep?" says Sheila.

"Are you?" says Marie.

"What I mean is she naps sometimes," says Sheila. "Then you and Lawrence should take time to yourselves."

"We're not—"

"Or leave her with me in Anchorage for a bit," says Sheila.

Marie does not answer.

"You don't want me to take care of your child," says Sheila. "Is that it? I can't have one, so I'm not fit?"

Marie's eyes are watching Sly, him bouncing Colleen, a flask in his other hand.

Sheila sees her looking, crosses her arms. "He'll make a great father someday. Sly would never harm anybody." She skates away and Marie tries to catch her.

"Wait," says Marie.

Sheila looks over her shoulder and says, "At least my husband wants me." She turns. "And I have a wedding ring." She skates faster, and reaches the fire, and walks on the blades toward Sly. She puts her arm around him and kisses his cheek. Marie makes another lap by herself, and on the far end stops and pretends to check her laces. How could she tell Sheila her fear, not that she did not trust her and Sly, but if something terrible happened she could not lose her ties to them as well. She and Lawrence had survived losing the first by the skin of their teeth, as they say. And Sly, a kind man, but not reliable in all his ways, even Sheila would admit. Colleen was not an easy baby and Marie does not dare tell Sheila how, even as a mother, she had little faith in herself.

Marie skates over and joins the gathering at the fire and warms her hands. Sheila and Sly, their attention on the baby, how happy one of their own would make them. Perhaps more than she and Lawrence. What of their life here? She could not catch her own feelings, not for months. Lying alone in the bed, her mind racing, arms heavy at her sides, hearing a baby's cries where there are none.

—+—

LAWRENCE SITS ON A stump near the fire, as close as he can without burning his boots. There is an ease seeing Sly because they had agreed on bygones. Course, no hunting this time, being stuck on a stand in the trees for hours waiting for a moose that never showed. He will ask Frank how they keep the meat, though someone in his family must have a freezer.

Marie sits down and removes her skates. He could admit he missed her, how they were, even as he knows she is right there. Last night he had crept out of bed to throw wood in the stove and for a moment everything and everyone was calm, and sleeping, even the baby, and he stood still in the middle of the kitchen. *All is well,* he said to himself. He remembered he had filed on the claim, the papers hidden, and someday he would have to tell her.

—+—

LATE AFTERNOON, AND THE sun has set. Time for an early supper, leftover ham and mashed potatoes. Marie feeds the baby a bottle and leans back in the rocking chair, treasures this moment. She has let Sheila take over before, but not this time. Sheila can do the cooking, Marie has a child who needs her.

After the dishes are dried and put away in the cupboard, Sly wants to play pinochle and Lawrence says the only way he can is if he has some whiskey. But Sheila is tired, though the time is just after five, and sits on the couch next to Sly. The decorated tree in the corner, a little spruce with the red wooden beads of garland. They raise their glasses. "To our health," Lawrence says. In the cradle the baby whines and Marie puts on one of the new records, a gift from Sheila and Sly, and cranks the Victrola.

"Here," says Sheila, and she taps the couch. Then she makes more room by sitting on Sly's lap, her arm around his neck. Marie takes the spot on the other side of Lawrence so she does not have to be near her sister. She knows what Sheila is doing, proving what she can. Marie places her hand on Lawrence's knee and he smiles. Sheila laughs, loud and booming, and drowns out the music.

"Let's leave them be," says Marie to Lawrence. "Have a smoke?" They put on their coats and stand on the porch. Lawrence lights his cigar and then Marie's rolled cigarette, the glow of the lantern behind them. No need for talking this winter night, the sky clouded over, the snow a gray in the darkness.

A yowl in the woods. Marie walks to the edge of the porch. "Did you hear that?" she says.

"I don't hear anything anymore," says Lawrence.

"A lot has changed," says Marie.

"Remember the quiet," says Lawrence.

"Remember when it was just you and me in the bus," says Marie.

"We could go there now," says Lawrence, and meets her eyes.

Then a shout from inside the cabin, and a crash. They rush inside and Sly is on the floor and two kitchen chairs are knocked over. Baby cries from the cradle.

"We found a bottle of your cherry wine," says Sheila, through her laughter, her grip around the neck of a bottle. Her lips and teeth are stained red.

"Been keeping it from us?" says Sly, and he stands.

"Saving it," says Marie. "Stash is almost gone." She reaches for the bottle and Sheila swats her away.

"You saying we're not good enough?" says Sheila.

"It's for pinochle," says Lawrence. Marie is surprised at his measured answer.

"Then let's play," says Sheila.

"Then you have to share," says Lawrence. He holds out a hand and she pulls away, then smiles and offers the bottle.

"Have something to tell you," says Sly, and he uprights a chair and takes a seat.

"Shhh," says Sheila. "They know we found the wine."

"Do you have news?" says Marie, earnest.

"News?" says Sheila, not understanding. Then her smile fades. "Why would you ask me that?"

Lawrence shuffles the two decks of cards.

Marie touches Sheila's arm and she bristles. "I'm sorry," she says. "I misunderstood."

"You can be so cruel," says Sheila. There are tears welling in her eyes.

Sly pounds the table. "This game starts now," he says.

Sheila turns away and passes behind Sly, and runs her fingers through his hair, and then sits at the table.

———

SHEILA AND SLY ARE up late, and rush to leave as the sky darkens beyond the ridge, a storm. A crooked line of sunrise underneath, as if a lid is about to slide off and fall above them. Marie hugs Sheila, but she pulls away. Sly keeps on about the cherry wine and will bring something special to make up for leaving them with only one bottle. "Don't worry about it," says Lawrence. But when they finally drive away, he shakes his head. "Both of them this time," he says.

Double-barrel stove ticks with heat and Lawrence opens the metal door and feeds the flame. Baby has been crying all morning and Marie carries her on her hip. "You trying to burn us alive?" she says. Lawrence, always cold, a chill through the long johns and the double wool socks. Marie opens a window with a *praise the Lord* on her lips. Her knees buckle and she leans on the sill, catches herself. "Take this baby before I drop her on her head." Lawrence sets the crying baby down in the cradle. "Will build a crib," he says. He heads out with a pot and comes back with a mound of snow and leaves the door cracked open. Shovels into the stove, steam and stamp.

He dresses, and Marie sits at the kitchen table, head in her hands. "The heat," she says, though the temperature keens.

"Let's take a drive," he says.

"Now?" says Marie.

Lawrence kicks the airplane tires and starts the army ambulance, the documents in a toolbox in the back. Marie holds the baby and he takes them for a ride, as fast as he can go, around the cabin, the hum of the engine, the roar of the gas. He slows and the tears have stopped slipping down the baby's little face. "I want a turn," says Marie. He brakes. "All yours," he says, and hurries to her door. And she drives them around until the blizzard arrives.

—+—

IN THE OUTHOUSE SHE sits on the slab of wood covering the hole, the flashlight pointed at the ceiling. Hours of the storm before it passed, she and Lawrence drinking the last bottle of cherry wine, and the baby will not sleep. In her pocket, a jar of canned salmon, a rolled cigarette, a match, a pocketknife. Provisions. Salt and oil—the fish she caught with Sheila. Pops the lid with the knife. Each strip tender and sweet, and she eats the whole jar, licks her fingers. Lights the cigarette with the match and the booze lifts that burn, and this is better. Not many left for the winter. And she still has a sense that he is keeping something from her.

The crying baby. Opens the door a crack to knock the ash outside, freezing snow and the dark. Branches scratch the roof with the sway of the wind. Then a clawing down the side. "Lawrence?" she says, and locks the latch. Something is out there. An animal circles the outhouse and here she is, smelling of smoke and fish. She snuffs the cigarette. A lean, a pressing on the door. She yells and bangs on the wood wall of the outhouse. Waits, her breath fast and shallow. Pricks of sweat on her neck. Her feet and hands announce the cold. She shivers, and she is tired, more than tired. If not for the cold she would sleep here, the sound from the cabin hushed. Another scratch. She could be mauled. Or she could set the outhouse on fire. Or run, if her feet will carry her. If there is an animal, so be it, kill her, she is beyond that care, already dead and waiting. She unlatches the door and shoves and it slams open with a bang. From the light of the cabin windows there are tracks in the snow. Larger than a fox. She bangs her fist on the outhouse, the noise hollow. Every tree and branch is a hiding place. She will take the chance, and rushes toward the cabin, and turns around with the flashlight and catches the silver of two eyes. She shouts for Lawrence. She reaches the back door, and quickly fastens the lock. "Get the gun," she says, and Lawrence is asleep at the table, the drained bottle of wine and two glasses, one filled for her and his is empty and the baby is crying. She hammers her fist on the table and he does not rouse, the glass shakes, the baby screams. She sits down. *Lord,* she thinks, and gathers herself. Chased and suddenly safe inside. If only she had quiet, her blood rushing in her head. *Lord forgive me.* And she soaks a cloth in the cherry wine, red and sopping, and drips the syrup into the baby's mouth until she suckles the rest, drowsy and calm. Marie drinks the pour of wine, fast and burning, what is he keeping from her, she cannot shake this, and she drinks until she no longer cares, is alive and more, and gives in to the warmth of the cabin and warmth in her throat.

—+—

LAWRENCE ROUSES TO MARIE kissing him, sweet taste of cherry, her hands in his hair, and she straddles the kitchen chair. The cabin dark but for the flash of her eyes. He resists for a moment, and then lifts her nightgown over her head. She undoes his buttons, peels away his long johns, and he remembers his scars, she has not seen the wounds since he could bathe without her tending to him, and in the moonlight they gleam, white and smooth, and he turns his face from hers, and she runs her fingers across every line, her hand over his thigh, and then her lips, her body against his, heavy breathing in the quiet, and carries her to the bed. He stands there naked, the flesh of his thigh marked and ridged, and her fingertips follow the skin, soft, and whispering, and he lays her back, mouth over her breasts, her stomach, and he wants to tell her, he wants her to forgive him, and he wants what is his, other men have words, and he kneels, his tongue between her legs, a howl in the night.

———

WHEN SHE WAKES, SHE is naked on the bed without a sheet or quilt, they are tossed to the floor, and Lawrence has a leg drawn over hers, a hand draped over her chest. Baby did not wake. But they did, she and Lawrence, god the heat, and not since the birth and before, this feeling, this pleasing, drowsing after. And things he did she had not known were possible. And what had he waited for? If she asks she might ruin how they are, how they were, forgetting themselves.

"Lawrence, wake up," she says, her mouth parched, and he startles, smiles at the where of his hand.

"Good morning," he says, and nuzzles her neck.

"I have to get the baby," she says. He lifts his arm and untangles his body.

"Did we?" he says.

Baby is sleepy but takes the bottle, a curled fist.

"Slept til noon," he says.

"I gave her medicine," says Marie. "Just this once. To sleep through the night."

"Worked like a charm," he says.

Windows are covered in waving frost and the winter light pierces the room. Lawrence stands on the porch. Every tree is glass and shine, the porch, the snow, the eaves of the roof, crystal from an ice storm.

Then Marie tells him the outhouse door is frozen open and Lawrence hammers free the hinge. Marie shows him the scratch. The tracks buried and gone.

"Wolves," he says. "And let's pray they've moved on."

They will have to be careful. And what of the two of them, she wants to say, the asking and not asking, are they still keeping from each other? All through the day branches fall and ice smashes onto the porch. Feathers of spruce weighted down in the melt, weakened and burdened, until they break. In her arms the baby is quiet and clasps her small hands together. A strange lullaby, these turns of cracking and splitting. "Listen," says Marie, as the woods fire another shot in the dark.

CHAPTER 32

STILL AND WATCHING

JANUARY 1959

WINTER TURNS, A WARM wind in the air, strong gusts and the snow begins to melt, puddles and dripping icicles, slush and rain. Lawrence drives to Knik for mail before there is another freeze. A letter from Joseph, asking after his granddaughter and Marie. These are answers he can give. As to the question about how he is taking to fatherhood, Lawrence does not know. He is learning, is all he can say. And he almost writes to Joseph to unburden himself about the papers he filed, but he knows his father, who prides himself on being a man of principle, would not approve.

He heads to the bar for news and he is early, but Jones is always around, and so is his truck, and someone else is already here. But the door is locked. He knocks and Jones answers, with caution, peering outside. "Not open yet," he says.

"I'll wait in the lot," says Lawrence.

"Come in," says Jones. And he lowers his voice. "But I don't want any trouble."

The door swings open and Lawrence takes off his cap. Two men are sitting at the bar, one older and one young, and they are alike in build, and are not drinking beer. They glance at him, and the younger one says something to the older in a language Lawrence has never heard, and he presumes it is a Native one. "This is Shem Pete, and his son, Billy," says

Jones. "They bring me birch syrup from Nancy Lake. Can't afford to buy it all at once."

Lawrence nods and offers who he is, and a handshake to both, and Shem accepts, and then Billy. He takes a seat, leaves two between him and the son, not one to crowd. The bar is too quiet.

"Lawrence is a homesteader in Point MacKenzie," says Jones.

"Dilhi Tunch'del'usht Beydegh," says Shem.

"We call it 'point where we transport hooligans,'" says Billy.

"Called them candlefish when I was a kid," says Jones. "You could dry them and then light them and watch the fat and oil burn."

Shem speaks. Billy says to him, "Do you mean fried?" Then Billy says, "Fried with salt. That's the best way to cook them."

"Been a while," says Jones.

"So are you homesteading in Nancy Lake?" asks Lawrence.

Shem and Billy turn to each other, amused. Lawrence does not know why. They talk back and forth, and then Billy says, "This has been our home for many generations. Even before it was a territory."

Jones holds up a stack of newspapers for Lawrence. "You hear we're officially a state? As of the third of January. The President signed a proclamation. I don't think you've been in since then."

"So it's a done deal," says Lawrence.

"For better or worse," says Jones. "Shem's been telling me some things."

Shem turns to Lawrence directly, and in English, says, "The state of Alaska took land. One hundred million acres."

"Not sure I follow," says Lawrence.

"Prime hunting and fishing land all around Alaska Native settlements now belongs to the state."

"One hundred million?" Lawrence says.

"People coming here brings trouble. The Russians, the Americans, selling and buying land that was not theirs." Shem clears his throat. "We know your government breaks promises." Billy and Shem take stock of Lawrence, who remains quiet. He has never heard anyone speak this way. Shem and Billy seem to disagree among themselves. But Shem insists. "My family has always lived here, and it is my hope they always will. But will they be allowed? When I was young, the stores in Anchorage had signs. The signs said NO DOGS OR NATIVES. A law had to be passed to stop them. And one hundred million acres taken. Why would I want Alaska to be one of your states? That's all I'm going to say."

"I wouldn't, if I were you," says Jones.

Lawrence nods, trying to grasp what he can.

"Shem knows all the history," says Jones. "And every creek, lake, and mountain around these parts. He's always traveling and sharing what he knows—it's like he has a map in his head with the names of places, how he knows them and we know them, the animals, the fishing, the hunting."

"The names, as he knows them, are Dena'ina Athabascan, and he is one of the last to speak the dialect of the Upper Cook Inlet," says Billy. "My father can understand you and he can speak English, of course, but speaks Dena'ina as much as possible to keep it alive. So I'm his translator."

Shem places a hand on Billy's shoulder and says, "A good translator and a good son."

The hand on the shoulder, something Lawrence's own father does, and he has the courage to ask. "I came across an animal I had never seen in March of last year," says Lawrence. He tells them what he has not told anyone, of the buried ashes, of what was digging in the snow, the creature he shot and killed.

Shem speaks in Dena'ina. Billy says, "I'm sorry to hear about your son." Billy waits and then goes on. "That animal is a wolverine—as a boy I was told 'Nełchish Tsukdu,' The Wolverine Story, and the wolverine has a tail and is very strong. And the wolverine is a thief."

"Yes, that must be it," says Lawrence. "Now I know."

"I've never seen one, but I've heard the hide is worth a pretty penny," says Jones.

"A good fur."

"And I see a tall mountain from my cabin, Pioneer Peak," says Lawrence. "I'm wondering, does it have another name?"

"'Denal'iy,' which means what is standing still."

"Well, I'll be," says Lawrence.

Shem stands, and then Billy. Shem says, "We must be going. Good luck to you, Lawrence, hunter of wolverine is how I will remember."

Lawrence offers his hand. And Shem takes it. As does Billy, and follows his father out the door.

When they leave, Jones says, "I've heard folks who live in the shadow of Pioneer Peak call it The Watcher."

"Standing still, watching," says Lawrence. "Makes sense."

"I wonder what he would have called you if he knew you'd been attacked by a grizzly."

"Foolish," says Lawrence.

"These things happen out here," says Jones. "I bet he has some stories. He always does. And how much he can remember, you would not believe." Then he looks Lawrence in the eye. "I was sorry to hear."

"What can you do?" says Lawrence.

"I can pour you a beer," says Jones.

Though he had never met one, he had heard of no-good Indians in Minnesota, and here Shem had shared what he could with a stranger. His own German name a following trouble, and his father said enlisting would bring honor. Shem was fighting his own battle and Lawrence could respect this even if he did not understand, besides what was being claimed by another. In the stack of newspapers he finds the published lines that name him and the tract and the witnesses, and tears them out to mail to the bureau. Sheila and Sly rarely get a newspaper, a Sunday if so, and will not see it. *A quiet title,* he says to himself, as a matter of fact.

And what could Shem tell him of his homestead land, the acres in his name, the cost of his assurance? In one way they were the same—the belief that there are things that should last, and be known, places and the names of a mountain. For all that Shem remembered, perhaps he was the only one. And Pioneer Peak was always watching, even if hidden by clouds, and he felt he had known this. If they ever crossed paths again, Lawrence knew what he would call him in return: *Shem, keeper of the map.*

———+———

THIS IS THE YEAR, is what she said to herself with the turning to a new one, another calendar from the Moose Lodge brought by Sheila and Sly. The blank days before her, and she has already marked the end of August, the proving up. The cabin built, and the time living here, and then the crops. Maybe these mild winter days mean spring will come in May. Though you would think it was here now, the snow dripping from the spruce. And Lawrence, what has changed, this wanting he has? Though she does not mind, this is what she had hoped for. Rain patters on the window and she makes more coffee. She had written Sheila an apology, asked how she was, said she was a doting aunt, thanked her again for the beautiful things she knitted for the baby, and truthfully, Marie is afraid of letting anyone else watch her. Though if she did, Sheila would be the first. She is waiting for a reply, an assurance this quarrel is no more.

Lawrence returns and does not have mail for her. She hides her disappointment and busies herself with sweeping the floor. He tells her of meeting Shem Pete and his son, of the wolverine, and what they call the mountain. At least she could name the fear, the strange animal in the woods digging at the grave. So there were wolves and bears and wolverines. And she thinks of the hook she buried so long ago. This Shem Pete might know how it was used, if she was right to say it was a hook. But she cannot tell Lawrence what she had done. This land belonging to someone else, before her, before him, before the Nike site and the other homesteaders, proof they lived here. This is why she could not hold on to it, with all of her keepsakes in her hatbox, where she has the prayer Joseph wrote out for the burial, and the map of the homestead, how she traced the lines over and over until they wore soft. And she could not recall where she had been standing, and now the white snow covers every acre. But she had found it near the dug pilings, and there could be more, and Lawrence, if he knew, might search. Better to leave alone what is in the ground.

"Can you imagine," says Lawrence, "if this land was claimed by the state?"

"But you have papers," says Marie.

"Why would the state need that much land? And the federal government already claimed ours for homesteading."

"Does there have to be a reason?" says Marie.

"I'm just saying," says Lawrence. "Trying to make sense."

"Now you know why it's important to me to sign my name," she says. "Let me show you." She brings out the map and shows him how she wrote, *Lawrence Beringer, Marie Beringer,* in the corner.

"When'd you do this?" says Lawrence.

"For after we have the crops. And to try my married name," says Marie. "Still takes getting used to."

"But a good one," says Lawrence, though he seems tense.

"Something else happen at the bar?" says Marie.

"Just thinking," says Lawrence, "that I'd like to talk to him again." He peers out the window. "Say we have some vanilla snow," he says.

The bottle of vanilla from the Nike site is long gone, but they have plenty of condensed milk stacked in the cupboard. Marie picks up the baby in the cradle, and spoons her a bite. And the baby flails her arms after the taste.

"She sure wants more of that," says Lawrence.

"She always wants more," says Marie.

And with the sun down, this day to rest, the baby falls asleep in her arms, and she dares not wake her by laying her down in the cradle. After supper, he is spent, he says, and so she leaves the dishes for the morning. He lowers the lantern and climbs into bed. She sits at the table in the dark, but she is missing something, or forgetting, and he has turned in so early, on a day without a long list of chores. She thinks of names, how she also has another. And what he said about Pioneer, still and watching, and re-members how the other mountains moved that day Lawrence was lost, and Pioneer did not, and she could admit, how the white peak would appear some days and make you feel small, but also chosen for that moment. And no one could take that from her.

CHAPTER 33

ICE, SNOW, TREE, SUN

FEBRUARY

THE BABY LAUGHS, A sound that thrills, with ears tuned to crying, and the cabin sleeps til morning, but Marie is wary of the ease. This is still new, this little face not red or pained. The head bald, with a fine down, covered in bright yarned hats Sheila crocheted for her. Eyes a gray-blue, dark mirrors, and Marie sees a flash of herself when she leans over the cradle. Hours of screaming and bawling ended, but then a day of rest and another after these slow and tired months, but will it last?

The baby smiles, at first Marie could not be sure, and then the smile every waking, as Marie bends down to say, *Good morning, little one.* And the baby laughs at her presence, the delight, belly and chubby legs. And that lightness, the heart making room, her child, her daughter, who she has fed and changed and washed countless times, the surviving, the passing of days.

A part of her, growing, living, breathing on her own, but helpless, screaming at the world. A tiny thing. And Marie knows all of her cries now, the hunger, the soiled diaper, the tiredness before sleep, as if she has known them her whole life, the startling wail and her answer. To be depended on, and in caring for Lawrence, the days after the hospital, the undressing and dressing of wounds. How much to be taken, and given, how much to be known, before calling this love, and will it be as sudden as a quiet hour?

———

LAWRENCE SANDS A SLAT for the crib, the rough paper, the cut wood, this is how he is a father, he stocks the stove, the kindling, he brings in the snow to boil, plows. A child growing, a child in health, and the baby laughs and he smiles as he works. Another snowstorm is over. Brightness in the windows, and dusty beams slant to the floor. He raps his knuckles three times for good measure. A new year.

At dinner, the baby sits in the high chair and eats oatmeal, and her hands smear cereal across her face. She watches Lawrence eat, and he chews with his mouth open, large chomps, and she squeals with delight, there is nothing better than eating, fistful after fistful, as much as a bowl that he would help himself. Marie reaches to wipe her messy face and she turns her head toward him and away from the rag and larks, her feet kicking wildly. "Little one," he says, "my little one," and she calms and drums her tray.

———

THOSE SLEEPLESS NIGHTS, THE sacrifice, and even now, so young, the baby charmed by Lawrence, and held on Marie's hip, the small hands hanging on to her, the sight of her is a given, is an always. How Valera would scold them, *Who puts a roof over your head, me, and you never listen, and then your mother shows and you're beside yourselves.* She was but a child when she had a child, and Marie could say the same. Daughters, Valera said, they will take everything from you if you let them.

How Lawrence took to the child, after the screaming, the ailing, came to an end. No one could settle her, the only quiet when she nursed a bottle of milk, tears in her eyes, Marie could feel her in her arms gathering strength. But she is already forgetting those pained months, the drag of the hours, as the time passes in favor.

———

THAT NIGHT OF THE last of the cherry wine, and since, Lawrence has a need. And he gives in, but waits for the sun to set, the darkness of the afternoon. This is how they could have been from the start, but he did not trust himself, how he felt he could break apart, the mayflies, the scattering. Everything is gathered, everything in one place, and he wants Marie, to be inside of her, to hear her breathing quicken on his neck, and her cries fill the cabin, on the bed passed down through the generations that can withstand this making.

If another child, so be it. But each time is another way of telling her, as she takes him, that he has a purpose, that this could be hers, each *you are* as he presses into her, her open hands under his, *you are,* let all doubt fall away, *you are my wife.*

———

WHAT IS HIS REASON? Because the baby is sleeping, and even the darkest days are beginning to lift? Why this longing for her, or is she mistaken? She turns to him. "Are you wanting another child?"

"Not the first thing on my mind," he says.

"Then what?"

"This is going to be a good year," he says. "I've decided." He begins to whistle.

She laughs, but shushes, and covers his mouth, *Don't wake the baby.* He holds her hands to his chest. So was this what Sheila had talked about, what being newly married was supposed to be, just a few years late? How did they survive the last winters? How did she? The early darkness and his distance. And now Sheila is her worry.

———

HE STANDS BESIDE THE door and breathes in the air. His children will grow up here with the acres of trees he has felled and chopped, years of firewood. His trees and land, and has he taken what has already been given, unnamed in blood? But there, in the waking of each morning, is the knowing, and Marie by his side.

His fills his arms with a load of wood for the bin, and when he turns around, he stops in his tracks. On the western bluff the setting sun is a diamond of light, drawn thin at the long points, and circled by a ring of bright and burning gold—God's eye, his father told him. Had not seen one since he was a boy. He should show Marie but stays a moment longer, a hush, alone in the sight.

"Marie," he calls from the porch, and empties his arms, "Marie," and she appears. "Look," he says. Her face, a spark, the spell of ice, snow, tree, and sun. And she rushes to return with the baby wrapped in a blanket, this silence, this ring of light around the sun waving over the ridge and falling, fading, and this is one day they will always remember, wintered and worn after the storms, and she rests her head on his shoulder. "Glory," she says, and he sinks with the weight.

CHAPTER 34

RATTLE
MARCH

A FUSS, THEN A cry, and Marie opens her eyes with alarm. Lights the lantern. Baby in the crib kicks her feet. A wail, and Lawrence groans and rolls over and covers his head with the quilt. Spoiled, the sleeping through the night, the waking when the body wants to rise. Marie sits in the rocking chair and dabs milk on her wrist to check the temperature of the bottle, and the baby, again, refuses, wrenching her head, and she holds her upright, stares at the screwed face, and the mouth opens, and Marie sees a speck of white, she searches with her finger, soft and slobber in the mouth, and finds a hard root, a bottom tooth coming in. She moves the bottle to the corner of the baby's lips, and this soothes. Marie's shadow stretches long into the early morning, a slow pull, an itch in the back of her throat.

Another wail startles her awake, and she clutches the baby in her arms, afraid of the slack. A louder cry. She fills a bowl with clean snow and rolls a small ball. Cold ice on the gums around the tip of the tooth, melts and drips, and the baby fights, then her eyes flutter. Marie lowers the sleeping baby back into the crib. Of a mind to pour the snow and icy water on Lawrence as he sleeps, but she crawls back into bed.

—

HINGE OF THE METAL door on the stove. Thud of the firewood, stack and fill. Marie calls for him, and he turns, but she is talking and dreaming as she does, babbling under her breath, and he listens.

Bed braces when he climbs in, and Marie moves her legs toward his cold feet. She does this without knowing, and this is what it is to be beside someone, day by day. "Tell me," says Marie, and she rolls over, unaware of his being there. Her eyes tightly closed. And he had already revea̶ so much, and at times regretted that he had. So instead he kisses ̶ neck, and her eyes open. "Sleep," she says. And turns from him, and he is stunned. She has never refused him.

———+———

OVER BREAKFAST THEY DO not talk of what happened in the night. But Marie says the baby is teething and shows him. And then places the quilt on the floor. They watch her crawl and she is fast, and when did this happen, the lift and strength, for so long her bald head a burden? They will need a pen for the baby. Keep her from the hot stove. Ah, says the baby. Ahhhh, and she shakes a rattle. Marie stands with her plate and as she passes by she touches his shoulder. But he brushes her off.

———+———

HE GATHERS NAILS AND wood, a saw, for the build. The weather starting to turn, the bite in the air less and less, through the brunt of winter, though a storm could prove him wrong. Sides of the pen will have to fit through the door, he assumes. And then he decides to build two, one for inside, and one for the porch, or wherever Marie wants to take the baby. To protect the baby from herself, her grabbing hands, her wanting to touch everything she sees.

What was Marie's reason? The baby's teething kept her awake. But he is wounded. Wasn't that what she wanted all this time? And would this happen again? What had he wasted by keeping from her? But he would let her be.

———+———

AFTER THE LONG NIGHT Marie walks to the bus for a bath. Sog, the ground, wet and frozen, the haze of clouds in the sky. A thud sounds, ground-shaking, a felled tree. Around her, no sight of one, and then she walks into the woods behind the bus, farther toward the ridge, and she knows, the eagle's nest. The split of the two large branches of a cottonwood, broken under the weight, the tree bare, the wreckage at her feet, the grave-yard of twigs and every year of returning, of finding. She spies the eagles in the safety of a birch, their heads bowed, the fallen nest before them, wings of mourning black.

There are other nests, but this was the first she knew, the oldest, a shel-ter in the wilderness. She does not know why she is crying—tears warm on her face. She bathes and visits the eagles on her way back, they have stayed in watch over their loss, the sun a leaving through the trees. How long will they be still? And silent. The hard freeze and the melting, again and again, the break and then the mending that will not last.

———+———

LAWRENCE WORKS ON THE porch, sawing and nailing. She wipes her reddened eyes and hurries past him.

"Why are you crying?" he says.

"The eagle's nest is gone," she says.

"What do you mean?" he says.

"Fell. Broke the tree," and she rushes inside.

So strange, and should he go after her, but he has this to finish. He knows what his father would tell him, but Joseph was not right about everything. And maybe she did not want to talk. What was talking to doing, to him making something useful for the baby, as she outgrows the crib? After the job is done he tells Marie he is headed to the post office for the mail.

———+———

THE EAGLE'S NEST IS a sign, a warning. What is built can be torn down. The baby cries again and Marie dips the rag doll in water and snow for her mouth. The first tooth, and how many more? She tries to count her own. Misery by misery. So soon after the baby started sleeping through the night. And Lawrence, what is behind his wanting? Surely, a lull by now, but she was the one who was kept awake and wanted nothing more than to rest a little longer.

Lawrence returns with a letter, not from Sheila, but from Sly, who has never written before. Addressed to them both. Before she can think the worst, he says Sly is asking them to visit. *Sheila is in a bad way,* Sly writes. *Marie, please come see her as soon as you can.*

"We'll go in the morning," Lawrence says, "when the ground is still frozen."

As he drives, they form a plan. They will go to Sly's shop first and Lawrence and the baby will stay there. Marie needs to see Sheila alone. Sly agrees, says she was feeling low and he made her come to the shop with him and knit. But she stopped, and for over a week, she has stayed in bed at the trailer, for all he knows. Not cooking or cleaning or knitting or seeing her friends or running errands.

Marie knocks on the door and notices the curtains are drawn. There is no answer, and then she yells, "Sheila, you better let me in or I'll make sure the neighbors hear." She hears footsteps and Sheila answers, in her robe. Hair unbrushed and more, she suspects. Eyes swollen. Smelling of whiskey. "I don't want to see anybody," she says.

Marie shoves her way past. The small sink is filled with unwashed dishes, which she knows Sheila cannot stand. "Sit down," Marie says. "You had your coffee?" and she does not see the pot on the stove. She decides to tackle the dishes first.

Sheila takes a seat. "I'm not talking to you," she says.

"I'll wait," says Marie. "Do you need a washing? Should I put water on?"

Sheila rubs her eyes and does not answer.

"You know Sly is worried about you."

"I just need to rest," says Sheila.

"From what I understand, that's all you've been doing."

Sheila shrugs at her.

"And drinking," says Marie.

Sheila turns on the radio. The announcer is relaying messages. "This goes out to Lorraine Smith of Anchorage . . ."

"Fine," says Marie. She cleans the kitchen. Scrubs the dishes. Makes coffee and sets a cup in front of Sheila and sits across from her. Lowers the volume on the radio. "I know how you took care of me," she says. "Let me be a help to you."

Sheila closes her eyes and sighs. "I'm fine."

"You are not," says Marie. "And I'm going to stay here until you talk to me. Until I smell like a frog in a jam jar."

Sheila has a mischievous look in her eye.

"And don't you dare say I already do," says Marie. "Because between the two of us, that would be you, and you know it."

Sheila sips her coffee, smug.

"You are going to bathe today," says Marie.

Sheila nods in agreement.

"And we're going to remember all the things we should be thankful for."

Sheila hangs her head. "I'm so tired of being happy for everyone else."

"You don't have to be happy," says Marie.

"I want to be," says Sheila. "But all anyone talks about is their children. And their men. You ever notice?"

"Now that I think on it," says Marie.

"And I try to bring up my knitting. Or the latest news on the radio. And both seem to turn back to babies somehow. Or how I can make something for their babies. And you've lapped me, twice over. Then you're talking about these women you met at the Waylon cabin."

"They can't knit like you," says Marie.

Sheila ignores her. "Then I was convinced Sly must be seeing someone. How could he be content? I can't give him what he wants. I wasn't myself one night and I told him he should leave me and he said he never would."

"See?" says Marie.

"That only made me feel worse," says Sheila. "I don't feel right. And I keep waiting for something to change. I thought I was fine after that day I told you. For a while I was."

"Remember how long it took me to come around."

"That was different," says Sheila. "You went through so much more."

"I would not have gotten through it without you," says Marie. "But I got my answer. You're still waiting. So tell me what I can do." Marie reaches over and places her hands on Sheila's shoulders. "Look at me."

Sheila raises her weary eyes. "You look terrible," she says. They both laugh and wipe away tears. "And where is the baby? Don't tell me she's with Sly and Lawrence."

"She is," says Marie. "At the shop."

"You think any of those men ever changed a diaper?" says Sheila.

"I was so worried about you," says Marie. "Didn't think."

"We've got time," says Sheila. "Well, should we go to Carr's for groceries so we can make supper?"

"The Lucky Wishbone?" says Marie.

"How about the Moose Lodge?" says Sheila. "About time I show my face again, and I think they're playing cards today."

"Well, first you better wash that face," says Marie.

"I hear you," says Sheila. "You know I do."

"Good," says Marie. "Because we'll be staying a few days."

———+———

LAWRENCE SITS IN THE office at the shop with the crying, teething baby. He has only been alone with her for short amounts of time. One mechanic at the shop says he knows what to do, as his mother was ill after one of his youngest siblings was born. So he helps with the changing. But Lawrence would rather stack wood for a week than ever have this responsibility again.

While he thinks of it, he should check his P.O. Box, and he borrows Sly's truck, just to drive, take a break, he says. "Sure," says Sly, looking down at Colleen's red face. "But don't be too long."

At the post office, Lawrence has one envelope waiting for him. His hand shakes. He reads: *The claim of Lawrence Joseph Beringer has been established. . . . . . .the area described contains 150.0 acres. . . . . . NOW KNOW YE, That the UNITED STATES OF AMERICA, in consideration of the premises, DOES HEREBY GRANT unto said claimant and to the heirs of said claimant the tract above described; TO HAVE AND TO HOLD the same. . . . . . Patent Number 1228092.*

He sits in the truck. The patent, the deed, is finally in his name. Must compose himself. Though this might be the most important day of his life. Yet, there is Marie, what he promised. But no matter what happens, what might befall him, the land, the homestead, is his.

———+———

WHEN LAWRENCE RETURNS TO the shop, Sly says he is taking a half day and they head back to the trailer. The baby falls asleep on the drive. Sheila and Marie are gone, have left a note, but Sly says the trailer has been cleaned. Lawrence lays the baby down on the mattress in the back bedroom, a pile of dirty sheets in the corner waiting to be laundered.

Sly makes eggs and beans for dinner. "Thank you for bringing Marie," he says, when they sit down to eat.

"Of course," says Lawrence. "You and Sheila helped us."

"She wouldn't leave the trailer," says Sly. "So her not being here is fine by me."

Lawrence chews slowly. Sly is troubled, he knows, if he is this quiet. And it occurs to him that he has spent more time talking to Sly than to his own brothers. "I didn't think Marie would come back from what happened," offers Lawrence. "But she did. And it can't be as bad as that. Sheila will, too."

"I just love her," says Sly, and his voice cracks.

Lawrence looks down at his plate. Sly composes himself. "Been meaning to ask, why'd you say you accidentally shot at me?"

"Why not?" says Lawrence.

"You're a hard one to know," says Sly, and shakes his head.

"And you know everyone," says Lawrence.

"But not everyone's family," says Sly.

"Thank the Lord for that," says Lawrence. And he laughs so Sly knows he is joking. And finally, there is Sly's boyish grin. "These women will be the end of us," he says. "We have to stick together."

"Can we drink to that?" says Sly.

"We can," says Lawrence.

———

WHEN SHE WALKS INTO the Moose Lodge after Sheila, Marie remembers the first time she went, the raffle, and how young she must have seemed. And now she feels a little worn, and many years older in the dim light of the afternoon. They pass the empty tables in the main room where all of those men were sitting, those possible lives that could have been hers. She was sure about Lawrence, but she did not know much beyond finding a means to stay, to have something of her own. Had he seen that in her somehow, in how she walked or what she said? That hunger he had, how could she forget, and was that what she was to him? If only she could pry into Lawrence, know his thoughts of her, of their life since, of being a father, and why he chose her that night—her life changed by a number, that quiet ticking to having the acres in hand.

CHAPTER 35

ALMANAC
APRIL

LAST DAY OF THE month, and Marie slices potatoes with a knife at the kitchen table, one bud, sprout, eye for each seeder. The cuts will cure and callus over for seven days on boards made to stack, an empty tin can on each corner so there is space for drying. Baby tries to stand in her pen on the floor, *Ma,* she says. Marie cannot believe her ears. *What did you say? What did she say? Ah,* says the baby.

Waiting for the words she wanted to hear. Her waking hours wrapped around this child. Close and there, and growing, and further, the hold in the arms, on the hip, the babbling sounds that fill the hours.

———

THERE IS NO ALMANAC, only the asking, the ways he knows of Minnesota, the advice of the homesteader in Palmer who sold the potatoes, the dirt that crumbles in his hands. His ear to the ground to test the warmth. Sun, soil, rain. The Old Cabin Still thermometer tells him. This year on track with the prior, warmer than two years ago with snow in May, and his timing has to be a few weeks before the last frost.

And where did he and Marie stand, and would they? Some days he wants to tell her. In the doorway he stops, and she is bent over the kitchen table with a knife, her hands sure, preparing for the planting. Happiness is in her face, the light at her back. And the baby in the high chair. He has never spoken to Marie of this, not out loud, and he says, "What do you think of having twelve?"

"Kids?"

"Us having twelve," he says.

Her eyes widen. "Where would we put them all? How would we feed them? And you looking for work?"

"We would find the means," he says.

She shakes her head.

He leans down to the baby. "And what do you say?"

———

WET DIRT, MINERAL SALVE, earth is the smell of the drying seeders, on the table, the floor, under the bed. Marie wakes to open a window, the air of rot, and finds blood on the sheet. She goes to the outhouse, her bleeding has returned to how it was before, a returning to herself, after winter and months of give and feed and wash and why. A coming back to never enough, empty and never filled the same. Split in two, that child to her life, to her. Twelve children, and this one who never slept, the colic for months, the heaviness in her bones, what did he know of carrying a child? *We shall see,* she will tell him, her name on the land after this harvest.

———

LATE LIGHT, AND A window is open, a breeze. Lawrence places wood in the stove, his palms callused and rough, skin thick against splinters. The baby's grasp, when she reaches for him at the table, and he sees the years and lines, the work. How he was a child, hands in a field, the hardened dirt. The weighing down when he carried a filled basket to the sack. And here he is, with the promise of the same crop on land he owns. This child, so small, but what could these hands grow and learn? A firstborn, no matter a daughter, who will know everything he knows. She will be made from this place he had chosen, in her eyes the shine of a lake.

———

A TIME FOR PURPOSE. A time to rest. A time for good. A time for tears. A time for stones. A time for music, a record on the Victrola. A time for keeping, and what is he keeping? A time for provisions. Canned beans, oatmeal, oil, fresh eggs after months without, she feels the crack of the shell in her teeth. A time for waiting. A time for cutting and halving. A time for planting. A time for giving. And what has been given? And what has been taken?

A time for yolk, the soak in the bread. A time for hunger. A time for salt. There will be a time for preserving. For jars. For every hurt to bruise. For spoil. For a dishrag to sour. There will be time to call hers. When the child is of age. If another is not already in her arms. Not for chopping wood. Or wringing laundry. Time to sit on the porch in the sun long enough to know the hour. To sing with no end. Time to be out of grasp, and sight. Time to be.

———

THIS CROP WILL BE the proving of his own accord. The shotgun close at hand. He watches for bear tracks, and signs. And every morning and evening, he drives the tractor around the cleared acres, a warning. Still waiting for the alfalfa yield this year. The second crop, the lie. The land, in his name. The fields, in his name. The cabin. His wife and child. What is a curse, but a name? But so is a blessing. These walls he built, the wooden floor. And the baby says, *Da,* and crawls toward him. *Dada,* she says, and he picks her up in his arms. The calling of and for, and he has a witness. "Did she say . . . ?"

"She knows you," says Marie.

"You know me," sings Lawrence, and he spins around, and the baby laughs.

———

SEVENTH DAY IS FOR planting. Cuts on the seeders have healed. In the cabin the baby sleeps in the crib, a rag doll in the crook of her arm.

Tractor tills four long rows near where the alfalfa was, and will be. Marie places the seeders in the trench, eyes facing up, two hands apart. A stoop in her back. Lawrence follows and buries them with the mound of soil.

Marie hears a cry, though from this distance she is in doubt. But she leaves the sack in the dirt and runs, and opens the cabin door, and the baby sleeps on, chewing on her mouth. In the rows the work begins again and Lawrence says nothing of the wait, the break for water. She had wanted to be a part of this, the last of what will make the land theirs. At the end they stand shoulder to shoulder in the field.

———+———

RAIN BEATS THE METAL roof and Lawrence places the boards outside for them to be washed. Marie holds the sleeping baby, a hum in the rocking chair. A slow afternoon. But the smell lingers, of dying, of rotting. He leaves the door open. And the shower is a mist on the porch and the fog rolls across the low. Brush piles of roots and branches, some from the first clearing, breaking ground, his father here, scraps to be lit and brought to ash, but not yet.

———+———

THE SCENT OF DEATH. Marie remembers rats dying in walls of the clapboard house. And that cannot be. She rummages under the bed, the crib. Baby mouths the skirt of her rag doll, the damp spot spreads on the cloth. Lawrence crawls into the attic and finds no trace of an animal. Marie pulls everything from the shelves. Their stock laid out before her on the kitchen table, cans and canisters. She wipes and cleans.

A rotting, even in the night. Marie washes the sheets. The diaper pail on the porch. Lawrence inspects the ends of each log. Marie traces her searching, finds a wet, molding lump in the bottom of an old burlap sack, and rushes to the stove, and an end to all of her misgivings, for this is a time to burn.

which he brings to the light, and there are woven rows of tightly knit straw or dried grass, and a design of dyed black triangles, the edges frayed. Will bring this to Jones, have him safe-keep for Shem, and see what he knows. No harm, as the land is secured, on record, and those who were here left long ago.

As a kid he looked for arrowheads at Blackduck Lake and the story was that a professor had come twenty years before and plowed the grounds, and found shards of Indian pottery and a burial ground with four graves. He took everything with him and left the scars on the land. But what of the bones, the taking of them, old as a mountain, and why not leave them to rest? All Lawrence had wanted for the ashes of his son. And when he is buried here, the land should remain, for his children and his children's children, and only then would he be forgotten in the flesh, though written in stone.

—+—

LAWRENCE IS SORE AND tired and Marie hangs a wet towel over the stove and then wraps the heat around his neck. She cooks oatmeal for supper, and stirs them with a wooden spoon, and for sweetness adds a can of peaches. Lawrence holds the baby by her raised hands as she toddles across the floor, happy and smiling, her steps more sure. Marie measures a good day—work and accord, the acres planted and growing, a baby in health. Here, steady, and Lawrence lets go and she takes a step by herself, small hands reaching. A step and another. "Colleen, you're walking," says Marie. "You're walking." And what did they know, before this, a daughter's first steps, of the happiness that can burst within?

She knows her own father was not there when she began to walk, and perhaps her mother in another room with her sorrow, but Sheila remembered. Had said so a few days ago when she was visiting. The baby had walked that morning in the cabin, Lawrence at the root cellar. And Marie swooped her up in her arms, and went to the door to tell him, but if she waited, he would never know, he would be there. He would have his chance.

And here, with her daughter in her arms, Marie could feel a thread pull from somewhere inside, a pain at knowing she was here now, but

CHAPTER 36

OLD AS A MOUNTAIN

MAY

SECOND YEAR OF THE alfalfa stand, and the green shoots sprout in broken rows, less than half of twenty acres of the first seeding have survived weeds and winterkill. Lawrence, for a healthy potato crop, begins work on the root cellar. Shovels near the side of the cabin and digs down to the pilings. He carries buckets of dirt up a short ladder and Marie brings him water in a thermos. Bucket by bucket, a shallow cave under the cabin, and he measures by the span of his arms.

He fills the truck bed with the shoveling and will take the load to the marsh. When the digging is done, there is room for storage, and he brings in saved wooden Blazo boxes. With the last, Marie appears and climbs down the ladder. Surrounded by dirt, they are shadows out of reach. Then she pulls at his sweat-soaked shirt and her lips find his mouth and he stumbles and her husk of laughter fills the air, and she pins his back to the wall. She leaves him there in the cool of the cellar, wanting. There is a lightness to Marie, a burden cast off, and he is not wise enough to know why. Though he remembers his mother, after having his youngest brother, not laughing for months. She did not as a rule, but would hold in until she broke, a loud and catching joy, and the whole house would laugh with her. And when that returned, his father said, *My Lois is finally back.*

He digs out a place for a board for a shelf, and unearths a torn scrap, would not always be, to tell her child, *I remember, your smell of bread, your eyes gray and then darker, the break of a tooth, the grip of your fingers in my hair, the sway of holding you as I stood, the rocking, there and there, the long nights, the two of us in the world as you cried yourself sick, and every day you lived, and I lived, and how it came to pass, the somehow and knowing, that you belonged to me.*

———+———

A CHILD WALKING ACROSS the floor, as he foresaw, the first teetered steps, and she has taken to pointing at the birch-bark call, and fussing, until he sounds the horn three times. The laughter over them, the walls echoing back. And what had he risked—this is how they could be, should be. The harvest is biding time. He has earned this land, he must remember. Nothing could wrangle this from his grasp—womenfolk, you had to watch yourself around them or you became a dog at their heels, said many a man in the war. And he counted himself lucky, then, to have no such ties back home. Only the farm and family he was born into, and he could tell himself he was rid of them, for a while. But if he had the homestead then, a wife and child, a place of his own, the passing of seasons framed by the windows over his front porch, Marie and Colleen, a part of his life, a part of him, the days and years of a marriage, of watching a child grow, he would have been eager to return. The proving of the land only the beginning, and he needed this to be his, perhaps he could make Marie understand, that if he had these two years, he could give her all those that remained.

———+———

THE LIGHT GAINING, THE night pushed back by hours and the ease of the evening sun. The plenty after the lack, the taking away. Days in a row above freezing, constant and counted on, so she has learned. And in the root cellar, room for the stock of a planting that will be brought to the full.

The baby falls back to sleep. And it is dust she sees, on the windows and sills, now that spring is shining through the glass, from having the door open to let in the breeze, too early for the bother of mosquitoes.

She fills a bucket with warm water and washes away what remains of the winter months, the panes drying clear, and she buffs the streaks with a handkerchief.

Inside, she starts again. A better view of the fields, the trees, and today, the very top of Pioneer, the mountain a mark through the clouds. And there on a shelf, the scrap of weaving Lawrence found. She holds it up, and pulls at an end, so delicate and strong, even she could appreciate the skill, from what she knows of knitting from Sheila. But what more is buried here? First, the hook she gave back to the dirt, and this. Lawrence will take his find to Jones to ask around, and the answers, if any, she does not need to hear. Or want to know, the living before, as she is staking her own.

———+———

LAWRENCE HAS A DAY set to see Shem Pete after talking with Jones. When he tells Marie she says he can go without her. "I want you to meet him," he says. "And I met his son, so it seems right he should meet my daughter."

He writes on the calendar and Marie seems displeased. "Be an hour at the most," he says. Marie opens her mouth to say something, but the baby fusses, awake from her nap, and she goes to the crib. She holds the baby and begins to hum and there is a pang in his chest, he knows what it is. Too late to turn back, the papers stashed in the army ambulance and not in the cabin, not here.

———+———

MARIE HOLDS THE BABY and follows Lawrence when they walk in past the CLOSED sign. Jones waves and there are two men sitting at the bar, one older. Lawrence introduces Marie and Colleen to Billy and to "Shem, keeper of the map," and Shem shakes his head. He speaks in Dena'ina and Billy translates. "No map. Stories and songs, old songs, and names of mountains and lakes told to me."

"How about Shem, the keeper?" says Lawrence.

Shem nods.

They sit down and Lawrence holds out the scrap of weaving to Shem, who inspects it and speaks, and then Billy says, "Part of a basket. And the weave is small. Could be for carrying water."

"Well, I'll be," says Jones.

"You should take it," says Lawrence.

Shem hands the scrap back to Lawrence and responds.

Billy says, "No, you should, so you won't forget. I'll remember."

"Beringer Homestead is the place," says Lawrence. "I'll let you know if I find anything else."

Marie turns her attention to the baby. She could say she found the hook and lost it, and tell Shem, but what would that mean for their land? One find is a stroke of luck, a second carries more weight. The baby fusses and Marie stands her up and she slaps the top of the bar.

"One beer coming up," says Jones. They all laugh.

"I'll take one," says Lawrence.

"Me as well," says Marie. "Only beer I like."

"You hear that, Shem?" says Jones. He turns to Marie. "I told him to try it, just this once. His birch syrup makes the best beer around. But this batch tops the rest."

Jones pours and then refills the waters for Shem and Billy.

Colleen grabs Marie's hair and shrieks with delight. Marie untangles and lowers the baby to the floor so she can walk, with Marie guiding and holding her hands.

Shem speaks to Billy, who says, "Can my father hold the baby? He loves children."

"By all means," says Lawrence, before Marie can answer. She worries, for a moment, if Colleen will know he is different from anyone else who has held her. She lifts Colleen to Shem and he balances her under her arms and lets her stand on his knees. He smacks his lips together and she gasps and reaches for his mouth. Then he begins to sing, his voice low and soft, notes held and then falling, and the baby is quiet, eyes fixed on him. There is an ache in the words, plain and beautiful, even without understanding. When the song is over, Shem looks at Marie and says, "I had a daughter, once." He holds Colleen out to Marie and she takes her. Marie nods and runs a finger under Colleen's chin. "A wife, too. Years ago. You make me think of those days."

"Never heard you sing," says Jones. "You've been holding out on me."

"Once he starts, he won't stop," says Billy. "Be warned."

Shem turns to Jones. "So when are you going to get a wife?"

"You ask me that every time," says Jones. "I told you that's not the life for me."

"Know anyone Jones can marry?" says Shem to Lawrence and Marie.

"He should go to the Moose Lodge in Anchorage," says Marie. "That's where we met."

"I will taste a beer if you go to the Moose Lodge," says Shem to Jones.

"I don't know," says Jones, and he shakes his head.

"How will I know the beer is that good?" says Shem.

"You try it," says Jones.

"Same with marriage," says Shem, and he laughs loud, head tilted back.

"You got me there," says Jones.

"I can recommend it," says Lawrence. He flashes a grin at Marie.

"And do you?" says Shem to Marie.

Marie, with Colleen in her lap, sips her beer, slowly, thinking. All eyes are on her. "Sometimes," she says, with mischief. The men throw up their hands.

Jones pours Lawrence another. "She has you there."

"I'm happy that I do," says Marie, and she raises her glass to Lawrence.

Shem and Billy have to leave for other meetings. Billy heads to the door and then Colleen, over Marie's arms, reaches toward Shem and cries. He holds out his hand to her, and waits for Marie to nod yes, and shakes her small hand goodbye. Colleen wails as the door closes, and while Lawrence finishes his beer, and only on the drive back does she settle. Marie rolls down the window, and they pass tall spruce, and the waves at the shore of the Knik Arm, water the basket could have carried. And that song, how she knew and did not know the meaning, and did not ask. Some things should be left alone.

CHAPTER 37

SOLSTICE
JUNE

IN THE FIELD HE leaves the tractor running, the shotgun slung over his shoulder, as he moves through the rows, piling hills of dirt around the thick stems of the leafy greens of the potato plants, the white flowers with yellow tongues. Alone in the field, the whine of mosquitoes in his ears, and he watches the trees for a sudden sighting of a bear, but land tilled, the alfalfa in return, and with the second crop he knows she will ask to have her name on the deed.

Tractor sputters, and he misjudged the time to run down a full tank on idle, but has brought gas to refuel. Even so, the pricks on the back of his neck are as cold as ice as he restarts the engine—the reminder of teeth and claws. Then the mayflies return, and the sweat becomes blood, their wings splashed with red as they crawl up his shoulder, and he brushes them off, even though he knows they are not there, and then lowers his head, breathes fast and deep, his hands resting on the metal tank track over the wheels, the surface hot, but not injuring, enough to bring him back to his legs standing on the ground. He knows this is a trick. One he will lick yet. He has three rows to finish, but they will keep til after supper.

Marie has coffee on the stove and they eat at the table, and the baby in her high chair, but he insists on holding her on his lap. A change that she allows. She expects Sheila and Sly in a few hours, the floor swept and mopped. He does not tell her about his spell, lets the baby make a mess on the table with his meal, her hands touching everything in reach.

"Here, I'll take her," says Marie.

"She's fine," he says. Marie is pleased. And it is her half smile, and the baby's laughter, that take him further away from the flies and the field.

———

NOT A CLOUD IN the sky. Lawrence is headed back outside, but Marie narrows her eyes at him.

"What?" he says.

"Let's go swimming," she says.

"And you need me to be on guard?" he says.

"I want all of us to go," says Marie. She looks down at Colleen, who is standing and holding on to the rungs of a chair.

"I have three more rows to plow," says Lawrence.

"Do you want to go swimming, Colleen?" says Marie. And the baby squeals. "How can you say no to that?"

"All right," says Lawrence. "But it'll be cold for sure."

"For you," says Marie.

On the walk she waves a few mosquitoes away from the baby's face. They stop to see the eagles and the site of the old nest. But the ground has been picked, and they look around, and Marie finds the new nest they have built nearby with the fallen twigs and branches, in a blooming cottonwood. "You see?" she says to Colleen, and kisses her cheek.

Marie turns to the path to the lake. Lawrence says he should clear a road so they could someday drive there. Marie shakes her head. The lake should always be surrounded by trees, as they first saw it, a hidden place. Though they pass a birch with a grazing mark in the bark, one of the shots Sheila took. Her sister is more herself these days, and talked about wanting her own cabin in her last letter. And of course she would want to be near them.

There are hoofprints on the bank, but no bear tracks. Lawrence sets the shotgun down and strips to his underwear, the scars on his leg have healed as much as they will. He wades into the water carrying Colleen, gasping with the cold, and stops at his knees. Marie undresses and follows, and sinks to her neck, and reaches for her. She holds Colleen on her hip and swirls around, Colleen's little hands slapping at the surface. "My waterbaby," she says. Lawrence makes a shallow dive into the water and submerges and shoots up, water dripping down his face. He swims around them, trying to keep blood in his toes, he says. Marie splashes him, and laughs, and he lies on his back and kicks water at her, and the baby squeals at the sound. Then Lawrence, shivering, says he needs to dry off and heads to shore. Marie brings the baby and wraps her in a towel, and they lie there, the three of them, in the warmth of the sun.

—+—

WASHED OFF THAT FEELING of flies, and he will have to remember swimming as a cure. The last three rows had been waiting and he piles the dirt around the last potato plant. Then he turns the tractor off and leans against the tire and takes a breather, his head cooled from his wet hair. So he is a homesteader, a farmer of potatoes and alfalfa, a father. And he begins to whistle and march the outer edge with the shotgun in the crook of his arm, and keeps going until he turns on all four corners around the crops, a boundary. He passes the seed-sack scarecrows drooping on sticks and he salutes them for guarding what they can as he spots nibbled leaves here and there. A testing, a trying, and he reaches the tractor once more. Wipes his forehead with a handkerchief. Dirt in his mouth, and he drinks from his canteen. Should have saved the swimming for after. But no need, for he is where he should be.

—+—

BREEZE SHAKES THE COTTONWOOD blooms, and tufts of white seeds float by. Sheila and Sly drive in. They bring in their bags and Sheila dotes on the baby, covers her in kisses. Remarks on her longer hair, a dark swirl, and says her eyes have found their color at last, a warm hazel like her mama's.

Sly builds a campfire and they bring the kitchen chairs out. He unwraps a roast from twined butcher paper and cuts the meat into a cast-iron pan over the flames, and when the meat is cooked, pours from an uncorked bottle, and drinks a swig.

"Cranberry lick," he says, and passes the bottle, sweet and tart. "Fixed a truck cheap and these are the thanks."

Meat is tender and lean, the flavor rich, and the baby fusses and Sly gives her a piece, and she mouths and gnaws, kicks her feet in delight.

"How's that for moose heart?" says Sly.

"You'll spoil her," says Marie. "And us."

"To spoiling," says Sheila.

Sly brought horseshoes and two stakes and he and Lawrence bet beer over the score, the shoes land with a thud until Sly throws a ringer. The baby fusses in Sheila's arms and Marie offers to take her.

"She's fine," says Sheila. She smiles. "I knew she would look like us."

"For now," says Marie.

"If she's lucky," says Sheila, and laughs.

"So you're looking at land out here, I take it?" says Marie.

"Tomorrow," says Sheila. "But don't get your heart set."

"I won't," says Marie. "Though you have to be near your niece, Aunt Sheila."

Sheila cradles the baby and wraps the loose blanket. The men return and the wood burns down. Sly tells them about the parcels he and Sheila are driving to in the morning. Lawrence meets Marie's eyes across the fire. She smiles and looks away. The sky is pale with ember of the low sun.

The baby falls asleep and Sheila says, "I'll put her to bed."

Sly yawns and says, "Have no idea how late it is, but time for me to hit the hay."

Lawrence raises his beer. "We'll stay a little longer."

"We will?" says Marie.

"Good night," says Sheila from the porch.

Lawrence kicks dirt on the coals and then grabs her hand. "Come on," he says. He walks with purpose and she tries to keep up with his stride as he heads toward the lake, the cottonwoods in bloom.

"We going swimming?" she says.

"Even better," he says.

At the hunting stand, he climbs first, and she follows, the lean of the ladder as she scales the height, taller than the cabin, above the swarm of mosquitoes. Lawrence stands on the platform, and she steadies herself against a branch.

"I wanted you to see," he says. "The land from here." Acres span far and wide, the alfalfa greens, the brown rows of dirt, the cabin and the smoke from the chimney, the marsh and the low, and the curved blue of the Knik Arm, and the lake beyond the trees. And, always watching, and looming, Pioneer Peak, alone, peering out from a clouded pall. Sun sinks below the ridge, and the alpenglow casts a gold sheen on the mountains, an endless day.

"I have everything," says Lawrence, and he pulls Marie close. A sway with the wind, then a strong gust, and cottonwood tufts float around them, snow in summer, and catch in their hair. Platform creaks and holds, and Marie is pressed to the floor, the weight of him in each breath, and rolls over and gasps for air, her hips over his, the bend in her back, the flock of white cotton silvers in the light, and they are no longer strangers in this place she can call home.

CHAPTER 38

HARVEST

JULY

A WEEK BEFORE THE harvest, and dark green spots shadow the lower leaves of the stalks. Blight. Lawrence pulls one potato from the ground. Skin has gray patches. His blood quickens. He walks down the line and inspects, snaps off leaves, and the spots become bigger, and brown and dry. Digs out another and his throat catches, this one is molding. Bites into the flesh to make sure and spits. The potato crop is ruined. He rips the bruised heads from the ground and throws them into the brush pile. There is kerosene and a match at the cabin. And Marie is there. He would have to tell her. How could this happen, the dirt, the rain, and so quick to turn? His dirt. His rain. His crop. What should be given to him.

He walks with the slap of years of picking sacks of potatoes on land that would never be his ringing in his ears. What will be his ruin. What is against him. And if this is, then she surely will be. He opens the door, and Marie is in the kitchen.

"We have rotten potatoes," he says to her. He pours a whiskey, and another.

She stirs stew in a pot.

A third pour to slow the ringing. "I'll burn them all."

"We can plant again," she says. She does not turn around. Baby sits on the quilt in the pen and throws her rag doll. "And besides, they said we had to grow the crops. Nothing about them surviving. We can still make the claim."

"We only needed the alfalfa," he says.

"You said we needed two crops," says Marie.

"Who says?"

"You kicked in the head?" says Marie.

"Something like that," says Lawrence. He hears a static, a splitting.

"Why don't you sit down?" says Marie.

"I'll show you," he says. He knocks over a chair and staggers out of the cabin with a bottle of whiskey in his hand.

———+———

MARIE WATCHES HIM FROM the window. Lawrence opens the back doors of the army ambulance. That morning they were talking of Colleen's first birthday and he left for the fields, a man to see about his crop, and returned as this. And why plant them if they are not needed? What could possibly be wrong? She supposes he wants to be alone, is sitting in the army ambulance and drinking whiskey. Maybe he is calming himself down. She does not know what else to do, so she serves two bowls of stew and sets them on the table. Hard footsteps on the porch stairs. She sits down and waits. The baby crawls on the floor. The door flies open.

He has documents in his hand. "This is all in my name," says Lawrence. "The proof. The patent. The cabin, the acres."

"What is this?" says Marie, and she stands and takes them. She reads the shock of white paper, then holds them to her chest, sick. He even has another mailing address. And she does not want him here. "You need to leave," she says.

"This is my homestead," he says. He stares into her eyes so there is no mistake. "Mine."

Marie drops the papers on the floor and picks up the baby, who is crying at her feet. "You don't mean that," she says.

"Every word," he says.

"Lawrence," she says, and he does not answer. This is not the man she married, the father of her child. And if he will not leave, then she will. Baby on her hip, Marie heads for the door and reaches for the keys to the truck. But near the keys is the pistol hanging in the holster. A choice. And she turns around. Aims the pistol at him.

"You wouldn't dare," says Lawrence.

Her hand shakes. She clicks off the safety.

Lawrence takes a step toward her.

"Get out," she says. She points the gun at a window and pulls the trigger.

GLASS SHATTERS, AND LAWRENCE drops to the floor. Baby screams. He opens his eyes and the barrel is pointed at him. "Take the truck and go," she says.

Lawrence stands, slowly, his hands raised in surrender. He walks, and he knows the pistol follows each step. Then the door closes behind him, and he hears her slide the lock. And it is that sound, more than the bullet through the window, that burns through him. He stomps across the porch and readies to throw the key into the woods. He is not leaving. She cannot keep him out. Or aim a gun at him. He will not let this stand. But he lied to her. But it is his land. But what can he do, besides drive to the Knik Bar, have time to think? Then he will be back this very night, in his own bed. He tries to put the key in the ignition. His hands tremble. He tries again. Things will be as they were. They have to be. He slams his foot on the gas to let her know he is leaving.

MARIE PLACES THE PISTOL on the table. "It's over," she says, and the baby cries. Her thinking she has a home, that he would keep his word, what she had asked for was a record, a knowing that he was holding a place for her, here, and in himself, in these one hundred and fifty acres.

The engine of the truck, a metal glare in the side windows of the cabin. A rev and a roar and the cabin lurches. A wall of logs bows and cracks. Marie rushes out, the baby wailing in her arms. The front of the truck is rammed into the cabin, and Lawrence sits in the driver's seat, a bloody bust on his lip, wide-eyed with the shock of what he has done. She hurries inside. He is on the porch, and banging on the door, and she will play every record on the Victrola until he stops shouting her name. Every meal cooked, every line of laundry, planting the field, the bearing of children, a son in the ground, and he would not pay for the hospital. "Marie," he shouts. He threatens to kick his way in.

The summer sun high in the sky, late, the light in the cracks of the logs. She checks the locks on the windows, covers the hole in the glass with a board. If he is thirsty, he can walk to the spring. Sleep in the truck or bus.

"Marie?" What is the meaning, the break, this life, the last two years, the belonging, the beholding—or so she thought, the days stretched out before her, with this man, and this child, and she saw the days and they were no longer thin. And she believed that marrying him, and sleeping beside him in the bed passed down, would mean more than a steadiness, a regard, a yoke around his neck.

The lie, and for how long?

She could have killed him, god help her.

———+———

A SLAM ON THE gas and the lurch forward when he meant to reverse, a mistake, and Lawrence has no one to blame but himself. The cabin he built with his father, one wall to fix. No telling what was in her mind, the pistol aimed at his back. The doors locked, for how long? One bullet, one pull of the trigger, a window to replace. He cannot say he was wrong, but what can he say? That he should not have made the promise, which he knew he could not keep? She cannot live here without him, this he knows. The child a bond between them for the rest of their lives. He will not leave. Here in the truck he will keep an eye on the cabin, and wait for a sign.

And the hours pass under the summer sky, the harsh light, darkness would be a mercy. The blood on his lip dabs dry, a smear on the sleeve of his shirt. A cut, a fault, a blow to the cabin. Has he lost everything he has with Marie? She is walking in the kitchen with the baby. He hears the cries. He should be with them.

The sun falls below the ridge and the dusk turns the sky gray. And he can no longer see inside. Marie and the baby must be sleeping. But for now, he will watch over them until morning.

———

MARIE COOKS OATMEAL AND spoons a bowl's worth onto the porch where he can see her. "If you act like an animal you can eat like an animal," she says. She slams the door. She would not be responsible for a starved man. The engine of the truck turns, and he is leaving, the satisfaction almost a smile on her face, and then the truck comes through the cabin wall as she stands there watching, the baby in the high chair, and the backing up, and the light streams through the splintered logs, and Lawrence appears, a shadow, and steps into the room. On the table, the proof and the patent, and she has added her name above his on both, and signed. He sits down at one end and tells her to do the same. She could run through that hole in the wall, she could drive the truck until the gas ran out, but she pulls the chair across and takes her place, the child and the pistol and papers between them.

They are silent, who will speak first? His hands flat against the wood, hers in her lap. How many meals at this table, pours of coffee, singes of cast iron, how many scratches, prayers over supper, settings and dabs of crumbs, how to measure the share of bread and store, the hunger? Could she spend her years looking at him, this man, and be without?

"You locked the door," he says. "You called me—"

"You lied," she says.

"I lied," he says.

"Here, at the homestead."

"I have sacrificed everything."

"And you think I haven't?"

He hangs his head.

"What is my life to you?"

"And what is mine?" he says. "You could have killed me." He holds the words on his tongue. "And you didn't."

"You will not lie to me again," she says.

"I will not," he says.

They both behold what is broken.

She stands and gathers the papers, the deed. "These are mine," she says. But for her, nothing has been given, nothing forgiven.

CHAPTER 39

FIREWEED

AUGUST

MARIE POURS KEROSENE ON the blighted crop in the brush pile, lights the match, a torching. The fire crackles as roots and stumps burn to ash on the edge of the field. They drove to Anchorage and let Sheila take the baby for a while—she did not tell her sister why. Work, not words, is her charge for the days ahead. Lawrence is on the other side of the pile, but he is a shadow surrounded by smoke when the wind turns. He has a shovel and she has a rake, and what falls away they send back to the raging heat, for no branch or root should remain.

—+—

SPRUCE FALLS BY AXE, and branches snap as the tree falls to the ground. He wants to drive the blade, learn to trust himself again, that fateful turn of the key, the accident, but the second time he meant to crash into the wall. He had mistaken himself for another man, one whose hands were for building and not tearing down. And he had wronged Marie, but he was not wrong in what he had done.

With the chainsaw he cuts off the branches. Only right that he repair what he damaged, but she insists on helping. She waits, then lifts one end and they carry the log to the cabin. Fresh cuts, no time to score and sap and dry out the trees.

———+———

MARIE SLEEPS IN THE bus. Hauling and holding up, and a soak in hot water with soap. What was and what will be. Divide the acres, their life. He could live here when the cabin is restored. Though he would never agree. One hundred and fifty acres in every ache and bruise. What did she know, before she came here, of the tallest trees and mountains, of colors in the sky she has never seen, of the wild places that hide a freshwater spring, of burying a child, of raising a daughter—these are hers to hold, to keep.

———+———

IN THE CABIN LAWRENCE guards the breach, lantern lit, gun at the ready, for a grizzly or any creature that would trespass. A wall he staked, and planned, and raised. Runs his hands along the buckled wood, built to last beyond him and his children and theirs. He found a window to match at army salvage, one with a lock and key. There were three, and he purchased all of them, not taking a chance. The first hit, one log cracked. If only he had stopped there. Marie had called him an animal. And that was his undoing.

———+———

FIREWEED IN BLOOM, THE fury of the blossoms scattered in the low. The years in between, and here they were again, and they dared to be so. What did she know now that she did not know then? Degrees of zero, and below, and a call in the night to come running to, and when to not answer, a fever in the mouth, snow to numb the cutting of a first tooth, to cry in the outhouse when the bleeding does not come. And what does she matter to this man she has a child with, to each pulled root and mouthful of dust, every log and splinter?

———+———

LAWRENCE STARTS THE CHAINSAW, and though he knows it must be done, he hesitates. He takes a deep breath. Then he carves a large frame into the side of the cabin. He knocks out the first log and Marie helps him with the rest. They line out the felled trees and he tries to match the diameters as close as he can to the ones in the wall, has an order. Cuts them to measure. And he and Marie place a new log and he drives in long spikes at an angle. One for the count, a toll into the late hours.

—+—

MARIE RUNS TO THE outhouse and is sick, and shaking, wipes her mouth on her sleeve. She has a hunger for salt and pilot bread and sits for a moment. Steadies herself. Why this, that night on the hunting stand? Before she knew the truth of the deed. She had her doubts, small and needling, but he was dishonest, and for how long, and surely he considered the harm.

Fine, fine, she says, on her return, hiding her weak stomach. The sky heavy with rain, and the fireweed reminds her summer is at an end. Come autumn, come winter. And come spring, there would be another child, and is that reason enough?

—+—

HE COVERS THE HOLE in the cabin with a tarp. The rain a patter on the windows. He stocks the stove with wood and through the mist he sees that Marie has done the same, the steam above the stovepipe on the bus. They will finish tomorrow, and then? A letter from his father sits on the table, unopened, along with a gift for Colleen, from Joseph and Lois says the package, in his mother's handwriting.

His footsteps across the floor make a hollow sound. How bare, how quiet the room is without a baby's laughter or Marie humming along to a record.

—+—

MARIE WAKES TO A glowing light. The rain has passed, the storm has moved on. A full moon shines, and then a thin cloud passes over the silver face, a delicate veil. The words of the priest, seemed so long ago. Would he take all the days of her life? Would she? In wanting the land, she wanted him, her aim as true as his, and as false, the lie of the lie.

For her children's sake, for her own—what would be the telling?

———+———

LAWRENCE SETS TO TEARING out the broken window while he waits for Marie. He knocks out the glass with the bullet hole, and sweeps this into a bin. The shards he picks out of the dirt, one by one, caught by the sun. Somewhere is the bullet, perhaps lodged in a tree. Maybe one day they will find it.

The morning gone, another pot of coffee. He stacks the busted logs in a pile to burn. Then he knocks on the door to the bus and Marie appears, pale and yawning. She assures him she will be there as soon as she can.

———+———

AFTER THE LAST LOG, Marie and Lawrence stand and run their hands over the bark of the completed wall, the old and the new. Cabin is a cabin, whole once more, the pieces fitted, the fault marked. Tired as they are, and their clothes are soaked through with sweat and repellent, but they will not tarnish what they have this day. Together they trudge to the bus, Lawrence following, and he gathers three fireweed stems blooming with purple flowers and offers them. The crush of the petals in her hands.

He opens the door. They lower their bodies to the floor, apart. How they slept their first night on the land. In this resting, the downing, Marie knows what she knows, the child to be growing inside. Her words break over them.

"There was a bear at the cabin," she says, and she places his hand on her belly.

Lawrence turns to face her, and he sees what she sees. "I was in the truck," he says.

"I was on the porch," she says.

"There was a grizzly," he says.

"There was a grizzly at the cabin," she says, and this is a beginning.

CHAPTER 40

RECKON
SEPTEMBER

LEAVES TURN GOLD AND yellow, aspen and cottonwood and willow, and there is no turning back to warmer days, and they fall, one by one, and float in the lake. Marie brings the mud to her mouth, a fever, a hunger for salt. Another child, and what will this bring? What will be enough? The water laps at her waist, and ripples with every reach.

Twigs snap, a thrash in the woods, and a bull moose is shoved into the clearing, antlers deadlocked with another bull pushing from the high ground. Their hooves scrape for footing against each other. They are tall, strong, with long white-tipped legs, smooth, brown on their sides that lightens to copper along their scruffy necks. Trapped together, they swing their tangled antlers side to side and circle each other, craning and turning. Her teeth ache as she steps toward shore. If she can reach the pistol she can shoot one for meat.

Circling wide, around and around, the bulls trample her clothes and boots and kick the pistol. Their legs slip toward the water, and they snort and huff, hooves dig in, the first bull lifts up his front legs and stomps the air for a moment, the other bull's neck bends back with the force. The first loses his hold and stumbles, boulders over to the side, and the other bull, antlers caught, must follow, neck yanked with the fall, kneeling down. The first struggles for a footing to get up, the other jerks, trying to free the antlers, back legs crouched, and with each striving they both groan, the other bull pulling back, the first being pulled, and then they both find a footing and rise up on their legs. They stand still, antler to antler, heads bowed. Flaps of their chins hang low. They are tired. They are bound.

No truce, or surrender. Sides heave with strain. Antlers drop, scratch the ground, and lift, and drop and rise for another count, and they circle each other again. Their back legs tense, hooves claw for a hold, and brow to brow they push and ram, pressed and locked, and they both slip, and are thrown by their own weight and fall over together, the crash and thud. She hurries out of the lake, splashing with each step, and retrieves the pistol. The moose keen with long, pained cries, and their legs kick and twitch. She stands above the back of the first, wet and dripping, the ends of her hair clinging to her shoulders and breasts, water streaming over the hard swell of her growing belly. Antlers are locked above the brow, a tine wrench around and another below—a ring woven under and over. There are broken-off points and small cracks in the long-fingered palms. The front leg of the first bleeding and split open below the knee, the hinge of knuckle will never recover.

Naked and trembling, she clicks off the safety on the pistol. She targets the white of the eye, and, with both hands, sights below the ear, the skull, and with no feeling, she pulls the trigger. Bullet hits the mark, and the first bull grunts, his back legs jerk, and then he tosses his head, and the antlers rake the ground, and then it is over. The other bull shakes, muscles quivering over bone, his neck bent at a sharp angle. There are no whites around his black, glassy eye, and she aims above the dark gleam, and takes the shot. A bullet wound opens and seeps with red. The bull's side heaves one last time. Fresh, bright blood trickles out of the nostrils and pools on the dirt. She crouches next to him and pats the patch of gray on his shoulder, and he is still, and she runs her hand over the neck to the soft open flap of his ear and slides her hand inside, the pulse slowing to the touch, the silken tufts of white fur warm against her skin.

Leave the baby safe in her crib. Knives, a bucket, burlap sacks, more bullets, meat after hash and canned beans and oatmeal, meat for the winter. Lawrence had heard the shots, thought hunting season had begun.

"No telling what animal will beat us to it," he says. They creep toward the lake, Lawrence with the shotgun in hand. Antlers on the ground, propped on their lain side. Gutted, entrails, stomachs ripped open, not a clean cut by knife, but ragged by teeth.

She runs toward them.

"Get back here," he says.

"They're mine," she says.

Not a heart, not one organ. Nothing to salvage. A burrowing through both chests. Trails of bloody tracks cover the clearing, a dance of death surrounding the two carcasses.

"Wolves," says Lawrence.

"I want the antlers," she says.

"We'll come back with the chainsaw."

"Go on and get it."

"Not leaving you here alone," he says. "You hear that?"

"Just the trees," she says.

The antlers are shackled together, but the fallen animals are not the same in injury. The one she touched, the eye is gouged out, the fur of the ear ripped apart—they found her scent. Her aim, her bullet, and they took this from her, ransacked the kill, a moose kill. Stolen from her, the first on this land, in their record, and she cannot abide. What will Lawrence do, by her and for her? What will be? Forget them, he says, the danger is too great. So much has been taken, how can he not see, how can he deny her, and she says, "I will not live this way."

The baby on her hip, and she stands on the porch. She will wait. For what has been earned. *I thought I was dreaming,* she will say, her whole life. *Can't tell by looking at him, but he's the strongest man I've ever seen.* Lawrence walking from the low. His hair black and shining in the sun. So dark, the brightest spot for miles, soaking up all the light. A tangled circle of antlers crests his shoulders and towers over him—how he can carry them, she cannot reckon—the width of them, the heaviness, the spread of their palms. Two moose heads, sawed at the neck, bowed nose to nose at his chest, must weigh a tree stump each, rust drips down the front of his shirt and pants, the pistol tucked into his belt. His skin slick with sweat. Each step a burden, a giving, a repenting. And she will forget the questions stinging her that morning. Every new day will be a staying, another set and rise, and what is between her and Lawrence, she has not come to her own, and his name is her name, their children, and this place will outlive them, and a territory becomes a state, a woman marries and becomes a wife, and what is the difference, what must be repaid—what is it worth, this water, this dirt? She will forget, then, and in every telling. His knees buckle and he kneels, the weight of the antlers tip on the ground, the sharp points of white stab the sun, a crown of blood and bone. *These are yours,* he says, a promise and a vow, and the years will pass, winter after winter, the antlers wreathed and nailed above the cabin door.

ACKNOWLEDGMENTS

I would like to thank the following members of my family: my parents, Constance and Michael Moustakis, for their love and support, Sonny Traxinger for sharing memories of his father and the homestead and answering mountains of questions, my grandmother Kathleen Traxinger (formerly Kubala, died July 21, 2022), who homesteaded in Point MacKenzie with my grandfather, Lawrence Traxinger, and who I interviewed for this project and gave me a copy of the homestead proof. Michael and Heather Moustakis, Melaina Moustakis, Sam and Kamal and Sophia and Olivia Traxinger, Kitty and James Mullican for moose tacos on the island, Mark Moustakis and Cynthia McMillin, and Shirley and Brian Saupe.

Much gratitude to my agent, Bill Clegg, who has encouraged this project for many years and patiently read many early drafts. My editor, Caroline Bleeke, for her insight and for bringing this book to the finish line.

Pam Houston and Jaimy Gordon for mentoring me as a writer at pivotal points in my life.

All the fellowship programs that have supported me over the years I was writing this book: the National Endowment for the Arts Literature Fellowship, the Hodder Fellowship at the Lewis Center for the Arts at Princeton University, the Kenyon Review Fellowship at Kenyon College, the Jenny McKean Moore Writer-in-Washington Fellowship at George Washington University, and the Rona Jaffe/Cullman Fellowship at the New York Public Library. And the Visiting Professorship at UC Davis.

ACKNOWLEDGMENTS

These friends of many years: Adeena Reitberger, Danielle Evans, Jennine Capó Crucet, Sara Ortiz, Tessie Prakas, Emily Stinson, Lynn Melnick, who is my Monday check-in, Katherine Zlabek, Rachel Swearingen, Jessi Phillips, Amber Dermont, Beth Marzoni, Leah Davis, and Jo-Jo.

From my time in Austin, Texas: Jordan Brown, Tim Bauer, Sarah Berson, and Tanya L. Stokes.

Davis, California: Katie Peterson, Lucy Corin, Kate Asche, Nick White for the inspiring pep talk, Mangai Arumugam and Manesh Patel.

Denver, Colorado: Lindsay and Pete Cooper, who gave me a place to stay, Danielle and Derek Swink, Kelsey and Reid Morgan, Sara Laimans and Watson, Ashlyn King, and Erin and Shane Glackin.

Gambier, Ohio: Sergei Lobanov-Rostovsky for encouraging the mess of early pages, Angela Haas, Natalie Shapero, and Kirsten Reach for Friday martinis at the Kenyon Inn.

Juneau, Alaska: Katrina Wolford, Matt Klosterman, and Ben Huff.

New York City: Molly McCue for her wisdom, Andrea and Aaron Adcock, and Beth McCabe.

Princeton, New Jersey: Chang-Rae Lee, Susan Choi, Amy Jo Burns, James Arthur and Shannon Robinson, Mirka and Kjartan Døj-Fetté.

San Luis Obispo, California: Susann Cokal, Kevin Clark, Bill Jenkins, and Virginia Bell.

Washington, D.C.: Jennifer Chang, Lisa Page, Jung Yun, Nate Brown and Thea Brown James Han Mattson, and Tassity Johnson.

Special thanks to James A. Fall, one of the authors of *Shem Pete's Alaska: The Territory of the Upper Cook Inlet Dena'ina,* who I consulted on the chapters that feature Shem Pete and his son, Billy. He knew Shem, who was a respected elder, and gave me invaluable advice on this fictional depiction. And to James Kari, another one of the authors, for pointing me to James Fall. *Shem Pete's Alaska* includes stories and personal accounts by Shem and displays his vast and intimate knowledge of history and geography. More information about Shem Pete's life and the Dena'ina history and language he preserved, as well as audio recordings (including Nełchish Tsukdu, The Wolverine Story) can be found on the Anchorage Museum website. I used *Shem Pete's Alaska* as a resource, as well as *Dena'inaq' Huch'ulyeshi: The Dena'ina Way of Living,* edited by Suzi Jones, James A. Fall, and Aaron Leggett. The two artifacts described in the book, the basket scrap and hook, are based on artifacts in *Dena'inaq' Huch'ulyeshi.* Also, thank-you to Aaron Leggett, senior curator of Alaskan history and Indigenous culture at the Anchorage Museum, who assisted in pronunciation of the Dena'ina words and Robert King at the Bureau of Land Management for a conversation about homestead documents.

Note that the law that Shem Pete refers to is the Anti-Discrimination Act of 1945 and was the first anti-discrimination law in Alaska and the United States. St. Michael's is based on a church in Herreid, South Dakota, but I moved its location to Blackduck, Minnesota, for fictional purposes. A few aspects of the homestead filing process have been expedited to fit the timeline of the novel. Billie Holiday visited Anchorage in 1954. Rosemary Clooney sang the mentioned version of "This Ole House." Frankie Lymon and The Teenagers sang "Why Do Fools Fall in Love?" George and Peggy Brown owned The Lucky Wishbone, and Walter Teeland owned Teeland's Country Store. Wilson, the medic, is based on Richard G. Wilson, of the 187th Regimental Combat Team, who earned the Medal of Honor for his bravery on October 21, 1950, in the Korean War. The radio announcement of "We're In" was taken from a headline announcing statehood in the *Anchorage Daily Times.* The article "Cruelty in Maternity Wards" published by *Ladies' Home Journal* in 1958 describes the common practices used on laboring women in hospitals. A poem about being blinded by small dreams, which I cannot find again, inspired a section in the chapter titled "Winterkill." The chapter "Almanac" was inspired by the poem *Sestina* by Elizabeth Bishop.

"Oh, to grace how great a debtor. . . ."

ABOUT THE AUTHOR

Melinda Moustakis was born in Fairbanks, Alaska, and grew up in California. Her debut story collection, *Bear Down, Bear North: Alaska Stories,* won the Flannery O'Connor Award, the Maurice Prize, and was a National Book Foundation 5 Under 35 selection. Her work has appeared in *American Short Fiction, Alaska Quarterly Review, Granta, The Kenyon Review,* and elsewhere and has been awarded an O. Henry Prize. She is the recipient of the Hodder Fellowship from Princeton University, the NEA Literature Fellowship, the Kenyon Review Fellowship, and the Rona Jaffe Cullman Fellowship at the New York Public Library. *Homestead* is her debut novel.

melindamoustakis.com

RECOMMEND *HOMESTEAD*
FOR YOUR NEXT BOOK CLUB!

Reading Group Guide available at
flatironbooks.com/reading-group-guides